The Debt of Blood,

By Charlie Revelle-Smith

For Kat,
Come home, town mouse!

"The hour of our departure has arrived and we go our own ways; I to die, and you to live. Which is better? Only God knows."

Socrates, (BCE 469–BCE 399)

"Many people die at twenty-five and aren't buried until they are seventy-five."

Benjamin Franklin, (1819-1880)

"Millions long for immortality who don't know what to do with themselves on a rainy Sunday afternoon."

Susan Ertz (1894-1985)

1.

Spencer Nordstrom knew exactly how he would die.

He would be old enough in body, but not so old that his mind had lost its edge, and he would know when that day was on the horizon and how to plan ahead for its arrival. By then he would no doubt be in possession of a substantial estate so he would ensure that his vast fortune was securely in the hands of those who most deserved it and all loose ends were neatly tidied away. On the morning of his death he would send letters to his sons or daughters and any grandchildren who had come along in the intervening years. Spencer was not a man for goodbyes in person but he knew how to express himself in the written word - his letters would be a permanent memento of his love for his family before he slipped into the eternal embrace of oblivion.

He would certainly be living in the country by then - somewhere grand and remote. His last meal would be venison, which he had never tried before but was certain he would develop a taste for in the twilight of his life. He would listen to a grand, tragic opera as he ate and sipped the champagne that had been chilling for many years. When he was finished, he would dress in his finest suit and retire to the garage where he would switch on the engine of his tastefully expensive car and gently fall asleep forever.

That was the plan, and it had given Spencer Nordstrom an enormous amount of comfort over the years - death was not something to fear, for it was up to him when it came to claim him. The dignity of a life opted out of, rather than gracelessly clung on to, was what suited a man of such character as he.

These thoughts were far from Spencer's mind on that October morning. At 44 years of age, death felt decades rather than minutes away as he strolled across the city under the chicken soup sky of a dusky Thursday. He was a chartered accountant at a firm he was sure he would one day be running and he always liked to be the first to arrive each morning - even if in these autumnal months that meant waking in the dark.

The streets were almost void of people but filled with the detritus of a debauched night. The students were returning to the city where mere hours before they had been spilling out of bars, smelling of too much cheap aftershave and cigarette smoke. Beer turning stale in the carpets beneath their feet, toilets blocked with vomit.

Such an undignified way to live. Such an aimless, pointless existence. For Spencer Nordstrom, life had always been a simple illustration - a lone arrow pointing skywards, driving him ever onwards to greater things.

A chill wind howled across Queen Square and the last of the summer leaves began fluttering down around him. He buttoned his overcoat and pressed on, these mornings weren't pleasant but were the price one must pay for excellence. His life was not about the simple pleasure of an extra hour in bed; that would come in later years - this part was to be endured as he lined his nest in readiness for his great fortune, until the day came that he finally believed he had made it.

These thoughts motivated him on mornings like this - away from the troubles of the mortgage that was far too large for his earnings - and his wife who was far too young to stay interested in him. This was how he controlled his direction; ever upwards until the final day came. He crossed the silent road and stepped onto Pero's Bridge - a pedestrian crossing over the waterfront that bore two huge concrete horns on either side. It was a peculiar construction and one that Spencer had heard had something to do with slavery. He was at the halfway point, between the horns, when he found he was not alone.

At first his mind could not make sense of what he was seeing. It was a human, certainly - a man, but one dressed so strangely that he could easily have dropped from another century into this one. A long black coat was draped around the man's shoulders - his body was as thick as an ancient oak, a huge mess of fiery red beard cascaded from his head, upon which sat a three cornered hat, the likes of which Spencer had only ever seen in...

...No. He stopped in his tracks. The man ahead of him was dressed as a pirate, and not just any pirate. Unnerved by the oddness of the moment, Spencer was about to call something dry and quippy to the stranger but found his mouth empty of words. An overwhelming sense of unease told him to turn and run, but instead he stood his ground and watched as the pirate reached inside his overcoat and presented a curious contraption, sturdy and familiar even in the mirthless light of the morning. The instant Spencer Nordstrom recognized the weapon to be a crossbow the arrow passed through his eye and into his brain.

Stumbling backwards, he fell to the ground and was suddenly gazing upwards into the morning sky with his remaining eye. His mouth was filling with blood and a chill was settling over his fingers and toes. The sky was shrinking away, narrowing, like looking through a telescope the wrong way round, the blackness swallowing it with every dull heartbeat.

As he died, Spencer Nordstrom thought only one thing.

This was not how it was meant to happen.

2.

The drive from Bristol to Cheltenham would take Franklin Gallow less than an hour but he had allowed himself almost twice that to make sure he wasn't late. He was anxious enough about this journey without competing with the clock adding to his mounting worries. He was only going to get a chance to do this once and he was going to have to do it properly; this could be the turning point in his life and future - if he could just get it right.

Approaching Gloucester, Franklin was aware that he was absurdly, almost rudely, ahead of time, so opted to stop at a service station on the M5 to refill the car and have an early lunch. In the car park he tapped the number of his assistant into his phone and she promptly answered.

"Morning, Franklin," Rowan chirped.

"Good morning. How's it going?"

"Nothing of note, in fact, I'm just about to leave. Peterman's dealing with the only been we have today"

"Been? What's a been?"

"It's what Peterman calls the bodies, you know, like has-been?"

Franklin sighed. "Please don't start talking like that, I've taught you better."

"I know. Sorry, I just thought a little gallows humour might lighten the mood."

Franklin rolled his eyes at the pun on his name. "How's Peterman behaving?"

"Same as always, it's hard to tell if he's drunk on power or just plain drunk. We tend to keep out of each other's way."

"That's the Rowan I taught," Franklin laughed.

"Talking of unspeakable little shits. How's the father-son reunion going?"

Franklin shook his head. He was quite certain that his dauntless, young assistant was the only person in the world he would let speak about his estranged son, Alf, in this manner. "I haven't heard from him this morning, but I'm assuming the plan is still on. I'm a little worried about it; I think I might have made a bit of a mistake. I was supposed to take the van this morning - Alf's got a lot of stuff he wants to bring to Bristol for university - but Peterman needed it to pick up the body."

"You can't put all of Alf's stuff in your Smart car, it'll never fit!"

"I didn't take the Smart car…"

He heard Rowan gasp on the line. "Oh Franklin. You didn't…"

"What else was I supposed to do? There's loads of room in the hearse."

"I know there is, because it's designed to carry dead bodies."

Franklin knew that this had been a foolish idea but hearing the words out loud only made it more obviously so. It was difficult enough patching up a lifetime of absence with his son without adding public humiliation to the list of wrongdoings he was responsible for. It had only been a few months since he'd discovered Alf even existed, due to an online reconnection with Verity Duke, his long ago love but only one time bed partner, which had resulted in the birth of a boy over eighteen years ago. Now this boy was a man and a man with a huge amount of resentment towards his missing father, added to which, he was now coming to live in Franklin's home city of Bristol to attend university. Nothing about this scenario was likely to run smoothly.

"It's the best I can do," Franklin admitted, defeated.

"You're just inviting more reasons for him to hate you," she replied.

"One more can't make that much of a difference can it?"

The moment of silence suggested that Rowan had said her piece and was ready to move on. "So I suppose you've heard the news on the radio?"

"No. It's just been me and Kim Wilde all the way up from Bristol." Franklin could picture Rowan's withering expression at this.

"There's been another murder," said Rowan, grimly.

Franklin pressed cautiously. "What do you mean by another murder?'

"You know what I mean… after the spring."

Franklin knew exactly what she'd meant. Earlier in the year they had found themselves inadvertently investigating a series of murders - duties far from ordinary for a funeral director and his assistant. It had started as a kind of morbid mystery for them both but had escalated rapidly into Rowan risking her life in capturing the culprit. Now, even months later, with the killer caught and imprisoned, the pair of them rarely spoke of that terrible day or the events that had lead up to it.

"You can't think like this every time there's a murder, Rowan. Bristol's a big city and violence can happen anywhere…"

"…They're saying it happened on Pero's Bridge this morning. Who would murder someone in such a public place?"

"I don't know Rowan, and neither should you. This has nothing to do with either of us, even if we end up arranging the funeral we are going to stay out of it this time. I am not Miss Marple and you are not Hercule Poirot."

"It's quite telling that you thought of us that way round, Franklin." Rowan laughed to herself. "Well, there's very little reason for me to hang around here and be sneered at by Peterman all day. If Meredy needs me she'll call me. I think I'm going to head back home. A storm is pitching over the city and I want to be ahead of it."

"Alright then, enjoy your afternoon off."

"I will. Oh, before I go, a parcel arrived this morning. It was addressed to you, I put it in your office."

"Rats. Did I drink too much and accidentally order something online?"

"Don't think so. It has a hand written address. It's heavy."

Franklin smiled to himself. "Is there anything more thrilling than a mystery parcel coming through the post?"

Rowan said her goodbye and hung up. Franklin strolled inside the service station in search of food, his mind excitedly racing through the possibilities of what his parcel could be.

3.

Rowan took the long route home on her bike so that she would pass by Pero's Bridge.

It felt less like morbid curiosity to her than it did duty. To have seen so much murder, to have had it come to her door and claim one of her own, to have found herself trapped on the backseat of a car as a psychopath drove her to where he wanted to bury her, had left murder a very familiar foe - so much closer than it should be.

Looking back to that dreadful day, what struck her more than anything was not the horror of her near death, it was her lack of horror at it. Sometimes she would remember little details, like the squeeze of fake leather against her face as she struggled to free herself from the backseat, or that musty, wet smell that filled the inside of the car, it would grab her late at night as she was drifting off to sleep, but other than that, there was nothing. It did not haunt her and that was what frightened her. Was it right that she should feel so normal about being almost murdered?

Pero's Bridge had been blocked at both sides and police officers stood guard at either end, talking grimly to curious passersby. Rowan scanned the faces of the men but saw none she recognised. In the centre of the bridge, between the twin horns that anchored the rising section to allow boats to pass underneath, stood a white tent that was too large for the narrow walkway and bulged awkwardly over the handrails. A sizable group of onlookers had gathered on both banks of the harbourside and were constantly being ordered to step back. "You don't want to see something that will haunt you for the rest of your life," a policeman grimly informed them.

Rowan passed through the throng, not wanting to be associated with the grief tourism that passed for entertainment in this cynical world. Her interest was not to take a peek into the chasm of death, or into another family's tragedy, it was almost an obligation - a respect for one who had died at the hands of another, while she had managed to survive.

She thought about the poor man's family. The news that morning had reported only the scantest details of the outrage. A middle aged man, a local businessman murdered on Pero's Bridge. Police were watching CCTV; anybody with any information should come forward. It was the stuff the public had seen a hundred times over - but what they had never seen was what happened away from the news. The terrified family waiting and worrying, hoping against hope that the knock at the door was their loved one come home and not a police officer with the worst news anyone could ever hear.

Her phone buzzed in her pocket. It was text message from her friend Lise.

"Have you heard about the murder?" it read.

"Yes. Do you want to meet up later?" she replied.

"No. I'm fine. Just need to get my head around it."

"Call me if you need to."

Rowan returned her phone to her pocket and cycled home.

With the kind of timing that rarely worked in her favour, the enormous dark clouds that had settled over the city broke open just as she stepped into the hall of her new home. Far away a roll of thunder declared the approach of a storm. She had lived in this house for a little over two months. Hers was the flat on the third floor with only an attic above her.

It was an old Victorian semi which had clearly seen better days. Its floorboards creaked, its windows let in the draft and the whole place ached and groaned after a hot day. It had once been all one house but had been split into four flats above ground and one in the basement. There was a small garden but it was too overgrown with weeds to even venture into. It was small and kind of squalid, but to Rowan, it was freedom.

She could almost see her parent's house from the window of her flat but she might as well have been in a different country. Away from her drunken mother and unreliable father and the ever-present stench of loss and mourning, Rowan felt like an adult for the first time in her life. She had moved out shortly after her 20th birthday, into the first place she could afford. Stokes Croft was once cheap but with an influx of artists and counter-cultural types came gentrification and a massive increase in rental costs - it wasn't much of a flat, but it wouldn't financially cripple her - and above all else, it felt like home.

It was a simple, spare space that she hadn't yet redecorated. Her landlord had said she was free to repaint as long as she returned it to the stark magnolia when she left, but she had not got around to choosing which colour best fitted her new surroundings. Save for the bathroom, there were no doors inside her flat, the living room, bedroom and kitchen were all divisions of the same space, with her bed elevated above the floor so she could fit a desk and computer underneath it - in a place so small, every square centimetre was put to purpose.

Something was certainly different. She had sensed it soon after closing the door behind her. There was a noise in the kitchen, a constant, drip, drip, drip coming from the area of the room that had Lino on the floor to allocate the space as a kitchen. A heaving wet bubble bulged in the ceiling from which water was steadily falling in big drops. Rowan quickly put a saucepan in the puddle it had formed and called her landlord.

"Yes?" Mr Shaw yawned.

"Mr Shaw. The ceiling is leaking."

"Um… Where do you live?"

"I'm in the Stokes Croft house on…"

"Oh yes, I remember. The coloured girl?"

Rowan frowned at the phone, more intrigued that Mr Shaw had answered his phone in the 1970's than she was offended.

"Yes," she replied. "The black woman."

"Yeah. The roof's leaking. The chap upstairs must have forgotten to change the bucket."

With that, the man was gone and Rowan was left with no option other than to venture upstairs to meet the chap who lived there.

4

The Georgian terrace in Cheltenham was verdant and classy, with ornate street lamps and hanging baskets bearing the last of the season's flowers. As Franklin pulled in to park outside the address Verity had given him, he saw her and his son seated upon the doorstep, holding hands sadly, eyes puffy and red. Both of their mouths fell open at the sight of the hearse.

"I'm sorry…" he began hastily as he stepped out of the car. "The van was in use and this was all I had."

Alf was rising to his feet. A soft smile was spreading across his face, which he seemed to be trying to hold back. "You're taking me to university in a hearse? That's … actually pretty cool."

Alf looked precisely as Franklin had at his age and the two men bore a remarkable resemblance that went beyond the slightness of their frames and the redness of their hair. There was no doubt that they were father and son, to the extent that looking into Alf's face, Franklin felt the eeriness of seeing himself staring back.

"Thank you for doing this," Verity said warmly as she embraced him. Her hair was tied back and her shirt sleeves were rolled up - it was the kind of earthy, homely look which Franklin thought suited her best; she really did seem to grow more beautiful with every passing day.

"Are you sure I can't tempt you to Bristol to see him off? There are four seats in the hearse so there's plenty of room."

Verity broke away from the hug and shook her head. "Today is hard enough without dragging it out. This is just about as much as I can bear." She looked over at her son who was investigating the back of the hearse as if it were some ancient, fascinating relic from another world. Her eyes filled with tears, which she wiped hastily away. "Keep it together, Verity," she hissed at herself.

"I remember when I left home for uni. I thought it was the last I'd ever see of that funeral home. I was so scared but

I didn't want to let it show - to this day I think my parents thought I was being cold or unfeeling but it wasn't true."

"Oh god," Verity wept softly. "He just looks so small, I feel like the worst parent in the world. I know he's eighteen but it just seems like he was a baby last week. How has this day come?"

"You can come and visit whenever you want, Bristol's only down the M5 and I have a spare room that you can use… as long as staying over a funeral home isn't going to disturb you."

Verity was wiping her eyes again. "Thank you, but I don't think Alf would want his mum visiting him every other weekend. I remember what it was like at university. But please Franklin, can you try and keep an eye out for him, you know, just try and see that he doesn't get himself into too much trouble - my little boy is going to be out drinking 'til the early hours, experimenting with drugs at wild parties, wild sex - all the kind of stuff we did back then."

Franklin smiled at her. "We never did drugs, not really - and I didn't have sex until my third year."

"And look what came of that," Verity nodded towards her son. "Pretty fertile loins there, Franklin."

Franklin laughed.

"Oh god. He's going to get himself a boyfriend isn't he? He'll spend all his time with him and won't want to come home for the holidays… This really is the end of everything, isn't it?"

Suddenly Franklin was hugging Verity again as she tried to stifle her sobs. Franklin often forgot that his son was gay - a fact that had been accidentally stumbled upon earlier that year. Alf had yet to confide this information to him and Franklin wasn't about to let on that he knew already, his son would tell him when he was ready.

"Are you two dweebs going to lend a hand, or do I have to do this all by myself?" Alf called out to them. He was already stacking the car with boxes of his belongings.

"Wow. I really did raise a charmer," Verity said with a smile.

With three of them working together, the back of the hearse was filled in a matter of minutes. Last to squeeze in

16

between the TV and speakers were several planks of wood bound together with string. "Alf's art project," Verity informed Franklin who nodded in response. Several months ago Alf had taken a photograph of him at the funeral home for this very project, but he had not heard a word about it since. "I think you'll like it," she said.

Franklin instinctively knew that this part of the day would have nothing to do with him. Verity thanked him again and offered him a tender kiss on the cheek before she and Alf sloped away inside the house and Franklin retired to the driver's seat. He waited patiently as Verity said goodbye to her son and found that he too had tears pricking at his eyes - it was a monumental day for them both and one in which he played no part. Nevertheless he found himself chuckling at the sight of the sticker placed in the rear window of Verity's car that was parked behind the hearse, the kind of sticker only a history teacher could have, it read: "Those Who Fail Their History Exam Are Condemned to Repeat It." - how he loved her.

When Alf returned his face was stoic but pale, he had clearly been crying but was not about to let Franklin see he had. He climbed into the passenger side of the hearse and simply said, "Let's go."

Franklin waited briefly to see if Verity would come to the window to wave them goodbye. When she didn't he was suddenly confronted by the horrible image of that poor mother sobbing at her kitchen table in a house that had suddenly become twice as big and half as full. Eighteen years as a diligent, single mother, she was now all alone.

"Is your mother ok?" Franklin allowed himself to ask his son as the hearse pulled out into traffic.

"I don't think we need to talk about it Franklin, do you?"

"I guess not."

"If you must know, she's pretty miserable actually, but thanks for asking dear, old daddy."

Franklin ground his teeth in silently exasperation. Every time he tried to reach out to his son, every time he thought he was making some progress, Alf would remind him that the pair of them could never be close.

"I know you don't want to play happy families Alf, and I certainly won't force you into doing it, but can you please try and be civil to me, at least until we get to your halls. You can tell me to piss off then if you want to, but I just want a nice steady drive back to Bristol."

"Fine," he huffed and the young man's attention was drawn lazily to the passenger window, where flecks of rain had started streaking in sharp bands.

By the time they reached the campus on the north side of the city, they were driving through an almighty storm. The hearse was lashed with angry rain that the wipers could barely slosh away. The whole vehicle seemed to tremble in the roar of overhead thunder as wind bore against its sides. Through the rain Franklin could just about make out the imposing precipice of the central campus building. It was a mighty, parliamentary looking structure made of Bath stone and bearing a huge clock on a tower that seemed to be daring the lightning to strike it.

"Bloody hell," said Franklin. "You didn't tell me you were going to Hogwarts."

Alf remained unmoved.

Nearing the building they were suddenly sheltered from the rain and the wind and Franklin began to notice how many people were peering out of windows at the approach of the hearse. He felt quietly confident that he had been right in choosing this particular means of transport to take his son to his halls - this was quite simply an unbelievably cool way to make his arrival.

Alf however seemed to think otherwise, as the second the car pulled into a parking spot behind the university building, he released his seatbelt, threw the door open and after stumbling out into the torrential rain, promptly vomited into an ornamental hedge. Franklin was frozen in his seat, temporarily at a loss as to what to do. He watched helplessly as his son dropped to his knees and began retching, at which time Franklin launched himself from the hearse and ran over to Alf and awkwardly patted and rubbed his back.
"It's ok to be frightened, I was terrified on my first…"

"…I'm not frightened." Alf barked as he got to his feet. "You're just a bad driver, I got motion sickness."

Franklin knew this lie was not meant to be challenged, so he simply nodded in agreement. Reaching into the pocket of his suit jacket he found what was left of a packet of Fisherman's Friends and offered one to his son. He took it and munched away at it before helping himself to another.

"Don't tell Mum about that. She'll just worry."

"I promise," said Franklin. "If it helps, I don't think anyone saw you throwing up."

Alf just shrugged as rain poured down his face. "I don't care."

Franklin followed him to the door of his new home. Two grand glass art deco doors swung into a small lobby with a staircase and a plump woman who sat behind a desk. Drying his hair as best as he could on his sleeve, Alf gave her his name and she in turn gave him a key, a map and a welcome pack before directing him up the stairs.

"Do you want me to come with you?" Franklin asked.

Alf seemed to ponder this question for a frustrating amount of time. "Yes, I think so."

"OK."

Alf led the way up the staircase that swooped over the lobby and around an expensive looking chandelier. These halls were far grander than the digs he was cast into over twenty years before. "Do you know who you're living with?" he asked.

"Three girls, two other boys. We've all friended each other on Facebook. They seem ok."

Franklin was impressed by this news. How much easier and less fraught with worry his first day would have been if he had known ahead of time that the three young men he was going to be living with were all as shockingly unpopular and socially awkward as he was.

On the first floor, Franklin was struck by the far off scent of pot drifting along the corridor that stretched out before him. Boxes on either side propped open doors from which students were dashing through in the process of unpacking. Walking past them, Franklin peered in through the open frame of one and spied a cluster of teenagers sitting around in a circle on the floor playing ukuleles. In another, beers were being passed around and clinked together against the sound

19

of loud music playing from an iPhone. Further on a young woman was pinning a rainbow flag to a wall. Alf was going to be safe here, Franklin thought.

Alf's flat was at the far end of the corridor. The door opened onto a bright, clean kitchen from which a narrow hall held the bedrooms and bathroom. His room was light and narrow and he seemed assured enough in it to even offer Franklin a tepid smile. With the help of his flat mates - five impossibly young looking students who already knew him by name and by sight, the hearse was rapidly unpacked and Alf's possessions were moved into his new home.

"That hearse is effing badass," one of the girls offered as way of judgment. "Where did you get it?"

"I'm a funeral director," Franklin replied casually. When the girl seemed not to respond he clarified with, "an undertaker." That did the trick, the girl's eyes widened with wonder.

"Authentic. That is so verified."

Franklin nodded in agreement, fully aware that a young person had just used slang in a conversation with him. It made him feel incredibly old.

The time had come to bid Alf goodbye, and in doing so, he found himself inordinately sad to be leaving him. For the first time in his son's life, Franklin had done something to help Alf and as chilly as relations between them might be, something beneath the surface might be thawing.

"That's the lot of it then," said Franklin with a sigh as the pair met over the threshold of the door. "If you need anything, feel free to call, day or night."

"Has Mum given you the details about my rent? She says you're paying, right?"

"Yes. It felt like the proper thing to do, after all, I missed out on…"

"…If you want me to say thanks then it's not going to happen. A few rent payments aren't going to make up for missing out on my whole childhood."

"Fine. Whatever you say, but you know I would have done more if I'd known you existed."

"Franklin, you've done your duty, now can you please just piss off." Alf slammed the door on him and he was left momentarily outraged and ready to hammer on the door in angry defiance. Getting the better of his senses, he concluded that rude as his son may be, at least he was true to his word and waited to tell him to piss off.

By the time Franklin left the campus, the skies were clearing but dark clouds had instead settled over his head as he miserably made his way across the city towards Gallow & Sons Funeral Home. Pulling up into the garage, Franklin inspected the damage the downpour had done to the garden in front of the building. The annuals had seen better days and were mostly on their way out already, the perennials were reliably stoic in the face of the onslaught.

Inside the reception, Meredy, the secretary of the funeral home, sat behind her desk, eyes fixed squarely on the computer monitor in front of her. "Afternoon Franklin," she said.

"Afternoon Meredy," his secretary was a short, round faced and kindly looking woman who had an almost supernatural ability to soothe devastated mourners just using her empathetic telephone voice.

"Have you heard about the murder?' she asked.

"A bit. Rowan called earlier, she did mention it. If we have to deal with the body, I'm saying right now that Peterman's doing the directing this time around. No more murders for me - or for Rowan. Not for a while anyway."

Meredy drew her eyes from the screen to meet his. "The police aren't saying much but people are talking about it online. They say he was killed with a crossbow. Who the hell gets killed with a crossbow? It isn't the dark ages."

"That is peculiar."

"People are mentioning you on Twitter," Meredy intoned, darkly.

"Crap. What are they saying?"

"That Franklin Gallow would be better at solving the case than the police."

"That isn't good at all. I thought the police said they were going to keep my name private and out of the reports - and Rowan's."

Meredy just shrugged her shoulders. "All it takes is for one person to talk, that little leak causes the whole dam to rupture. At least nobody's mentioned Rowan - and to be honest, most people are calling you that undertaker who solves murders."

"My barber asked me the other day if I was the one who caught that murderer earlier in the year."

"Like I said, the dam's burst. Nothing can be done about it now."

"If only I were Peterman, I could use a drink right now."

"That bad a day?"

Franklin just shook his head and left her in peace. It was only when he opened the door to his little office that he remembered the mystery parcel that had arrived with the post that morning. It sat on his desk, enticing and demanding his attention, too tempting to resist for even a moment. It was wrapped in brown paper and string - a pleasantly antiquated form of dressing, thought Franklin. The address was written in beautiful, ornate calligraphy; such a shame, he sighed, that calligraphy had died an unceremonious death. The package was heavy, clearly a book of some sort. Who did he know who would send him a gift out of the blue? Who did he know who had mastered such handsome penmanship?

With a pair of scissors, Franklin cut the strings and carefully opened the package at one end - such ravishing wrapping needed to be treated respectfully. He slid the book out into his hand.

There was no detail on the cover. It was plain and bound in a grayish white leather that was oddly loose. The book was hefty and expensive looking, with gold leaf along the edge of the pages, he turned it over in his hands and spied something unusual on the back; a dark round circle with a little raised dimple on it. He leaned in closer to see what it was. Tiny hairs surrounded it, tiny hairs which sprung from pores.

Franklin released a roar of terror and dropped the book to the floor. It was a nipple - the book was bound in human skin.

5.

Rowan had never ventured to the top floor of her building, and there was a certain thrill in doing so, like when she and her sister were little girls and her father would open up the attic and the pair of them would be amazed that their house contained an entire, secret room that they barely knew about.

The narrow staircase twisted upwards from the landing and stopped abruptly when it met the door of her upstairs neighbour. She knocked on it and was surprised that instead of the door opening, a voice called out for her to let herself in. What kind of person just invited a complete stranger into their home?

A rather odd one, she concluded upon opening the door. The man who lay on the bed, softly strumming away at an acoustic guitar, wore nothing but a pair of boxer shorts. His long blonde hair hung like a mane of curls about his strikingly angular face. His torso, as Rowan was quick to note, was toned and bronzed - she hated the flurry of excitement it gave her, for this man was clearly a vain idiot.

"Hi," Rowan began. "I'm from the flat downstairs. I just called Mr Shaw because my ceiling is leaking and he said you need to change the bucket up here."

The young man just winked at her and clambered off the bed. His flat was nearly identical to hers but had been painted a royal blue. She watched her neighbour pad barefoot across the carpet to the kitchen area where he swiftly emptied the overflowing bucket of water into the sink. The rain had stopped falling outside but it still fell in drops through the roof.

"Mr Shaw really has to do something about this," said Rowan.

The man just shrugged his naked shoulders. "Makes no odds to me, as long as I have a roof over my head then I have a home."

"But you won't have a roof over your head. It'll all come crashing down eventually."

The man seemed to ponder this for a moment. "Then I was never meant to have a roof to begin with."

An awkward pause filled the room and Rowan once again found herself gazing at her neighbour's torso. "So," she blurted suddenly, "I like the colour of your walls."

"I like the colour of your skin," he said with a grin and a wink before seating himself on the edge of his bed and returning to his guitar. "Ooooh," he sang, seemingly without a care for his own dignity. "Hot Chocolate Girl..." Rowan remained unmoved by the spontaneous song, so he repeated the refrain. "See, that's what I do," he said. "I write whatever I see. The whole world moves me to create, you know, it's just like a series of energies we take from the world - if it's food or drink, or like... nature. Sex even. It just fills me up and I start to create - beauty, that is the greatest inspiration of them all; all the greatest art, the truly profound world of the great masters is all about beauty."

Rowan thought about her own favourite work of art, Picasso's Guernica, but was in no mood to prolong a conversation with this faintly nauseating man who was clearly desperate to wrench a compliment from her.

"I'm kind of a free-wheeling drifter, you know - I'm a poet and musician. I'm kind of like a leaf on the breeze, just going wherever the wind takes me."

"I work for an undertaker." Rowan deadpanned, enjoying the sound of her words crushing his lofty nonsense beneath their weight.

"Oh. I see," the man seemed suddenly self-conscious as if only now aware of just how idiotic he must sound. He stood up and threw a dressing gown around his shoulders. "I don't suppose you work for that guy who solved that murder do you?"

Rowan hated this question, but it was one she was confronted with at an increasing rate. Not only was she expected to deny that she did, but the truth was that she had played a much larger role in capturing the culprit than Franklin had, and yet she could never brag or enjoy that fact. "No," she said. "I think that was just a rumour."

"My name's Jude, by the way. Jude Tyndale," he said as he held his hand out to her. Rowan shook it and introduced herself.

"How long have you lived up here?" she asked.

"Just over a week. I tend to keep to myself mostly, but you're welcome up here anytime you like. I brew my own cider," he said with a nod to an elaborate set up of huge glass bottles and tubes in his kitchen. "You're welcome to try some once this batch is done, or if you want to come here and just listen to my music sometime all you have…"

"…No thanks. I'll be fine,"

"Or if you want to see some of my paintings. I'm working on a portfolio of nudes at the moment"

"No. That won't happen either. Just keep your bucket empty and try not to play that guitar too late into the night."

"I write my poetry at night."

"Great. Good for you."

After exchanging phone numbers, in precaution of a similar event occurring again, Rowan left her neighbour and immediately heard him strumming away and singing "Ooooh, Hot Chocolate Girl."

Back in her flat, she arrived just in time to spot the light vanishing from the screen of her mobile, indicating that she had missed a call. She had in fact missed five calls, all from Franklin, and a text message.

"Please get here now. I need you."

She was out the door with her bike in an instant.

6.

Franklin didn't know much about forensics, but he knew enough not to allow any more of his fingerprints to contaminate an investigation. From the steel walled room in which he and Rowan worked on the bodies, which had been morbidly dubbed, "The Death Chamber," Franklin retrieved a pair of latex gloves which he stretched over his trembling hands before placing the gruesome object on his desk.

Whoever had sent this to him was clearly sending not just a book, but a very strong message along with it too. The police would be here to take it away in no time, so as horrible a task as it may be, he would have to record its contents before it was gone. With a cold, white hand, he flipped open the cover of the book where the words, "A gift for Franklin Gallow, from an admirer." were written in that same studied hand. He took a photograph of the page and turned to the next one.

This page bore the words "The Necropolis" in bold letters at the top, followed by a body of text:

"The necropolis sleeps tonight,
A debt of blood is owed.
I wait in every quiet house,
Down every darkened road.
Blood of thousands run the streets,
A promise here is made.
I will not stop nor be restrained,
Until the debt is paid."

Franklin clicked his phone camera and tried not to let the words sink in. This was more than a simple warning. This was a promise.

The following pages were reproductions of illustrations he had seen before. One was a drawing of a black slave with his mouth bound with an iron bit. Another was a diagram of a slave ship, the likes of which once left Bristol for Africa. The diagram bore the figures of countless hundreds of slaves crammed within the hull. A more modern photograph was of the statue of Edward Colston that stood upon St. Augustine's Parade in the centre of the city - tucked away far enough from the waterfront as to go unnoticed by most, but there all the same. The man had been a wealthy merchant and a generous benefactor to the city, but he had made his money through the trade of human beings from Africa. Solemnly his statue stared out of the page and into Franklin's camera. Try as he might not to speculate, it was impossible not to imagine how all these images were fitting together - the only true question was what in the world did it have to do with him?

The next page was another modern photograph but reproduced in black and white. It showed a man, probably not much more advanced in years than Franklin's own forty, leaving the front door of his Georgian townhouse; one of the ornate pastel coloured ones on Redcliffe Parade that overlooked the city from high above the waterway. The man seemed oblivious to the fact that his photograph was being taken. The next page showed the man crossing Pero's Bridge on the harbourside. This time he was dressed in a different suit, and again seemed unaware that he was being watched. Someone must have been following him for a while.

Next came a drawing etched in pencil and with some skill. It showed the huge horns of Pero's Bridge rising like trumpets at either side of a man's body, an arrow piercing through one of his eyes. After that, the pages were empty.

It had been about twenty minutes since he had last called Rowan, insisting that she came over. Poor Meredy was not made for this kind of stuff and Rowan would know better than he what to do next. He had rang his brother Edison immediately afterwards. His brother was a policeman and he would rather deal directly with him than an anonymous officer who would no doubt look upon his involvement in yet another murder with alarmed suspicion.

Rowan arrived first. Her Brompton bike was carried under her arm in a pretzel of metal and her helmet still rested on her head. "What's happened?"

Franklin just closed the book so she could see its binding. "Don't touch it," he warned.

"Is that? It looks like human skin."

Franklin turned the book over so she could see the nipple on the back. "I think it's fair to say it is. It came through the post this morning."

"Who sent it? Who would send something like that?"

"Someone who wants to give me a scare, I'd imagine. Did a bloody good job of it, too."

"Have you called the police?"

"Edison's on his way."

Rowan took a step closer to the book. "Can I see inside?"

"I've taken photographs of all the pages. I don't think we should touch it unless we really have to."

Rowan nodded in agreement. It was strange. The pair of them had touched countless bodies through their work, to the extent that the sight of a corpse no longer troubled either one - but this book, this intentionally sinister tome was something far beyond what they had encountered before. This death had been for them.

The pair agreed that the best place to store the book before Edison's arrival was in the refrigerated unit in the death chamber. It was designed to keep bodies from decomposing in the funeral home and it would certainly protect the binding until the police came to collect it. Once it was stored away, Rowan followed Franklin to his office where he brought the images up onto his computer. Rowan read the poem aloud as she downloaded the images onto her phone. "What's the necropolis?" she asked.

"It's an old, old word for a cemetery. It's Greek, I think," said Franklin. "Some graveyards still use the term - it means city of the dead."

"Do you think the writer means Bristol? A city of the dead?"

"I have no idea."

"This is really bad," said Rowan as she clicked through the photographs of the man in the suit.

"I know. What's taking Edison so long?"

"No." Rowan had come to rest on the drawing of the body on the bridge. "I was at Pero's bridge this morning. This is where the murder happened."

"I know, it's from the killer for sure - he must have taken it just before he killed the man."

"I know that, but think about the rest of it too. The Colston statue. That bastard's got streets and pubs and schools named after him. Why do you think people are so furious about that?"

"Because he was a slave trader." Franklin said. He was in no mood for a history lesson.

"Of course, but look at the bridge. Do you know why it's called Pero's bridge?"

Yes," Franklin nodded. "He was an African slave, he lived in what's now the Georgian House Museum."

"And look," Rowan clicked through to the photograph of the man leaving his town house. "Redcliffe Parade. Those buildings were constructed with money earned from slave labour. This murder, and this book isn't just a statement - it's a manifesto. The poem says a debt of blood has to be paid - here it is. Whoever sent this book wants to take revenge on the city for its past."

Franklin narrowed his eyes incredulously at Rowan but pondered what she had said nonetheless. "Bloody hell," he concluded. "You're right."

It took almost a full hour between Edison receiving the call and arriving at the funeral home. He was a couple of years senior to Franklin but his white hair and years of smoking made him appear considerably older. Today he looked haggard.

"Sorry it took so long, it's been a busy day."

"Right," Franklin huffed. "I tell you I got sent a book covered in the skin of a dead person and you take your time."

"It's just a prank Frank, and yes, it has been a busy day. Unless you haven't heard somebody was murdered in the middle of the city this morning."

"It's not a prank. Follow me and put on some gloves in the death chamber."

Edison, having grown up in this very house, when the funeral business belonged to their father, showed none of the unease most did when entering the room. They had been eight and ten when they had first seen a body - a peaceful looking old man dressed in a suit in an open coffin, and steadily over the months and years the coming and goings of corpses in their house became as normal as the daily milk delivery. Death for them bore no secrets. Edison himself tapped in the password to the lock on the door, 1-7-7-6.

Franklin opened the refrigerated unit and slid the book from the top shelf. He handed it to his brother who turned it cautiously over in his hands. "It looks so real," he marvelled.

"That's because it is real."

Rowan, who had been waiting patiently, interrupted, "We think it's a manifesto. It talks about taking revenge on the city, for the slave years."

"What's a necropolis?" Edison asked. Franklin told him. It was not until he turned to the image of the man leaving his house that Edison responded. "That's the man. Spencer Nordstrom. I've been with his family all day."

Franklin felt a little pang of guilt for being so irked with his brother earlier. "Turn the page."

The moment Edison saw the drawing of the body on the bridge, he slammed the book shut and pulled out his phone. "Rhonda, this is Edison. I'm going to need you to organise a forensics team to come to Gallow & Sons Funeral Home in Bedminster… yes, he is my brother… No he didn't solve that murder. Frank, did you keep hold of the packaging this arrived in?"

Franklin nodded. "Paper and there was a bit of string too."

"Good, we can get DNA from where he licked the stamp. What do you mean stamps are self-adhesive now?" He almost bellowed down the phone. He hung up. "I need a drink. How long is this day going to go on for?" He pulled an electronic cigarette from his pocket and drew from it.

"Can you not do that in here please? It's a sterile environment, you can't smoke in here!" Franklin immediately snapped.

"It's not smoke, it's vapour."

"I don't care what it is, just don't do it in here."

Edison just rolled his eyes childishly as he returned the tiny, black clarinet like stick to his jacket. "What I don't understand though, is what any of this has to do with you? Why send your manifesto to a funeral director? Why not us?"

"Maybe he wants to get caught and has heard I'm more likely to catch him than the police…" Franklin sneered.

"Who actually caught that murderer last time around. Was it you in your tiny little Smart car, or the dozens of police with their proper cars and helicopters?"

"Please. You would still be trying to catch him if it weren't for me," Franklin turned pleadingly to his assistant. "Rowan, tell him!"

Rowan just stared appalled at the two brothers. "You're unbelievable."

"I know!' said Franklin.

"I meant the pair of you. You should both be ashamed of yourselves - this isn't the time for stupid sibling rivalry and I am not your mother!"

The two brothers apologized and waited in stony silence in the death chamber until they could hear the approach of police sirens. All the while Rowan quietly relived that day in the car, the trapped quarry of a madman intent on killing her, peacefully assured that it was she who brought him to justice.

7.

Later that day Rowan sent a text to her friend Lise and invited her over. It had been a long time since they had last met but she knew her teenage friend would be in want of company in a manner that only she could relate to.

The pair had met earlier in the year when Rowan and Franklin had been working on the funeral of Lise's older brother, Henrick. At the time it had only been Rowan who had harboured doubts that the young man's death had been due to suicide, until this sixteen year old girl, with plaits in her hair, had timidly confided that she too believed it had been murder.

The plaits were gone now, replaced with a boyish, messy Peter Pan cut - the kind of radical departure from the norm that Rowan had considered in the months after her own sister had been killed. A physical manifestation of the end of the life she had once known. Lise sat on the edge of the bed and sipped on a glass of wine.

"I know it shouldn't get to me," she said, with an attractive Danish lilt to her words, "but it always will. I can't stop thinking about that man and how his family must be feeling tonight. I hope he didn't have any kids."

"He didn't," Rowan replied. "I mean… on the internet they're speculating about who he might have been." She was not about to let on how much she knew about the case already or how Franklin had been purposefully drawn into it. Murder was already the unlikely tie that bound each of them together, the murder of a sibling, no less; this poor girl did not have to know just how close murder still was.

"So tell me about this… cult again," Lise asked with a slight smile as she finished off her glass and helped herself to another one.

"It's not a cult. It's a church and I'm just trying it out. They meet every other Friday and I thought I'd just give it a try. It feels right, you know. Like I'm supposed to be doing this." Lise did not respond. "A couple of weeks ago, I was just sorting out some of my things, I hadn't unpacked properly after I'd moved in and went through the last of my bags and I found these jeans. They were the jeans I'd been wearing on the day I got kidnapped by... that man. I had thrown out the t-shirt because it was caked in blood - his blood - but I had kept the jeans I wore as a kind of memento of my survival, plus my bum looks really good in them. I'd also been wearing them the day before, when this woman handed me a leaflet about a church in Bristol - not like a regular church, but one that offers actual proof of life after death."

Lise shook her head. "It still sounds like a cult to me." She read aloud from the pamphlet: "A Bridge to Another World Church Ministries of Spiritualism. ABTAW Church offers hope and peace to those who have lost loved ones. Spiritualist mediums from around the world offer their services for free to allow YOU to reach out to the dear departed on that heavenly plain. They await some company as we await yours." Lise looked up after reading. "This sounds really dangerous, Rowan."

Rowan shrugged her shoulders. "It could very well be, and I know I must sound as if I've lost my mind but I promise you I'll be safe. I need to see what it's about, just this once, and if it's a load of bollocks then that'll be it."

"So why are you even telling me about it then?"

"Because... I thought it would be best for somebody to know where I was going tonight. In case anything does happen."

Lise raised a cynical eyebrow. "So the thought has crossed your mind that they could be dangerous then?"

Rowan snatched the pamphlet back from her friend. "I just know the importance of being careful - more so now than ever."

"Well okay then, but promise that as soon as they try and get you to drink a load of mysterious punch, you get out of there at once."

Rowan agreed. She knew Lise would have doubts about ABTAW but was certain she would at least understand. The four years between them in age would usually seem vast at sixteen and twenty, but nothing forces you to grow up faster than the murder of an older sibling, and often Lise seemed like the more level-headed and mature of the two, possibly because her parents were themselves far more stable than hers.

"What do you think about death?" Rowan asked her bluntly.

"Death, or the afterlife?" Lise was quick to clarify.

"The afterlife, I suppose."

"Well. I have no reason to believe in it. There is not a single shred of evidence supporting the theory that we have a soul or that we are anything other than walking bags of chemicals. But I hope that's not what it's like - I really hope there is something more, forever is an awfully long time to be dead and I just want to believe that somewhere out there, Henrick is still around and remembering all of us."

It was not uncommon for Rowan and Lise to slip easily into these discussions and Rowan was certain that this was not the first time Lise had pondered the answer to life's greatest mystery.

"That's all I hope for too,"

"However," Lise went on, "I think the church you're going to sounds like a massive con and there will be some way that they will try and swindle you. People like that make me feel sick with rage."

With a hug and a tenderly sweet kiss to the cheek, Lise left Rowan soon afterwards. She had promised her parents she would be home before eight and promises to grieving parents about your whereabouts were not to be taken lightly. Rowan helped herself to a final half-glass of wine and left for the bus. Ordinarily she would have cycled but her own promise to her parents had been never to do so once it had turned dark.

The bus was unexpectedly on time and only half full. She took a seat by herself and slipped her earphones in. Some girls were singing drunkenly at the back and she was in no mood to enjoy their bleary cover of "Call Me Maybe." Sometimes she listened to music of her own but in recent years she had favoured the spoken word - audiobooks and podcasts on every subject imaginable. She did not always understand or even listen to what was being said but there was comfort in that private conversation in her head that staved away the loneliness and more desperate of her thoughts.

There was however only so much listening to words could achieve, and very soon Rowan was musing over Lise's hope of an afterlife. How fundamental it was to the human experience to try and make peace with the concept of oblivion - scores upon scores of religions were founded upon that existential panic that strikes at three in the morning, when the thought that death is unstoppable and will claim every life in the world, that only time keeps it at bay. How strange to think that the lives of everyone around her, everyone she had met and would ever meet, would not only die but had inner lives every bit as rich and profound as her own.

The bus pulled to a stop at the midway point of Whiteladies Road where an old, once abandoned art deco cinema had been transformed into a theatre space for local artists. It was here that ABTAW met. Stepping from the bus Rowan looked up at the imposing tower before her. Part of her knew how stupid and possibly dangerous this entire exploit was, but an even larger part had to see what any of this could mean. Maybe in some other realm, where such things are possible, her older sister - now a full year younger than her - was fixing things behind the scenes, invisibly pulling strings to drive her on to this moment and place in time. Maybe this would be the night when she could reach across the chasm between the living and the dead and hear proof that something lived on beyond our bodies.

She checked the pamphlet once more, nervously certain that she had misjudged the night or the hour or the building. Ahead of her she could see a couple of people propping open the doors and welcoming a handful of friends with hugs and well wishes. They looked sane enough.

The time had come.

8

"I don't care what anybody says. It isn't the same," Edison complained as he puffed on his electric cigarette. "Where's the stinging eyes or that burning sensation in the throat and nose? Do you know who's to blame for all of this? The political correct brigade and those… health and safety people. Do you know they're trying to stop us doing this now? Can't even have fake cigarettes anymore. I reckon they know everyone's having more fun than them and want to see it stopped."

Franklin was mostly ignoring his brother's protestations. Every Friday night, with the exception of their work getting in the way, he and Edison met in the Tobacco Factory - a bar that accompanied a theatre and drew the kind of hip-yet-poor-yet-arty crowd the south of the city had become renowned for. "Do we have to discuss this every week Edison? At least we don't have to sit outside in the cold and rain anymore."

"That's true, it's just… enough is enough, when are we going to fight back against these fascists? In 1930's Germany it started with book burning, soon these little Hitlers will have outlawed everything we enjoy."

"Yes, Edison, you really are as heroic as the German Resistance movement, and yet where's your medal?" Franklin was tired of this conversation. "So are we just going to ignore what happened today? The book and that man on the bridge?"

"I was kind of hoping that we could," said Edison. The pub was crowded but the pair had found a table in the corner. Even so, Edison seemed a little wary about discussing such sensitive matters in semi-privacy. "Did you know his parents still live in the city - they're the ones who took it worst of all. His wife… she was sad but not half as much as you might expect."

"Does that mean that she's a suspect?"

"That is privileged information, Frank and you know it."

"Hey, I didn't ask to be involved, but guess what? I am."

Edison finished off the last of his beer with a resounding belch. "Well, at this point anybody who's ever met him is a potential suspect as we have no leads - except for that book. Forensics are going over every page but it could take a while - I can't imagine that whoever sent it wouldn't have known how to cover his tracks."

"Will I be directing the funeral? I could see what I can get out of his wife," Franklin suggested.

"You know it's not up to me. I can only suggest you to them but they get to choose their funeral home themselves. I really don't think it's her though - she's one of those glamour wives, you know. Never worked a day except on her suntan; not the type I'd expect to be proficient with a crossbow."

"CCTV?"

"I've heard nothing about it so far. They'll have hours of footage to get through. We still don't know exactly when Spencer Nordstrom died."

"How about the other murder?" Franklin asked.

"What other murder?"

"The book, Edison. The killer must have taken a huge strip of skin from some poor person and I'm pretty sure they couldn't have done it without killing them."

Edison shook his head. "I hadn't even thought of that. Crap. This whole thing just looks like a huge, scary mess."

Franklin bought two more pints and returned to the table. "Anthropodermic bibliopegy," he declared as he sat across from his brother.

"Pardon?"

"It's the process of binding books in human skin. It was never common but it happened a few times in the UK - mainly in Bristol, did you know?"

Edison just shook his head.

"I looked into it last year. One of my clients had stipulated in his will that he wanted the family bible bound in his own skin. There's no specific law saying it's illegal but the laws around the sanctity of the corpse pretty much made it impossible. There's a book bound in human skin in the M-Shed Museum."

"Really? Is it on display?"

Franklin nodded from behind his pint of cider. "Isn't anywhere near as fresh as the one that came in the post, and it's properly tanned, to last like leather. It was from a hanged man called John Horwood - he was sentenced to death for murder but what he had done seemed far from premeditated. He saw his ex girlfriend with another man and was so furious that he threw a stone at her and struck her on the head. She was fine for a couple of days but died of aneurism a while afterwards. The notes on his case were bound in his skin and his skeleton was in a cupboard at Bristol University up until a few years ago - still with the noose that killed him around his neck. He was given a proper burial in about 2012 I think."

"How do you know all this?" asked Edison, dumbfounded by his brother's knowledge of all things morbid.

"Because some of us actually go to museums and read books."

"So where's the body that goes with the skin?"

"That's your job to find out, not mine. I'm pretty sure I would have noticed if I'd worked on a body with a square foot of skin missing from his torso though."

Edison shuddered at the thought of it.

"Talking of murder," Franklin went on. "Ruby Kaplan - Rowan's sister. People are still looking for her killer aren't they?"

Edison eyed his brother cautiously. "The case is still officially open, yes."

"That's not what I asked. Is anybody actually doing anything?"

"I've told you, Frank. We already know who killed her, it was her dad."

Franklin shook his head irritably. "No, you said the police haven't been able to verify his whereabouts on the night she was killed and that he has changed his story. You don't know he did it. I don't believe it's him - what kind of father would do that to his own daughter?"

"There speaks a man who hasn't worked as a policeman for the past twenty years. I've seen my fair share of subhuman parents who would kill their babies for a can of cider."

"It has to be someone else. I don't believe it - he sounds like a good man."

"Now you're just being naive."

"He's a… pharmacist…" Franklin was certain that wasn't much of an argument.

"More than most," Edison replied, "you should know that killers can come from anywhere - and they do come from everywhere. Murder knows no boundaries of class - and you are sounding like a bit of a snob."

Franklin sank in his chair. How he despised it when his brother was right. "Anyway, Rowan is settling into her new place nicely, so she's not even living with him anymore."

"And did you help her find her new place?"

"I upped her pay and lent her some money. Everywhere's so bloody expensive."

"So you had your doubts too then?" Edison asked, "About her dad?"

Franklin met his brother's eyes. "If you tell me that my friend may be in trouble, then I have to do what I can to help."

"And she still doesn't know?"

"I don't know how to tell her. It's driving me barmy knowing what I know. Every time she talks about visiting her parents I have this snap of pain in my belly - guilt for knowing more than I should."

"Well, you'll just have to live with that, Frank. I'm sorry but if Oscar Kaplan knows that he is the prime suspect in the murder of his daughter then the whole case could go to shit. Trust me, we're going to find something to get him on. It just takes time."

Oscar Kaplan. It was only in that moment that Franklin realized he had been defending a man he had neither met nor knew the name of.

"It's not going to be like last time," Edison continued. "I'm not going to be doubting you this time around - if you see anything or something weird comes through the post, you tell me at once. I'm letting you in on more than I should, but only because I don't want to mess things up again. That third guy in the spring…"

"…Ben Tramor. The hit and run?"

"Yeah him. I think about him a lot - if I'd believed you I might've been able to put the pieces in order quicker. Maybe I could have saved him."

"Maybe," Franklin said bluntly. "But it's not your fault he died. You didn't kill him."

"I know, but I could have done more." This was the time of the evening where alcohol got the better of Edison and he either turned angry or maudlin. He had clearly chosen the latter.

"Well it's nice to know I have you on my side this time around," Franklin offered with a gentle pat to his brother's shoulder. "Anything I see or hear, I'll share with you. Scouts honour."

"Maybe this is all that will happen. Maybe it's all over and the killer's got his revenge already."

"Maybe," Franklin said, but neither brother for a moment believed it to be true.

9.

There were probably fewer than fifty people in the auditorium of the cinema. Where the screen had once been, a small stage had been erected upon which a man with a microphone stood.

Rowan had a clear idea of what she imagined their spiritual medium would look like. She had seen her as grey and wispy of hair, with a flowing, flowery dress and pale, ancient skin - someone who could reach out to the afterworld as very soon she would be among its population. Instead, the man on the stage could not have been much more than thirty, with neat dark hair and a clean-shaven boyish face. Far from the old crone she had imagined, this man looked vibrant and fun - kind of hot, thought Rowan.

He wore jeans and an untucked shirt and as he paced about the stage, Rowan caught glimpses of lime green socks. He was likable in an approachable camp way with a singsong Welsh accent. Rowan quickly warmed to him as he strolled back and fourth before the audience of mostly old, white women who were no doubt there to hear from their husbands.

"Is there a Rose here?" The man, Tegwyn Jones, asked the assembled crowd who swapped expectant glances. "No? I'm hearing Rose. Not to worry, I'll come back to that one."

The woman who had introduced him, the Bristol minister of ABTAW, had informed them that Tegwyn Jones was one of the most respected in all of Europe. He had just returned from a tour of America where he had sold out mega-churches. "We are," she informed the sparse audience, "exceptionally lucky to have him in our midst this evening."

Rowan was surprised to find that snacks and drinks had been laid out in the lobby of the cinema. She helped herself to a paper plate of mini pizzas and vegetarian sausage rolls and tried her best not to be noticed as the congregation filed into the auditorium. The minister had offered her a glass of sparkling wine but she declined - not for fear of it being laced with poison, but because she had already had two and a half glasses earlier and wanted a level head for the proceedings - plus she really didn't want to have to be getting up to pee every twenty minutes.

The group had been led in a brief prayer, the words had been projected from the old cinema booth onto what was now a bare wall. The rest of the congregation seemed to require no such help. There was no mention of God or of Jesus, or even of heaven. Just the concept of the "Universal Good" watching over us from the sweet hereafter. Rowan liked that idea.

"I want to hear from an Emily," Tegwyn Jones continued as he wiped his brow with a handkerchief. The stage lights bounced fiercely from his forehead.

"My sister is called Emily!" a woman exclaimed as she leapt to her feet. Rowan was in the back row and could see only the back of her white hair.

"What's your name, sweetheart?"

"I'm Milly."

"And when did your sister pass on to the hereafter?"

"Oh!" the woman exclaimed. "She's not dead. She's in Keynsham."

There was a light smattering of gentle laughter among the crowd.

"Sweetheart, I don't think this one's for you, but give my love to your sister."

The woman sat down, seemingly unabashed by her misunderstanding.

"I've got another voice here…" Tegwyn leant into his shoulder as if being whispered to by an invisible presence. "He's a man, he died an old man but he's showing me himself as a young man. He's wearing a suit with a flower in his lapel… he's laughing!"

Rowan looked at the empty space beside the medium, not allowing herself to believe that there could be an invisible man standing in the shadows.

"It's his wedding day," Tegwyn continued. "He was so proud to stand beside his bride this day. He's saying she was the most beautiful bride in all of Bristol. He'd just come home from the war… John. That's his name."

A shriek erupted from the audience and another woman found her way to her feet. She swayed uneasily upon them. "John? Is that you?"

"What's your name, Petal?" Tegwyn asked into the microphone.

"Lydia. Oh John - I knew you'd come back to me!"

"That's the one. He says he's so pleased to see you. Did you know that he still drops by to see you from time to time? He has never stopped loving you."

The woman was trying her best to speak through her tears. Her shoulders trembled as her friend, seated beside her held her hand. "I knew you were near. Please tell him that I miss him every single day - sometimes it feels like I can't go on without him!"

A wide smile spread across the medium's face. "I don't mean to sound insensitive, but John is laughing right now. What a laugh that man has! He's laughing because he says he never left you. He might have passed to the hereafter, but he has always been with you. He tells me that you need to stop grieving for him and to get on with your life. He wants you to enjoy the time you have by yourself and he is so proud of how you have coped. He will wait for you and one day, when your time has come you and he will be together forever."

Rowan wiped the tears from her eyes but more came to replace them.

"Do you have a message for him?" asked the medium.

"Tell him I love him," she wept.

"He says he knows, and he loves you too. There, he's gone now - the walls between our worlds can only last for a little while."

The elderly woman sat down and fell into an embrace from the woman beside her.

"I'm still hearing from someone called Rose? Nobody? No it's not a flower, it's a plant, a tree." There was silence. The audience needed more. "I have another name, oh, it's so hard to get a hold of it. The walls are weak and she's showing me symbols, some... they look like rocks... no, stones. Precious stones. Bright vivid red... They look like rubies."

Rowan threw a hand to her face to stifle a shriek.

"Ruby. That was her name - and I'm seeing her now... big wide smile, perfect teeth. She has dark hair and dark skin and this red woven into her hair. She's showing me this ring she wore on her finger - there's a big ruby on that too. That was her joke, it was a big old plastic one like you'd get in a Christmas cracker but she wore it everyday."

Rowan was trembling in her seat. From the corner of her mouth a bead of saliva began to drip. She wiped it away. This had to be a dream. Wake up Rowan!

"She has a message for her sister. She's pointing her out to me as she's here in the crowd." Tegwyn leant into the invisible person behind him. "Rowan. Rowan Kaplan, she's telling you not to be afraid."

"Oh god!" Rowan screamed as she slowly rose from her seat. Her legs were trembling so much she did not know if they could hold her weight.

"Are you Rowan Kaplan?"

"Y-Yes, I am." The whole audience gasped.

"Ruby loves you, Rowan. She's telling me that she always loved you. They never caught her murderer did they?"

Another gasp from the audience. Rowan could only manage to nod her head.

"Oh you poor little cupcake. She says it doesn't matter who killed her and you need to stop thinking about it. She's happy where she is and if she could live that night again then she wouldn't change a single thing about it. She just wants you to let it go and to be strong. She is always by your side and she is always in your heart."

Rowan was openly sobbing now. Huge tears rolled down her cheeks and her breathing came in heaves. Someone was beside her - the minister who had introduced the medium. She put her arms across her back to steady her and moved a microphone into her face. "I miss you Ruby," was all she could manage in her grief.

"I am so sorry for your loss, petal," Tegwyn said. "She says that you should never miss her though. She says you have a special song, she likes to play it for you whenever she can, DownTown, by Petula Clark. You know it, don't you?"

Rowan gasped and filled her lungs with air. Yes, she knew the song. It had been the one Ruby had been rehearsing on the night she was murdered.

"I'll take that as a yes, then." There was a peel of kind, gentle laughter. "She says that whenever you feel sad, you must listen to that song and think of her. She is always with you when you hear that music. She loves you so much but you must stop trying to unravel her mystery - it doesn't matter."

"It matters to me!" Rowan suddenly blurted out. Her voice echoed throughout the auditorium, the silence which followed it was icy. "Who killed you, Ruby?"

"I'm sorry," Tegwyn said. "The curtain has drawn, the wall is no longer thin. She's gone."

Rowan fell back into her seat. The medium excused himself from the stage and the audience burst into spontaneous applause. The woman beside her offered her a tissue; she wiped her eyes and nose with it.

"I should have warned you," the woman said. "It can be brutal the first time you make contact. It's not always what you'd expect and sometimes it can be quite disturbing."

Rowan simply shook her head. "No. It was wonderful. Do you know what this means?"

The woman stroked her hair lightly. "Yes, I do."

"Ruby lives on… we all live on."

"I know."

Rowan had never been one for physical affection but the hug that this stranger gave her was the most fulfilling and wonderful she had known in years. Into her shoulder she wept and let the tears keep flowing until it felt as if there was simply no more left. Patiently the minister waited and it was only when the house lights were raised in the auditorium that Rowan realized that she was expected to leave.

"I expect I can count on you next time, can I?" the woman smiled affectionately. "We have a special Halloween congregation this month too."

"Of course," Rowan beamed back at her.

As she left the old cinema she felt so light that a soft breeze could have sent her soaring. It all seemed like a dream - a wonderful dream but one that she wanted to hold onto for as long as she could. The night felt full of enchantment, as if suddenly she had discovered that magic really did exist in the world.

As the bus took her back to Stokes Croft, Rowan did not listen to the podcast she was half way through, instead she scrolled through to the music and played the Petula Clark song that held her sister's spirit. She closed her eyes and was certain that she could feel the sister she loved and missed so much, seated beside her as she made her journey home.

10.

John MacGregor did not believe he would ever die. Rationally he knew this to be nonsense - every living thing must die eventually, tens of thousands of people died every day with every tick of the clock. He had even had a woman die on his bus once. She had been old and riding to the supermarket one Wednesday afternoon. She stood up as the bus reached her stop, clutched her chest and fell like a marionette that had had its strings cut.

Like all people who witness death, he still thought of that woman - such a public, undignified place to die, and yet he would not allow himself to believe that the same would ever happen to him. It was simply too ghastly, somebody would sort the whole sorry business out in the future, that was how he made it through the day.

As a child, his first experience of death was that of a pet - his small, ginger cat named Tiger who was hit by a car and died a couple of days later while having surgery. When he had cried - and he had cried a lot for his cat, it wasn't just the realisation that he would never see him again, but the terror of nobody being able to prevent it - his mum and dad who looked after him with studied diligence could not save him, nor the vets and their clever operations. A greater, darker force lived in the world that stole life and one day it would come for him. So he chose not to believe it - to lock away that fear and to hope that he would grow as old as time and live forever.

Like most boys, John MacGregor had liked toy vehicles. Not just cars, but trains, tractors, trucks, anything that could be pushed along the carpet of his bedroom floor, but above all, he liked buses. Unlike most, this odd fascination did not fade with age nor did his ambition to drive them. At twenty-one he had become fully licensed and operating throughout Bristol. The politics of pay and unionising were frustrations, as were the passengers who seemed convinced that he was personally responsible for every fare rise and late arrival throughout the line, but when he was on the road, behind that big wheel and panorama of glass, he was where he belonged - no longer a husband or father, just a boy in his bedroom with simple dreams of an easy, honest life.

Weekend nights always proved to be the most troublesome. The late shift involved a long route that ran well into the morning and the passengers themselves were the most difficult. .Rarely had they the right money, often they had none at all. Rude and drunk and quick to temper - or to vomit all over the seats, it was a rowdy, unpleasant route that was meted out across the bus drivers so that none would experience more than one such evening a fortnight.

One of the university campuses was his penultimate stop and the one which haemorrhaged most of his passengers and this evening was no different. They had been mostly well behaved with the worst of their shouty, sweary conflicts between each other. A student girl had called him handsome as she filed past and he pretended not to hear her - almost fifty but he could still turn heads he reminded himself.

There was only one passenger left for the final stop, a curious looking man in fancy dress, no doubt returning from a party in the city to his home in Fishponds - a self-contained neighbourhood in the north of Bristol. He spied him in the rearview mirror and called: "Bit early for Halloween isn't it, something to do with fresher's week?"

The man did not respond. It was quite possible he had fallen asleep, which was not rare on these late journeys. Not to worry, he would retrace his route soon and drop him off at his stop on the way back to the city. It was hard to tell as the man wore a red beard and a pirate's tricorn hat that obscured his eyes. Perhaps, thought John MacGregor, this man did not speak English. Fishponds was becoming increasingly international as gentrification of inner city areas pushed new immigrants farther away from their once traditional areas of St Pauls and Stokes Croft. He would not pursue the matter further.

As the bus pulled out onto Fishponds Highstreet, John MacGregor felt a tremendous blow strike the back of his head. The man had punched him. Utterly perplexed and instantly terrified of a violent confrontation, he crushed the brake pedal and spun his head around - the pirate was still in his seat, gazing out of the window. His hand went to the back of his skull, where to his horror, he felt the spindle of something narrow and firm gorged into his bald scalp. His eyes were growing bleary and red, his face suddenly felt wet. When he saw himself in the reflection of the window in front of him, he watched in a state of confused madness as blood began bubbling and cascading down his face from an arrowhead that had passed through his temple.

John Macgregor's death came quickly after that. He fell forwards into the steering wheel over which the last of his blood poured. He was not alive by the time the pirate rose from his seat, so he would not have known what his killer did to his tooth. The murderer released the close mechanism of the door and slipped away into the quiet, dark night.

John MacGregor's last thoughts had not been of his wife, or his children, and how he would never see them again, they had not even been of the terrible fate that had befallen him. They had been of a little boy, pushing his bus across the carpet of his bedroom - a little boy with all his life ahead of him.

11.

By nine in the morning, news of the murder had spilled over the borders of the West Country and was being given blanket coverage across the nation.

Rowan had noticed the curious spectacle of journalists lining up one at a time to offer to-camera pieces from Pero's Bridge as she cycled past on her way to work. Vans and temporary filming units were bustling for space with one another like angry vultures fighting over the stripped carcass of a fallen animal.

She had heard of the second murder upon waking. She had fallen into the habit of consulting her iPad immediately after her alarm had gone off and the local BBC page was bristling with speculation. Details seemed thin on the ground - she had learned from watching the police drip feed information to the press after Ruby's murder that the way to keep the media interested was to keep the public constantly hungry. Offering them a few crumbs in those all important early days of an investigation was the best way to increase the profile of a crime - to let them dine upon it all at once would leave them sated enough to leave the table altogether. The easiest way to solve a murder was to have the public in a state of famished vigilance.

Rowan spied a tall, spindly woman approaching her with a smile. She instantly seemed familiar and Rowan found herself mentally scrolling through her mobile phonebook, trawling for her identity as she glanced away self-consciously.

"I love your bike," the woman smiled. Her smile was broad and framed by scarlet lipstick, some of which had rubbed off onto her impossibly white teeth.

It was the voice that suddenly launched a name from Rowan's memory. "I know who you are," she gasped. "You're awful."

The woman simply smiled, but her eyes pierced sternly at her from between the curtains of her expensive looking shaggy haircut. "I have been called far, far worse."

"You're that horrible woman who writes articles for the Star, and that blog about immigrants and poor people." She was indeed Ellie Sutton, an inflammatory columnist who had learned that thoughtful articles on social trends were no match for the financial rewards of spitting vitriol in electronic text. On once reading a tirade of hatred on the subject of gay marriage, Rowan found herself signing online petitions to have this dreadful woman banned from speaking at university societies, until she realised to her horror that Ellie Sutton's career only ascended higher with each act of notoriety.

"I aim to give a different slant on the news of the day, aside from the usual liberalism we are used to. I used to live here, did you know? That's why I'm here looking into the murders."

"I honestly couldn't give a flying fuck about what you're here for. Why are you even talking to me?"

"I know all about you, Rowan."

Her words turned Rowan's skin cold, a flashback to the morning when her would-be killer had said the same to her. "I…I'm not Rowan."

"Yes you are," the woman's smile was now contorted into a grimace. "I know all about you and Franklin Gallow. He's your boss, is that right? At the funeral home? I was wondering when you'd make an appearance at one of the crime scenes – it must be terribly hard to keep away after what you went through, and of course your sister."

"I'm sorry, but I don't know who you think I am."

The woman reached into the pocket of her grey blazer and retrieved a business card featuring her face and a nauseating lipstick kiss beside her name and email address. "If you do happen to remember who you are and perhaps wanted to talk about what happened earlier this year, I'm just a message away. I can make it financially rewarding for you, and of course, drum up some publicity regarding your sister. I could make Ruby Kaplan trend on Twitter, I could bring her back to the evening news. In exchange, you could tell your story of how one teenage girl managed to thwart a madman."

"Don't ever use my sister's name again." Rowan hissed. She snatched the card from the woman's fingernails, which had been manicured to the brink of becoming talons, and was fully prepared to tear the card to shreds before her eyes, but instead she acted on impulse and pocketed it before cycling away from the horrible vulture-like creature.

On her way Rowan decided not to mention the encounter to Franklin, aside from him having enough things to fret about, she felt a very real worry that he would contact his brother. The court case had been troubling enough and the very last thing she wanted was to have to relive her attack for an inquest into a potential police leak.

By the time she reached Gallow & Sons Funeral Home, Rowan was surprised to find that Meredy was not in her regular spot behind her desk in the reception. Peering along the corridor which led from it, she instead spied her standing in the open doorway of Franklin's office, from where she could hear the drone of a TV set.

"Oh Rowan, Isn't it terrible?" Meredy exclaimed as she saw her approach.

Rowan just nodded as she pushed past her into the office. There she found not only Franklin, but Peterman - Gallow & Sons other, much less personable, funeral director. All three were transfixed by the rolling news on the wall-mounted television.

"Morning Rowan," Franklin said, his eyes not moving from the screen. "Have you heard?"

"Yes. A bus driver in Fishponds - are they saying that they're linked?"

"Yes," Franklin nodded as he pointed to the screen. "Blackbeard the pirate did it…"

On the screen a police inspector was being interviewed from high upon the Avon Gorge. Over his shoulder the backdrop of the Clifton Suspension Bridge immediately alerted all of the country to exactly what city was in question. He wore a thick, walrus moustache and the heavy bags under his eyes suggested he'd not managed much sleep the night before. "We have very strong evidence that suggests that not only are these two crimes linked, but that there is reason to regard them as a form of terrorism."

On the screen appeared a heavily pixilated image in black and white of a man standing in the aisle of a single-decker bus. He was dressed as a pirate - like a movie version of a pirate - with a hat and buckles and an outrageous beard that tumbled almost as low as his navel. "Police," a voiceover informed them, "have released this image which appears to show a man dressed as a pirate who has been spotted on CCTV at both crime scenes. They are asking the public to come forward with any information about who this person is or where the costume may be from."

The story seemed so farfetched, so elaborately evil and calculated that at first Rowan's mind blankly rejected it. Yet the story was being reported as if it were not only feasible, but that it had really happened. Franklin leaned into her ear, "Meredy and Peterman don't know about the book," he whispered. "Edison wants it to stay that way, ok? We'll speak later."

There was some further talk from the inspector about expert archery skills before two images, side by side of Spencer Nordstrom and John MacGregor floated upwards against a dark background.

"Fishponds," Peterman huffed. "So it's students then - some kind of initiation prank on one of the campuses I reckon. Bunch of monsters the lot of them, I tell you, a bout of national service would see them right." Peterman seemed to mull this over. "Or immigrants; that place is swarming with them - probably something tribal. They're always throwing spears about and making arrows out of bamboo - that was one hell of a shot to hit them first time. They should all be sent back to where they came from, and they should sink the boat as it's going there!" the fat, red skinned old man hollered to himself but the rest of the room ignored him. "Present company excepted," he offered to Rowan, who could not even bear to look at him.

When it was apparent the reportage of the story was now repeating its loop, Peterman and Meredy returned to their work and Rowan and Franklin were left alone in the office. Franklin clicked the TV off with the remote. "Bloody hell," he said.

"They're saying a lot to the public. That's unusual,"

"I think they know that there's going to be more. I got a call from Edison last night; I think they're talking about a serial killer."

"They called him a terrorist on the news."

"That too. I think he's trying to hold the city hostage for its past crimes. There's nothing in the world quite as dangerous as a madman with a mission."

"That's for damn sure," Rowan said, recalling the events from the spring. "What are we going to do?"

"We're going to do nothing at all. We've played our part and have done all we can. It's for our own safety that we stay out of this one."

Rowan looked at the blank screen of the extinguished television. "I think you're right this time around. I feel like we're too much involved - I don't even like the idea that the killer knows the address of this place."

Franklin nodded in agreement. "The news didn't say anything about the book."

"They always like to hold things back. When the investigation into Ruby's murder was going on, we were always trying to get the police to use a more recent picture of Ruby. The one they had was a few months old and was from before she had added the red weaves to her hair. But the police said it's what they always do - they always have to hold something back so they can prove a witness really did see her and wasn't just giving a description of the photo. They also told us it's for branding her…"

" Branding her?"

"Yes. If you have a single image, people are more likely to have that face burned into their memories. Think about what happens whenever a child goes missing - they keep the same image in the public's eye at all times because it turns her into a brand. There's a reason why Coca Cola has stuck to the same logo for more than a hundred years…"

Franklin nodded and then sighed. "I just hope they catch him - and that they do it soon. Anyway, onto the matters of the day - how do you fancy working on a once in a lifetime body?"

Rowan looked puzzled.

"That storm on Friday? A man was struck by lightning…"

Rowan's mouth fell open. "Are you joking?"

"Not even slightly. Think you can handle it?"

"Of course. I just… didn't believe that anything like that really happened, it just seems so…biblical."

"Not biblical - pagan. The man in question was…" Franklin consulted the note Meredy had written for him. "Teagen Thorn, High Priest and Witch and Servant of the Gods. He was born Ken Miller, died aged 68 on Blaise Castle Estate. He was conducting a ritual when his staff was struck by lightning."

Rowan was certain she had woken up in some kind of parallel world. None of this morning was making any sense.

"Don't look so alarmed, I've conducted Pagan funerals before. They're a little unconventional but nothing we can't handle."

"But he was a witch? That's the bit that's alarming me."

Franklin shook his head. "It's a religion like any other Rowan and one that deserves the same respect. I can walk you through this one, I promise you that they're nice people - you will not end up cursed."

"We've only really done secular and Christian ones before. How often does something like this come along?"

Franklin shrugged his shoulders. "We get a handful of Jewish ones every year - they can sometimes prove problematic just because so many of the burial grounds are full and there is still a big tradition for burial rather than cremation."

"I can understand why Jewish people might want to avoid the image of being incinerated in a furnace."

"Quite," Franklin nodded. "Muslim funerals are rarer because lots of people like to go with someone who specializes in Islamic traditions. Some of the more orthodox traditions have strict rules about people touching a body after death… especially women."

"Have you ever directed a Spiritualist funeral before?"

Franklin thought for a short while. "I don't believe I have. I remember that being a bit of a thing in the late 80's, early 90's - my dad probably did some at that time."

Rowan did not want to press the matter further. She knew telling Franklin about the night before would be the undoing of the spell it had cast upon her. He was a logical, rational man who had no time in his personal life for fantasies about an afterlife. Her encounter with Ruby in that auditorium had been so magical, and yet so fragile, that exposing it to even a tiny bit of cynicism could cause the whole miracle to scorch before her eyes. She would save it for someone who needed to hear it, someone whose need to believe would outstrip their immediate skepticism. Her parents did not need to know yet, it would have to be Lise.

12.

Teagen Thorn, High Priest, Witch and Servant of the Gods, was in a much worse condition than Rowan had been anticipating. She had imagined that being struck by lightning would end life in a manner similar to the flick of a light switch. An almighty thunderbolt would burst from the heavens to electrify the victim - whose heart would stop before he even knew what had happened.

The result on the steel shelf before her told a different story. The man's entire right arm had been blackened and burnt. The remnants of the metal staff he had held aloft had melted and fused with his fingers. Unable to completely free the tool, it had been sawn away as close to the hand as possible by the mortuary attendants.

The lightning bolt had jolted diagonally through the man's body, burning his ceremonial robes as it went in a rip down to his right leg, almost exploding his foot from his ankle. All pieces of metal that had been on his body - pieces of jewellry, a belt buckle, a watch – had fused with his naked skin. The poor man still smelled as if he were burning.

"That stench," the burly mortuary attendant grimly informed them, "is what human flesh tastes like. Believe it or not, we taste like pork - according to those in the know. If you ever attend a barbecue with firemen, you'll see that they never serve anything from a pig - no bacon, no sausages, nothing. They know what that smell means, you see."

"Fascinating Roger, now can we take the poor man away?" said Franklin.

The mortuary attendant shook his head disbelievingly and presented him with the necessary papers which Franklin dutifully signed and Roger counter signed. Each took a copy - Roger the original, Franklin the carbon replica.

"I don't suppose you're working on either of those murder victims are you?" Roger asked, a little too enthusiastically for Rowan's taste.

"They won't be released for ages, "Franklin replied. "But even if I was, I wouldn't be able to tell you."

"Imagine the skill. That's a hell of a shot to get someone in the back of the head on a moving bus - or walking over a bridge. I bet the police'll be going after the Olympic archery team, it has to be one of them."

"I have no idea." Franklin sighed.

Once the remains of Teagen Thorn had been discretely placed in the back of Franklin's van, he and Rowan were on the road leaving the hospital behind.

"I'm sorry, Rowan. I didn't know he was going to be in such a state. I didn't know lightning could do that to people."

"Thanks, but I'm fine. It was pretty horrid but it's so much easier when it's just an accident - nobody to blame but the gods. Murder is different."

"No arguing with you there." Franklin did not even try the radio as he knew it would be full of more lurid coverage of the murders. He instead opted for his regular Kim Wilde CD. Rowan rolled her eyes but didn't complain, she knew it didn't help, and besides, she had grown rather fond of these journeys with Franklin and Kim.

Once Teagan Thorn was safely stowed away in the cold unit in the death chamber at the funeral home, Rowan and Franklin swapped from the anonymous black van to the compact Smart Car that Franklin favoured for city trips that did not involve human corpses. Rowan typed the address of Teagan's home into the SatNav and a woman's voice instructed them towards a little village near Blaise Castle Estate.

The estate itself had been designed under the instructions of a wealthy Quaker merchant named John Harford who had a flair for the theatrical, constructing a quaint castle folly on a hill, a hermit's cave (for which he employed his very own hermit) and a fairytale cottage in the forest, from which a constantly fed fireplace would allow wood smoke to billow dramatically through the trees. It was eventually gifted to the city and had become a popular spot for dog walkers and cyclists - and a handful of pagans too, who were drawn by its enigmatic history to worship there. It was where Teagan Thorn, High Priest, Witch and Servant of the Gods had heard what the gods had made of him.

The village itself was small and plain with nothing more than a post office, a pub and a general goods store, but the cottage in which Teagan and his wife Sora Sky, High Priestess, Witch and Servant of the Gods, had made their home was a charming cob construction with a garden overflowing with well-tended flowers. Franklin silently admired their ability to keep their blooms alive so long after the end of the season and knocked on the old warped, wooden door.

Rowan had no idea what to expect from meeting a high priestess for the first time, but as soon as she saw Sora Sky, the woman made complete sense to her. She was tall and slim with long hair that was somewhere between dusty blonde and grey. She wore about her neck a chain of semi precious stones. From her shoulders to her bare feet, a cascade of an unadorned peach dress covered her.

"Welcome!" the woman beamed. "I didn't know there would be two of you. Come, come inside!"

Stepping over the threshold, Rowan had the peculiar sensation of stepping into a different world. An agreeable smell of burned incense drifted through the air, whilst beams of sunlight sliced through the open windows onto a coffee table on which the paraphernalia of an extraordinary life were placed. Tarot cards lay in a cross, melted candles stained the glass around them, little trinkets scattered here and there along with symbols Rowan had never seen before. Shelves were lined with books about the occult and statuettes of curios from around the world. There was no unifying world order here - bits of eastern religions brushed up against Native American folk art. Images of crop circles from the Shires sat alongside those of African deities. The only thing to spoil the ethereal beauty of it all was the 42" flat screen TV in the corner of the room, from which a news report was again showing the image of the pirate on the bus.

"Isn't it awful," the woman tutted as she turned it off. "Can I get you anything to drink? Tea?"

"Chamomile if you have any," Franklin suggested. Rowan was momentarily taken aback by this peculiar request until she remembered how diligently her boss knew his clients. Of course this woman would have chamomile tea. Rowan asked for the same and she and Franklin sat beside each other on a sofa before the tarot-laden coffee table. Rowan produced her iPad and opened up a page to take notes.

"Ms. Sky," Franklin began upon her return. "First may I say how deeply sorry I am for your loss."

"That's very kind of you to say, Mr. Gallow, but please, it's Helen Jones the rest of the time." She offered them both a kindly smile as she passed them mugs of warm tea. Rowan liked this woman. "I know it sounds a little ostentatious but Teagan Thorn and Sora Sky does help us get into the mindset somewhat. Nine tenths of every religion is just about how we dress up the same old customs. Names just help us connect with our past a little easier. Gallow... it's unusual, is it Scottish?"

Franklin blushed a little about the origins of his own fabricated name. "It was Italian originally. My father is something of an obsessive when it comes to America. When my older brother, Edison, was born he Americanized the spelling by adding a "W" at the end."

"Oh, how wonderfully different! Edison and Franklin - your father really is an admirer." The woman smiled but Franklin simply nodded. "And your assistant?"

"Rowan Kaplan," she replied.

Helen clasped her hands together joyfully. "Rowan! That's a proper pagan name - all of the trees are; Willow, Holly, Ash, Hazel. How marvellous! And Kaplan?"

"Jewish, I think," then by way of an explanation. "We have something of an unusual family tree."

The two women swapped friendly smiles and Rowan sipped her tea. It was peculiar, not unpleasant, but earthier than she had imagined it would be.

"Now," Franklin pressed, "on with the unfortunate business of arranging a service. I'm not sure if you've had time to give much thought to what you'd like, but this will not be the first pagan service I've worked on."

"Fortunately none of that is up to me. My husband left very strict instructions on how he wanted his farewell service to be. We spoke of it often you see. We always knew of course that one of us would go first, I just don't think we could have imagined it would be quite so... sudden. We were hoping that we could have an outdoor service. There will only be a handful of us, just the members of our coven - maybe ten, twelve of us. He had requested an open coffin but given the circumstances…"

"I understand, of course," Franklin said softly.

The woman sighed. "It happened right in front of us. We'd heard the thunder coming closer but it just added to the drama of it at the time. It was exciting… electric, for want of a better word. It was just our standard ode to nature that we do once a month. I don't think any of us thought it would be anything special at the time. You should have heard the sound of it - I've never heard anything like it before."

Franklin cleared his throat. "I'm very sorry, there are laws regarding outside ceremonies in the UK. Funerals can only be performed on licensed premises… I can make an application on your behalf, to see if a religious exemption can be made, but that can take time and can cost an awful lot of money."

Helen nodded slowly. "I see,"

"We could perform a religious service at a crematorium."

"Is that inside a building?" she asked.

"I'm afraid it is. All registered places aside from cemeteries and graveyards are indoors."

Helen wiped her mouth and seemed to be blinking away tears. "I see, it seems a little unfair, but it's not your fault."

Franklin nodded in agreement. "Some of the rules about services are unfair. Earlier this year I worked on a funeral where the wife wanted to have "God Only Knows" by the Beach Boys played at her husband's service and it wasn't allowed as it was secular ceremony. It had been their first dance at their wedding."

"Oh how awful," said the woman compassionately.

"I have an idea. A little compromise that I think might work within the law - well, within the hazy bits of the law anyway."

Helen smiled. "I think my husband would certainly appreciate the idea of his funeral being only partly within the law."

"I'll see what I can do," replied Franklin.

On the drive home from Helen Jones' cottage Franklin decided that enough had been achieved that day and he'd collect Rowan's bike from the funeral home and drive her to her flat. Rowan felt enormously touched by her boss' generosity of spirit, not for saving her a cycle ride, but for his willingness to bend the rules for a client.

"So what are you going to do for Teagan?" she asked.

"I have no idea yet, but I'm going to go online and chat to some friends, see what they've done in the past."

"You have funeral director friends online?"

"I belong to a message board for my profession, yes… It's called Funeral Friends."

Rowan laughed. "Do you swap stories about the latest embalming practices or where to buy the cheapest caskets?"

"There's a bit of that, yes, but mostly it's just people chatting about their lives and how they cope with it all. I've started talking to funeral director in Edinburgh, we've swapped emails and stuff… a female funeral director…"

Rowan gasped excitedly. "No way! Tell me more!"

"That's all you get to hear for now, I don't want you interfering."

"That won't stop me, I hope you're aware of that."

"You know too much already," Franklin replied. "So, let's change the subject… You never told me you were Jewish, I didn't know they came in your colour too."

Rowan thumped him on the shoulder. "I didn't know you'd have a problem with it."

Franklin suddenly turned serious. "Oh no, Rowan, I was only joking, of course I don't…"

"I was kidding Franklin. I'm not sure what we are as a family now. I think we're just that kind of Christian where you think there's probably a God but you don't really care about it."

"Oh, so Anglican then."

Rowan laughed. She loved these silly moments with her boss. Light and friendly and just on the right side of being mean - or even worse - flirtatious. "I don't know that much about my history, but I'm actually trying something new… as far as religion goes."

"Do you care to elaborate?" Franklin pressed.

"You know too much already," she replied.

13.

There were no murders the following weekend but the mood of the city did not edge any farther away from the brink of hysteria. The students remained on their campuses, the bars empty of all but the most hardened of boozers, the streets by night were eerily quiet with not a soul to be seen, save for the occasional worker making their way hurriedly home - even during the daylight hours the city felt fearful. An electrostatic buzz hung in the air as the population went about their business with a cautious vigilance - no longer wearing earphones to block out the world, it paid to be watchful and wary of the people around you.

Franklin woke early that morning, not to the sound of his alarm clock, but his phone. With a sense of dread that there had been another death, he reached for it and consulted the screen; it was Verity.

"Franklin?" she asked the moment he answered the call.

"Morning, what time is it?"

"Have you heard from Alf? I sent him a text message last night and one this morning and he hasn't got back to me. I tried calling him but his phone is off."

Franklin blinked at the clock beside his bed. "It's seven in the morning…"

"I know, but I haven't really had much sleep. I just wondered if you'd heard anything."

"When did you last hear from him?"

"Yesterday afternoon, we spoke on the phone just after four."

Franklin cleared his throat and sighed. "Alf is fine, I promise you. I remember you at university, you were never up before midday if you could help it."

"I know, but it's just…"

"You're worried about him?"

"Can you blame me? It's all over the news, and that bus driver… he was killed near Alf's campus. Can you imagine how frightening this is for me? You say goodbye to your kid on the same day a serial killer shows up?"

"Verity, I understand, but he probably won't appreciate you smothering him like this. It's his first weekend on campus, he'll be settling in with new people and getting to know them - going out to the student union every night. He's probably sleeping off a hangover - it is fresher's week after all. For all you know he might have... he might have turned off his phone if you were phoning him around the clock..."

To his horror, he heard Verity suddenly collapse into a fit of sobs. "Oh god, you're right. I'm a pathetic, scared mother who's pretending her son isn't an adult. He's ignoring me."

"I didn't mean to upset you, I'm sorry. He probably isn't even ignoring you, he just wanted a few hours with his new friends."

Verity's breathing seemed to be steadying. "I must sound like a crazy person."

"A little bit," Franklin smiled. "It has only been a few hours since you last spoke to him. How else have you been?"

"A bit manic," Verity replied flatly. "I've been cleaning quite obsessively - the whole house feels suddenly gigantic and... full of ghosts. It's weird, in every room, at any time there can be ten different things to make me cry. His old shoes or old books, pictures on the walls, everything. I think I might head down to London for a few days, visit my sister. I haven't seen her in a while - I feel like I owe her a visit and a change of scenery would be nice."

"How's Alf doing?"

"Horribly well," she said. "I'm so pleased he's settling in but I wish it had taken him a little longer to completely forget me. I think he's really enjoying himself."

"You can't take that personally," Franklin laughed. "Imagine the alternative - he could be living in your house in his forties... like me."

"That's different. The house came with your job and your parents don't even live there."

The alarm clock had only a few minutes before it sprang into action, so Franklin turned it off and got out of bed, no point in wasting the morning if he was awake already. "I saw the campus - it was lovely, like something out of Brideshead Revisited or Enid Blyton. His flatmates seem nice too. Give him a few days to settle in and try not to worry about him too much. Yes, there's a crazy person in the city, but there are half a million people living in Bristol. All of the university campuses are stepping up their security and have patrols throughout the night. He really is safer where he is than just about anywhere else."

"I suppose so. I feel a little stupid now."

"As you should, but I think that's par for the course as far as parenting is concerned. It drives people crazy - look at my parents, I think me and Edison managed to break both of their hearts, and now they live in a flat in the middle of Bath, pretending that they're in America."

Verity laughed, Franklin was not sure if she knew that he wasn't joking; that was precisely how his Mum and Dad lived. He made the bed as best as he could while his cat Felicity stayed sound asleep in the middle of it. His aged pet, eternally just one step away from death's door, was an inheritance from an old woman who had died many years ago, Felicity, a nervous bag of skin and bone who was prone to fits of ill health that had cost Franklin many thousands of pounds, was in many ways his most loyal companion.

After stepping into his slippers he made his way down the stairs to the funeral home that was beneath his flat. The mornings were growing cold - autumn had taken up residence within the city.

"I'll give him until this evening," said Verity. "After that, would you be able to drop by... just to check."

"I will, but just this once. You can't let your fear get the better of you - plus, I'm trying to win my son over with my charm and natural coolness, he won't take kindly to me showing up on his doorstep every other day."

"Thank you."

Franklin spied something poking through the letterbox of the reception room. It was an envelope, nothing unusual in that, but his blood turned to ice when he saw the writing on it - that same studied hand bore his name on the front. There was no address.

"Verity, I have to go. Bit of a work emergency, I'm very sorry."

"I understand," she replied.

After hanging up, he immediately tapped the passcode into the electronic lock of the death chamber. From inside he slipped a pair of latex gloves onto his hands and tapped the code to release him from the room – the double locking mechanism that required a code to pass through in either direction was an invention of his father's - after a pair of hysterical parents had once attempted to flee the funeral home with the corpse of their son in their arms. He made his way heedfully back to the reception.

He opened the envelope in his office with trembling fingers. The contents were no more than a handwritten letter in that now chilling hand:

"Dear Mr Gallow,

The police shan't have any luck in finding me, but I imagine you have a better EYE for this sort of thing. You may think you know too much already but you do not know the half of it. I have sent to the police the TOOTH I pulled from the bus driver's mouth. If they have any doubts I am sure the man's dental records will prove my legitimacy.

I need your help, Mr Gallow. I won't be stopped, so you will play this game with me. I cannot come to your door as I know the police will catch me sooner than I intend. If I am caught I shall be caught only by the means I decide upon. At the bottom of this page, you will see the address of a YouTube video - the content of which is not of my devising. Beneath it, you will see a comments section. There you will write your private email address so I can contact you when I need to. The police must not know about this - nor must they know of this letter.

If I hear word that they have been contacted I shall kill a member of the public everyday until I am caught. The police will receive a note from me this morning but it will be quite unlike yours.

The city has asked for this Mr Gallow. They cannot pretend that they were not warned - I shall make sure that they pay through blood and through fear. If I am caught, the game will be over and I shall face my punishment - my revenge will be worth it.

Yours truly,
Jenkins Protheroe."

Franklin stared at the note, dumbfounded. His first instinct was to call his brother, Edison would know how to be discreet, but then what if the killer found out? What if this would be his chance to kill with abandon, each death adding as much blood to Franklin's hands as his own? He called Rowan.

"Morning Franklin," she answered. "Do you need me in early today?"

"I need you in right now. I think I might be about to lose my mind - the killer left me a note… and I can't tell the police, he says he's going to kill somebody every day until…"

"…I'm on my way now. Just stay calm."

14.

The wait for Rowan's arrival was a torturously long one for Franklin, who paced the length of the corridor as he agonised over his choices. He didn't like being left alone with either the note or his thoughts - the idea of being responsible for another person's death was one that had troubled him every day of his life. The fear that gripped him late at night, that perhaps he hadn't been paying proper attention when a child ran across the road or that he had somehow left an unscrewed bottle of paracetemol on the floor of a child's nursery. In a lot of ways he was glad he had never known Alf when he was growing up, as the daily responsibility for a child would have been enough for him to never sleep well again.

When Rowan arrived her first words were, "Stop panicking."

"I'm sorry, I just didn't know what to do." He suddenly felt acutely aware that he was still in his pyjamas - not his best set either, with the tasteful stripes - but the pair with fluffy sheep and "Zzzz" printed all over them. "What do we do?"

"I don't know. Where's the letter?"

Franklin led the way to his office, where the note lay on the desk practically radiating evil into the room like toxic waste. Rowan looked at the envelope it had arrived in. "There's no address on it. So he delivered it by hand?"

"Yes. He must have been here. What a horrid thought."

"Have you called Edison yet?"

"No," Franklin shook his head. "Should I?"

"I don't know. Give me a moment to read it." She read it aloud, the hate filled words that tumbled from her mouth seemed at once alien yet at the same time strangely familiar. "That is some messed up crap."

"I know, I feel as if the words have already been burned into my soul. So what do we say to Edison?"

Rowan leaned in closer to the letter, singling out lines as she read them once more. "The police will receive a note this morning. Maybe they will be as aware of things as we are. This could all be part of some sick game - like those fake letters sent to the police during the Jack the Ripper murders. Perhaps it's just a prank to get the crime solving undertaker involved..."

"But it's the same handwriting as the skin-book."

"Do we know that the bus driver had a tooth removed?"

Franklin shrugged his shoulders. "The news reports haven't said anything about it, but that's the kind of detail they'd try to hold back I'd imagine."

Rowan read the last line from the letter. "Jenkins Protheroe. Where do I know that name?"

"That's where I can help, I remember when we were kids and Edison used to scare me with ghost stories. That was the one that frightened me the most, Jenkins Protheroe was a highwayman. He was less than four feet tall as an adult and so ugly it was said that his own mother abandoned him at birth. He was probably what we would call a dwarf nowadays - a small person. In the 1870's he would wait in the dark in the streets around the Downs and lie in the shadows, crying like a child to trick passersby into thinking that he was an injured boy. Whenever they came to his aid, he would slash their necks and rob them. He was captured a few years later and hanged up in Clifton. They left his body hanging there as a warning until it was pecked apart by crows. People used to say he would climb down from his gallows at night and dance around in the moonlight."

"The evil dwarf of Clifton, I remember that story too! It wasn't true though was it?"

"Apparently it was - well, some truth mixed with a fair bit of folklore. Some people say the stories are massively exaggerated and that he probably never killed anyone. In fact, some go as far as saying that he was simply a beggar with a deformity and was hanged only because people were scared of him."

"An ambiguous historical character…" Rowan pondered aloud. "Do you see a pattern here?"

"No, please explain." Franklin asked.

"Jenkins Protheroe… John Horwood… the guy you told me about, the one who killed his ex girlfriend and his trial notes were bound in his skin? People executed in Bristol who may have been innocent, or at least not entirely evil."

"The pirate!" Franklin gasped. "He's not just any pirate, but Edward Teach - the most feared pirate on the seven seas. Blackbeard! He was born in Redcliffe and is a bit of a hero to some - a kind of Robin Hood of the ocean if you strip away all the myths."

"Edward Colston…" Rowan added. "The only reason we have a statue of him is because he donated a load of money before he died. Some people think that the slave trader is a Bristol hero." Suddenly through the confusion, the killer's motive seemed to make some sense. "Do you think this is how the murderer wants us to see him? Ambiguously evil? There will be people who think he's a hero, I've seen them on Twitter already. Righting the wrongs of our past and making us pay. He's an outlaw, not a villain - a hero, not a terrorist."

"Every terrorist is a hero to someone." Franklin conceded. "It's outlandish, but even a madman can show logic. The first victim, Spencer Nordstrom, was killed because he was a rich man living in a house built with the proceeds of slave labour. People don't like rich people, but what about John MacGregor? He was just a bus driver on his night shift, it's hard to see the reason for killing somebody like that."

It did not take Rowan long to rifle through the files of her memory. Something she recalled from her schooldays. "The Bristol bus boycott!" she blurted out.

"The what?"

"We did it in history class. It was sometime in the 60's. White bus drivers across the city said that they wouldn't work if they had to do so alongside black ones. The head of their union said something about how if a single black man was employed, every bus in the city would be stopped. It was a huge thing at the time. There were counter protests and the decent people of the city boycotted the buses. The whole thing was really divisive and needed intervention from the government. None of the racist bus drivers were ever disciplined for it…"

"…So he killed one of them?" Franklin said. "That was his revenge. It seems a little extreme considering John MacGregor probably wasn't even born when the boycott was happening."

"I don't think our killer is one for subtlety - or mercy," Rowan slipped into the chair in front of Franklin's computer. "Have you seen the YouTube video he sent the link to?"

"I didn't want to. Not by myself anyway, I was worried it would be something disturbing."

"Then look away, I'm going in." Rowan carefully copied the website into Franklin's computer and pressed return.

Franklin turned away from the screen. "Tell me if it's awful."

"It's a dog playing in the water. It looks like somewhere in Cornwall - St. Michael's Mount."

Franklin peered over his shoulder to the computer. "I bet something bad is going to happen to that poor dog."

Then the video ended. Rowan replayed it and studied it closely in case some clue had eluded her, but no, it was simply a cream coloured labrador tearing through the surf. "It was uploaded in 2009," she informed him. "We're only the sixth person to ever view it."

Franklin moved another chair to sit beside her. "So you don't think the killer uploaded it himself?"

"No. I think he just found the dullest, most generic video possible for you to contact each other on. The video is so old now that not even the person who uploaded it will get a notification if people start discussing it. It's kind of a perfect way to cover your tracks…"

Franklin took the mouse from Rowan and scrolled the screen upwards. Just as the letter had informed him, there were no messages. He typed his email address into the empty box, "franklingallow@gmail.com" and pressed enter. Then, emboldened by the fact that this had not caused his computer to explode, he added "Jenkins Protheroe. I will do as you ask and will not tell the police." After which he added his mobile phone number and pressed send.

"Do you think that was wise?" Rowan asked.

"Probably not, but what choice do I have? He's trying to get me to hold my silence for a ransom and I have to pay attention. If he does email me, can't the police trace it using that… thing that says where his computer is?"

"His IP address? Maybe, if he's been really stupid - I think he'd be more than capable of using a VPN to mask his whereabouts though." Franklin looked at her dumbly. "It hides your location and provides a fake IP - you can download them for free on the internet."

"How do you know this stuff?'

"I'm twenty, that's how I know this stuff, we're born with this knowledge, Franklin."

They repeated the video again and the pair watched all twelve seconds of it once more. "So, do you think this is a race thing then?" Franklin asked. "Black slavery, Pero's Bridge, then the bus driver. It sounds like he's one of those people who thinks we should tear down the Colston statue as it makes us all look racist."

"Would that be such a bad thing? It's a memorial to a monster, why on earth would we want that in our city? It doesn't make us look racist, it makes us look like we don't care about how awful our past was."

"Rowan, I don't like the man either, but it's a historic statue. It's been standing for over a hundred years - it only means as much as you want it to. Perhaps it was built to celebrate a wealthy merchant who traded slaves, but I think of it now as a reminder of our dark past - never forget and all that. You wouldn't say we should tear down the gates to Auschwitz would you?"

Rowan pulled a disgusted face. "Don't try that revisionist bollocks with me, Franklin, I thought you were smarter than that. There are schools in the city that are named after him, where the kids still celebrate his birthday - our biggest music venue is called Colston Hall - and you don't think that feels like a slap in the face every time me or any other black person walks past his statue, or down one of the streets with his name on the sign?"

"I don't think you rewrite history by demolishing your past, it's just bowing to the…" Franklin trailed off.

"Finish your sentence… bowing to what?"

Franklin sighed. "To the PC brigade."

"Isn't that exactly what your brother would say about it too? That everything's too politically correct? Isn't that what all straight white men eventually say when anyone wants to question the things they feel comfortable with? Call them the PC brigade so you don't have to take them seriously or even listen to what they have to say?"

"Rowan, you know I'm not like that at all. I'm very liberal - I have a gay son and… I employed you, didn't I?" At the sight of her mouth dropping open Franklin instantly wanted to take the words back.

"Do you want a medal? Should I feel grateful that you hired a black girl?"

"No, that's not what I meant, I just meant that I'm not one of the bad guys, I'm just…"

Franklin was relieved that his mobile phone had suddenly begun vibrating on the desk before him - he really hadn't been sure how he wanted to end that sentence. It trembled around in a circle before him whilst "Number Withheld" glowed on the screen.

"It's him," Franklin gasped.

"Answer it!"

"I don't want to." Franklin picked up the phone and switched on the speaker. After thirty seconds of ringing the voicemail cut in.

"Hello Mr Gallow," said the voice, it was a deep, gargled voice that sounded strangely artificial, as if it were being disguised mechanically; he had heard of apps that could be downloaded that altered your pitch. "Thank you for your message, I trust you will be responsible and show patience. I will not harm you unless you misbehave. I will not show mercy if you go to the police and do not think for a moment that I will not harm the ones you love if you do not play fair. I shall get back to you as soon as I need you. There will be no more deaths this week."

And then he was gone.

15.

Whenever Rowan and Lise walked together it was always with the same aimless meander. They could walk and talk for hours, just drifting through the city like leaves on the breeze. There would be no destination, just a walk for the sake of it. Often they found themselves climbing Park Street, the notoriously steep hill that led from the waterfront to the museum. That afternoon they ventured upwards further until they reached Whiteladies Road - a curious name for a wide thoroughfare -, popular with student drinkers from wealthier families. It had never occurred to Rowan until now to question its origins, or why the street eventually filtered into Blackboy Hill. She was certain that whatever the story, Jenkins Protheroe would not be pleased with it. She would investigate further when she got home.

Conversation between the two young women came easily, but, just as they unconsciously avoided the areas where either of their siblings had been murdered, they rarely spoke of Ruby or Henrik, strange considering that was the strongest tie that bound them. Murder itself felt ever present as they walked - as if it were their constant companion - a third friend who neither would ever address directly, always there but hidden just out of sight.

"I know I shouldn't," said Lise, "but I can't help but feel scared. My dad said most serial killers get sloppy in the end and with DNA and such it isn't like the old days. People get tracked; people leave a footprint all over the city. I trust the police."

"Perhaps it's naive of me, I know, but if we can't trust the police, things become a lot more frightening when something like this happens. What kind of monster kills for pleasure?"

Rowan nodded along thoughtfully. "That's if it is for pleasure. Have you heard any of the rumours online?"

"People reckon he's a madman - that he gets his thrills by dressing up in costume and killing people. Sick bastard... Someone on Twitter says it's a vengeance thing - for slavery in the past, I don't know, something to do with the Colston statue."

Rowan felt compelled to push her friend gently into this way of thinking but knew that she couldn't. "Yeah, that statue's pretty offensive. Plus, all the clean ups it has to have every year, you'd think that someone would have torn it down by now. Every month or so it gets bound in chains or covered with red paint."

"People will be even less likely to take it down now if that's what the killer wants - it's like bowing to terrorism of something. People don't like that. It'll probably just make the killer angrier and he'll like... kill a bunch of us." Lise shuddered and zipped up her coat. Dusk was falling all around them.

The street, half as full as it ordinarily would be at that time, began losing its populace - escapees from a city that now belonged to a murderer. They cantered out of closing shops and immediately into stuffed buses and taxis. Nobody would likely admit it, even to themselves, but this was a city gripped by fear and handed over to a madman.

Lise checked her watch. "I should probably give my dad a call, he doesn't like me out late at the best of times - he said he'd pick me up, he doesn't want me walking home alone."

"That's understandable. My parents aren't keen on me being out at night either, but they don't have much of a say in it anymore. Just imagine if they knew everything that happened in the spring."

"Are you still telling them that you work in a supermarket?"

"Yes," Rowan nodded. "It's just easier that way. If they knew I was working in a funeral home they'd try and get me to a shrink."

"I've given mine up," said Lise. "I don't think she was helping me at all. She just wanted me to talk about Henrik all the time. Who decided that was the healthy thing to do? It just made me sadder and sadder and I'd just dread the meetings all week long. Who says that bottling things up can't be healthy? Besides, nobody can relate to me as well as you can, if I need to talk I always have you."

However touched Rowan felt in that moment was immediately undercut by her sense of guilt. It was completely within her power to tell Lise everything she knew, including how she had heard directly from the killer that there would be no more deaths this week. How she wished she could relieve her friend of her fears, but she must stick to the rules - lives were at stake.

Once Lise had finished her brief phone call with her father she turned to Rowan and said something most unexpected, the likes of which she had never heard from her friend before. "Rowan, I know you must be scared too - you don't have to be brave just because you're older than me. When murder comes to your family it forces you to grow up - maybe we should talk more about Henrik and Ruby. I really do believe they will catch your sister's killer and when they do… things will start to get better for you."

It did not take Rowan long to recover. "Perhaps you're right, but do you know what, I've been feeling a lot better about things. I wasn't going to say anything about it, but remember that church?"

"The cult?"

"A Bridge to Another World Ministries. I went on Friday night."

Lise sighed. "I was hoping that because you hadn't mentioned it you'd changed your mind or seen some sense or… something."

"Lise, it was wonderful."

"Did they ask for money from you?"

"Not a penny."

"That means that they're waiting for the right time to do it."

Rowan immediately felt this slight like a wound. "You weren't there. You didn't hear what the medium said - and if you were there, you'd have been begging to hear from Henrik."

Lise stiffened visibly before her. "And what did they say? That someone's dead Mum had returned from heaven but couldn't remember if her name began with a P or an S?"

"You must think I'm a complete idiot. The medium, his name's Tegwyn Jones… I looked him up and some of his online testimonials are astounding… he knew she was called Ruby Kaplan - and who I was. She knew she was murdered and how. He even knew the song Ruby was rehearsing on the night she died."

"Really? Are you sure that you aren't just remembering it weirdly?"

Rowan was astonished that her friend seemed so underwhelmed. "It wasn't just me, she told this old lady that her husband had come to visit, he was called John and said he loved her and she should move on and enjoy her life."

"Did he tell her this or did he take a lucky guess that in an audience filled with old women one of them would have a dead husband called John? It's called cold reading - all the fake mediums use it. It's just making guesses that are likely to hit home with somebody." When she noticed how curiously Rowan was looking at her, Lise added, "I used to be a bit fascinated by Houdini a few years ago. He uncovered charlatan mediums after he retired."

"Well, it wasn't a lucky guess with me."

"I bet it wasn't. There is all out trickery too - that's hot reading. When you found that pamphlet, did you just turn up or did you email the ministry before you went."

Rowan didn't want to answer. She knew where this was heading. "There was a Facebook group…"

"So they had your name already then? All they had to do was Google you and everything's there in news reports. I've tried it with you before. There are dozens of articles that mention you by name, and from your Facebook profile they can see that video clip of Ruby singing DownTown. It's like a paper trail, people can find out more than you can imagine if they look hard enough - and are immoral enough."

Rowan felt herself begin to tremble as she stumbled away from her friend as if she had punched her. Lise could have looked triumphant in that moment, but she was too thoughtful a girl to do so. "Rowan, I'm sorry, I didn't mean to sound so brutal. Maybe I'm wrong…"

"I don't think so. But Tegwyn gave me so much hope. Who would do such a thing?"

"Look, take me along to their next meeting. Maybe there is something to this."

Lise's father, handsome, but still wearing a mask of grief that only fellow sufferers could spot, was parking his car a few feet away from them. He waved at Rowan, it was the first time they had met since the day after Henrick's killer had been arrested and he'd visited the funeral home, Lise and her parents were among the few to know the full story of her and Franklin's involvement in his capture.

"I have to go, I hope I didn't upset you," said Lise.

"I've been through worse," Rowan replied with a smile as her friend kissed her on the cheek.

Her walk back to Stokes Croft was all down hill, a blessing considering how fast night was falling upon the city, Rowan all but ran home, acutely conscious of how eerily quiet the streets had become and suspecting every passerby of being a potential murderer. She unlocked the front door to her building and bounded up the stairs to her flat.

She opened the door and let out a scream when she saw the man standing in her kitchen.

The man jolted and spun on his heels, but smiled warmly at her. "Evening, Hot Chocolate Girl."

"Jude. What the hell or you doing in my flat?"

"I thought you were in, I just came down to give you a couple of bottles of my homemade cider." Her upstairs neighbour unzipped his rucksack and pulled a couple of corked glass bottles from it.

"You can't just let yourself in whenever you want to. Haven't you seen the news?"

"I don't have a TV," he said proudly. "Rots your brain, stifles the creative juices."

"Big surprise, you don't have a TV," said Rowan, sulkily. "Now get out of my flat, you aren't welcome."

Jude just smiled, he had surprisingly flawless teeth which Rowan resented noticing. He was still wearing his dressing gown with nothing but boxer shorts underneath. She hated noticing that too.

"I'm on to you," he said. "Don't pretend you haven't noticed it too… this electricity between us. You don't want to admit it but you've got a big old crush on me haven't you?"

"Piss off Jude, go back to your flat and… make music or write poems… or whatever the hell you do instead of proper work, I have TV to watch and brain cells to rot."

"Don't worry, the feeling's more than mutual, I've always had a thing for dark skin," Jude winked and Rowan found her heart racing. Why was she like this?

"Do you want me to call the police? Get out of my flat!"

"Will do, Hot Chocolate Girl." As he brushed past her she caught scent of his aftershave, something rich and surprisingly classy. "But just remember, if you're ever feeling lonely, or bored… or horny, I'm just a staircase away."

Rowan slammed the door behind him and slumped angrily into her couch. How obnoxious to presume so much and feel at liberty to enter her space whenever he chose? How absolutely infuriating that everything he had said was true.

She hated him for making her feel this way. She stood up and helped herself to a bottle of cider.

16.

It was rare that Rowan found herself enjoying dressing up and even rarer for a funeral to offer her the chance to do so, but on the morning of Teagan Thorne's crematorium service - the first of a two-part "celebration of his life," Rowan had dressed in a long, loose clover green taffeta dress she had found in a charity shop, and twirled in front of the full length mirror in Franklin's bedroom.

Teagan's wife, Helen, who would be going by the name Sora Sky throughout the service, had insisted she and Franklin wore colour to the funeral and the pair had enjoyed researching appropriate clothes for a Wiccan ceremony, for Rowan it had been this green dress. She was waiting to see what Franklin had settled on. He knocked on the door and asked to come in.

Rowan could not help by smile at the sight of her boss and friend. Franklin wore a fuchsia suit with a purple shirt underneath, in the buttonhole of his jacket was a sprig of ivy. "Franklin! I've never seen you in colours before - you handsome fox, you!"

"Check out these cufflinks," he beamed as he flashed the matching pair shaped like the figure "8" of infinity. "You're looking rather fetching yourself - you don't think we've gone overboard do you?"

"Her words were the brighter the better - and think about the visitors last night… for mourners they weren't exactly toning it down."

The previous evening friends of the dead man had come to visit him in his wicker coffin. It was, according to his wife, an ancient custom to visit the deceased and to decorate the casket. The injuries to his body were so catastrophic that he was bound like a mummy in strips of brightly coloured cloth. His mourners had sung folksy songs and exchanged homely proverbs on death before each placed a flower, a trinket, or some such token of fondness around him in his casket. His wife placed in his hand a scroll tied with a red ribbon, "My words of love for you," she had declared as she kissed his bound forehead. A toast of mead was offered, which Rowan and Franklin were invited to join, Rowan had never tried this peculiar drink before and found it warm, sweet and incredibly pleasant. It had been a fine celebration with friends who had nothing but words of genuine kindness for their friend.

Once the final details had been sorted on their outfits, Franklin and Rowan returned downstairs to where some of the day labourers - the workers who attended the funeral home on service days - eyed them peculiarly as they slid Teagan's casket into the back of the freshly waxed hearse. From there the pair formed the first vehicle of the procession which would meet at Helen's cottage near Blaise Castle and would lead to the crematorium high on the edge of the Bristol Downs. Unlike most services, which Rowan and Franklin were expected to stay away from once they had begun, they had this time been warmly invited inside to watch first hand the conventional stage of the ceremony.

Rowan contemplated this invitation as they left the city on a bright, gently breezy October morning. She had often heard the idea that a funeral should be to celebrate the life someone had lived, rather than mourn their passing, but she had rarely found this to be true. The best intentions were so often ruined by reality and stood aside for genuine grief and loss. This service, or at least the second part of it, was to be a celebration of his death.

Death was nothing to fear, Helen had told her, it was simply another stage in the process of life, just as birth was. Just as wakefulness needs sleep, just as every butterfly needs a caterpillar, so life needs death.

Sora Sky was sitting on a bench in her garden when the hearse arrived, flanked on either side by two women about her age. She was dressed in a deep blue dress that was bound with a belt like a tourniquet in the middle; she wore her hair down in tumbles of greying curls. She met both Franklin and Rowan with warm hugs and cheek kisses before turning her eyes to the hearse. Her husband's casket was draped in red silk and topped with an abundance of seasonal plants - evergreens had seemed right.

"Oh look what you two have done," she wiped away a tear, "I simply can't say thank you enough."

Rowan watched as a rag-tag trail of mourners, dressed as brightly as a field of meadow flowers, emerged from the cottage. The hearse led the way with Helen and her two friends not far behind as the procession moved back towards the city. Maybe, thought Rowan, today really could be a celebration.

The crematorium was a huge construction on the edge of the Avon Gorge. Rowan had never before been inside and had always waited politely with Franklin by the back doors, they were met by the day labourers who had driven ahead and were waiting awkwardly in ill fitting red suits and opened the door upon their arrival. Seating had not been allocated so she and Franklin sat at the back - this service was for those who had known Teagan in life, after all.

The Wicker casket, now free of the silk covering and knotted with little bows and ribbons that Teagan's friends had tied on it the night before, entered the room with a small boy walking in front dropping autumn leaves from a basket, like confetti at a wedding.

The service room had some of the trappings of a church - long pews and vaulted ceilings but none of its overt symbolism - a massive window, which took up the entirety of a wall and overlooked the gorge, gave a wondrous view of spectacular natural scenery that Rowan suspected Teagan Thorne would find most befitting of his final journey from the caterpillar stage of his life.

Once the guests had taken their seats the officiant, a somewhat conservative woman with a sensible haircut and no-fuss spectacles who had nonetheless donned a flowery summer dress for the occasion, gave a brief introduction to the service before stepping down from the podium and welcoming Sora Sky to offer her eulogy.

Sora smiled and stood up to face the room. A light smattering of applause came from her friends. "I had some notes," she began, "but I know Teagan would have preferred it if I just spoke from the heart and said what he really meant to me. I know how he died was horrible and some of us saw it happen, but in many ways he probably would have wanted to go that way - it's hard to imagine a more fitting way for Mother Nature to take you back to her womb. Now, I know that this is a secular ceremony and I'm not to mention religion... and don't worry, I won't." To this there was only a slight murmuring among the assembled guests. "I will instead talk not about Teagan Thorne, but of my husband, Ken Miller.

"I think I fell in love with him the very first day I saw him. He had long blonde hair back then, he looked like a Viking! He shook my hand and kissed it and declared that he and I had been married before, in another life, he told me he'd been waiting for me to find him. I laughed, of course, but I believed it - because I could have married that man right then and there!"

Helen Jones told the story of how the pair had not just met by chance, but had met by chance over and over again, each time he had joked that they were being pushed together by fate. The audience laughed warmly and cried openly. Rowan sat transfixed by their tale and was touched by Helen's strength and conviction in her beliefs.

"We never had children. I suppose the universe saw fit that we should serve another purpose, but there was not a single day that we were unhappy - our lives were filled with joy in that little cottage and our hearts were full because of our friends. The days we had together were our treasures and I shall remember them, every last one for the love that we shared. I know I should never be sad because I will always have those memories - but Ken?" She turned to the coffin, her eyes now pouring with silent tears, "I shall miss you, my sweet love, my Viking. Goodbye. Until we meet again," she blew him a kiss and sat down. Rowan who had been fighting back tears of her own was unsurprised to see Franklin wiping his eyes with a handkerchief. She nudged him kindly in the shoulders just as a rapturous applause filled the room and the mourners leapt to their feet.

It was the most unexpected outburst of jubilance that Rowan had ever witnessed. People were cheering and punching their fists into the air, hugging and kissing and whistling. Peering over their heads, Rowan saw that the casket had begun to sink slowly into the stand on which it had been placed and his friends and family were cheering him on to wherever he was going next.

Rowan and Franklin rose to their feet and in a moment, he was gone, it was as simple and final as that. After filing from the service room, the pair joined the mourners outside where friendly chatter filled the air, alongside cigarette smoke - and some other smoke that Rowan and Franklin pretended not to notice. Gradually the mourners left one by one to attend the second part of Teagan's grand send off.

It took more than an hour before the crematorium was able to provide Franklin with the ashes. He had arranged a faster than usual handover but it had still taken longer than Rowan had expected and she chose not to think about how long it might take an entire body to burn. She held the wooden urn in her lap as they drove to Blaise Castle, fighting the temptation to peer inside all the way.

"I bet you weren't expecting that, were you?" he asked.

"Wasn't it wonderful?"

"I suppose it was. I'm glad we went."

The castle at Blaise Estate was where the ceremony was to be held and by the time they arrived they could hear it was fully underway. Drumming and singing filled the woodlands leading up to where Teagan Thorne, High Priest, Witch and Servant of the Gods met his end.

At the top of the stone steps by an opening in the trees where the castle folly stood, Sora Sky met them with a hug and warm greetings. Over her shoulder Rowan caught glimpses of wild dancing to drum beats and instruments that looked like museum pieces. She wanted to stay and see more, but knew that this part of the service was for those who truly knew Teagan.

"Merry meet and merry part and merry meet again." Sora Sky smiled as she curtseyed slightly before Franklin and Rowan. Franklin repeated the words to her and then Rowan was being led away from the jubilant ceremony, despite that curious beast within that wanted her to stay.

"It's a Wiccan proverb," Franklin informed her, though she had not asked. "Not quite as old as many would like it to be, but most Pagan things are 20th century ideas... the truth is we really have no idea how people in the old days used to..."

But Rowan was not listening, not to him anyway. She instead found her mind drifting through the music that filled the forest as if beckoning her to stay. Trees like the rowan - her own name; the name of a witch…

17.

The killer had stayed true to his word. There had been no more killings that week, nor had there been any the following weekend. Gradually the populace of Bristol was returning to the streets and the first bloodless weekend since the rampage began seemed to bring some semblance of normality.

On the Monday evening after Teagan Thorne's funeral, Franklin had settled in front of his computer with his Indian curry and a bottle of cider. This was his ritual and had been for many years - a service required a treat and the simple pleasure of a takeaway and medium strength cider was usually enough to clear away the residual gloom of the day - not that much remained that evening. The services, both of them, seemed to be such joyous occasions that it was almost churlish to feel glum, he would, like the Wicca, celebrate the evening - by flirting online with his Scottish friend.

"Evening Nell," he sent, the moment that he saw that she had come online.

"Good evening. How was the witch's funeral?" He always loved how quickly she responded, she was an enjoyably dependable woman in that way. On the dating sites he frequented he often found the women enjoyed playing games that he just didn't understand, one day seeming nice and flirty, the next claiming he was being obsessive or stalking them because he had messaged them twice in a single day - then furious when he stopped replying to their messages.

Then there were the questions about his height. Two or three messages into a new conversation would come a question about how tall he was. "5' 10" - 178cm," he would reply; measuring bodies for caskets meant that he could automatically switch between imperial and metric measurements in his head. The replies could be as blunt as; "Sorry, I only date men over six feet," or "I could never be with a man shorter than me." Franklin had taken to answering these questions with equal bluntness: "I'm 5' 10" - 178cm. How much do you weigh?" It didn't make him feel any better about himself but the brief release of irritation made him feel less defensive.

Nell seemed different. Not only had she never asked about his height, she had only compliments to offer him. "That's quite some hair - are you sure you're not Scottish?" or "I love a man in a suit, and you wear yours well!"

Conversation came easy and bubbled along flirtatiously. She enjoyed gardening and foreign films and baking her own bread. The photos on her Facebook page revealed that she had a wholesome, open face, with radiant green eyes and messy dark hair. She also had a six-year-old daughter from a previous marriage. In so many ways she was perfect, save for the fact that she lived all the way up in Edinburgh - that and not being Verity Duke.

She was a funeral director though, so that was one problem he wouldn't have to deal with - most women fled at the first mention of his profession - but that would clearly not be the case here. He had not joined the message board looking for love, in fact, there were so few female funeral directors that it had not even crossed his mind.

"Witch's funeral was wonderful. Quite an experience, I wore a pink suit!"

"Pics or it didn't happen ;)" she replied.

"Any chance we can chat on Skype this evening?"

"Sorry to cancel again. I promise we'll do it some time soon. Angel hasn't gone to bed yet, she's protesting because there was a spider in her room earlier."

They had been chatting this way for over a month and Franklin tried not to get too downhearted that she didn't want to speak directly online. Always there had been an excuse, which Franklin tried not to think too deeply about. "You're missing me in my favourite pyjamas, Wallace and Gromit print."

"Pics or it didn't happen," she repeated. In reply Franklin turned on his computer's camera and took a screen shot of himself with Felicity asleep on his lap and a bottle of cider in his hand. He sent her the photo.

"You didn't tell me they were such sexy pyjamas!" she replied, and Franklin laughed out loud causing Felicity to wake with a start.

Suddenly Franklin's phone buzzed into life on the desk before him. At first he thought it might be Nell, but then he remembered he'd never sent her his phone number; then with dread he remembered that the killer did have his number. Finally he noticed, almost with a sense of disappointment, that no, it was just Edison.

"Evening."

"Hi Frank. Sorry to call you late, I just thought you'd like to know. We've arrested somebody for the murders - he's confessed."

18.

Edison Gallow had once heard that nervous people were always the ones best equipped in times of crisis. They may spend every waking moment fearing the worst, but in doing so, they were preparing for it - mulling over every worst case scenario and possible outcome, so that when the worst really did happen, they are ready for it.

Edison hoped this was true, perhaps being in possession of a superhero-like power in times of trouble would make up for all the late nights and shredded fingernails.

Not many people knew he was a nervous man. Years of practice had taught him how to cover his anxieties in such a way that only those who were looking for signs would notice them - that hastily downed vodka on arrival at the awkward social event, the tell-tale sign of nicotine stains between his fore and middle finger, those extra lines around his eyes that had aged him terribly.

Perhaps it was true, because amidst the panicky, electric atmosphere of the police station that evening, Edison felt a Zen like calm as the flurry of nervous anticipation spiraled out of control around him. Arrests always caused heightened emotions around the building, but high profile ones such as the Blackbeard Killer threatened to spill over into hysteria. Edison took a few more puffs on his electric cigarette, before noticing to his dismay that the battery was out of power, and returned inside to frantic activity - people dashing to and frow with paperwork, press releases and assorted scribblings on the murders that had gripped an entire city - an entire nation.

"Are you ready Ed?" asked D.I. Gladstone, the investigating officer who was heading the case. The woman was nearly a full decade younger than Edison but held herself with a great deal more poise and confidence than he had ever mustered. He used to find himself grumbling about her to Franklin with alarming frequency. "Political correctness gone mad... A woman, an Asian woman. No wonder she got promoted so fast; white men hadn't got a chance next to that…" he'd said it but he'd never believed it; Trish Gladstone had two things Edison had never been in possession of; ability and drive.

"Yes Ma'am"

"After you." She pushed the door to the interview room open and Edison stepped in before her.

The man seated behind the table in the deliberately bland interview room immediately stood up. "No way I'm having one of them interview me," he barked, pointing his finger at D.I. Gladstone who simply took a seat coolly across from him and told him to sit down.

"My name is Detective Inspector Gladstone, I have been assigned to your case and I can assure you that whether you want one of me or not, I shall be interviewing you."

The man complied, grumpily. He was everything Edison had imagined a member of a far-right nationalist group would be. He had a shaved head and wore a t-shirt emblazoned with the cross of St. George over which a pair of red braces held up his cargo pants. His face was held in a permanent snarl.

"This is my colleague Officer Gallow who will be sitting in on this interview."

Edison took this as his cue and pressed record on the almost comically outdated cassette recorder that was the only furnishing on the table. D.I. Gladstone audibly marked the time and date.

The man was Karl Kitson, no stranger to the police after several charges of drunk and disorderly and a string of convictions for low-level assault and breaches of the peace. He had never served time, always skimming that line, as angry thugs were wont to do - between casually illegality and serious crime.

Earlier that evening, he had appeared at the police station with a collection of 800 hand written pages he had referred to as his "manifesto" which he had handed over to the police after confessing to both the murder of Spencer Nordstrom and that of John MacGregor. He was arrested immediately.

"I understand you have opted not to have legal representation at this interview, is that correct?" Trisha Gladstone asked.

"Yeah. What of it? Just another waste of the taxpayer's money. Just another tool of the government, that's what those lawyers are. Probably give me a black one of them and all." Karl Kitson then directed himself to Edison. "Aren't you embarrassed mate? Having one of them higher up than you? Telling you what to do and stuff. It's against the natural order."

"Not at all," Edison said flatly, though in truth he had never liked having women as his superiors. He would never say so of course and he knew it was childish and wrong.

"So, Mr. Kitson, I would like you to tell me everything you know about these murders. Let's begin by you telling us why you did it?"

Karl Kitson smiled and folded his arms across his chest. "Because I had to, darlin'. This is about more than just me - this is about starting a fuckin' race war!"

"Go on," Trish remained undaunted.

"See, everyone knows that this is a race thing, right? Ask anyone and they'll tell you why that rich guy got killed on the bridge - 'cause of racism. And that bus driver was over that protest in the sixties. Everyone out there thinks a darkie did it - so what's gonna happen next? Rights for whites, that's what'll happen. The white people of the city… of the country, will rise up and fight back - take what's theirs and send them packing and headin' back to where they came from."

"Tell me Mr Kitson, how much do you know about Bristol history?"

"What? Slavery and stuff? A bit - more than most."

"What do you know about John Horwood?"

"John Horwood? Never heard of him - why is he another one of your lot?"

Trish pressed on. "John Horwood was a 19th century murderer who the killer seems to know a great deal about."

"Oh right, yeah. John Horwood. He was this killer, right, from the 19th century who… killed a load of people."

"Would it be fair to say that you had absolutely no idea who John Horwood was until a few seconds ago?"

"Are you fuckin' deaf, woman? What did I just tell you?"

"Moving on. What can you tell me about the process of anthropodermic bibliopegy?"

"You what?"

"Binding books in human skin."

"Nothin' much. Wasn't that book in The Evil Dead done up like that?"

"The Necronomicon Ex-Mortis" said Trish. Edison tried his best to hide the surprise on his face at her demonstration of horror film trivia.

"Sounds like some messed up thing from the dark ages."

"And how many people do you claim to have killed, Mr Kitson?"

"I told you, two. The rich man and the bus driver."

"I see."

Edison found himself impressed by her skill, how quickly she unpicked his story with information that had never been released to the media - adeptly unraveling his lies.

"And you did this with a crossbow?"

"Yeah." Karl shifted awkwardly in his seat.

"That was pretty impressive, have you had training?"

"I guess I just got lucky, right. Next question?"

"And the bus driver - John MacGregor. What did you take from the murder scene? We know what's missing but we just want to hear it from you."

He shrugged his shoulders and stared at the desk. "I dunno, probably got his wallet or something."

"No, that's not right is it?"

"Look, Miss. It's not just me out there, there's loads of us. I'm just the one who came forward. Maybe someone else took somethin' from the bus. We're like an army you see, fightin' to wipe the streets clean of scum like you."

"Very well. Interview terminated at 11.15 PM." Edison pressed stop on the tape recorder.

"What? That's all I get?" Karl asked, incredulously.

"Mr Kitson, you will be held in a cell until more information can be gathered. You'll be interviewed in full tomorrow." she stood up from the table and Edison followed. "I don't know why you're saying this, but you know as well as I do that there's no way you killed either of those men."

Karl Kitson merely stewed in a silent fury and glared at the woman as she turned and walked away with Edison following closely behind.

"He's definitely lying, right?" said Edison as he almost jogged to keep up with her.

"No doubt in my mind."

"But why would he do that? He's what, thirty-five? Any judge would throw the book at him - this would be one of those cases where you'd never get out - no appeals, no nothing. The Home Secretary would get involved and make sure he's locked away for life…"

Trish just shrugged her shoulders. "Buggered if I know. Fame? Notoriety? You know what these thugs are like, he probably thinks he'll be a martyr for the cause - maybe lead to an all-out riot - he probably thinks he'll even get his war."

"Sick bastard," said Edison as he followed Trish outside and watched hungrily as she lit a cigarette. She offered him one but he declined. "You know, it's wrong what he said, I really don't mind working under you. I was very impressed by you in there."

"Thanks. Anyway, he knew nothing about the book or that John MacGregor had one of his front teeth yanked out. You'd have thought he would at least have mentioned that detail, wouldn't you?"

"Yes, definitely. And he doesn't strike me as the kind who would be an expert with a crossbow."

"Exactly. Have you ever fired one of those things? It's hard enough to be accurate at the best of times, let alone on a moving bus."

Edison allowed himself a moment of passive inhalation as a cloud of cigarette smoke drifted towards him. "He doesn't seem all that bright either. Our killer definitely knows his history. Do you think it's true though? About a legion - an army?"

Trish seemed to roll her eyes through a curtain of smoke. "Do you mean are there other far-right scumbags like him in the city? Of course there are - and it's not always who'd you'd expect either. They don't all look like him - advertising their hatred for all the world to see - in a way they're the safe ones

- the ones you need to worry about are the ones who know how to hide it…"

Edison pondered her statement for a moment before he drew in a deep breath, not of passive smoke this time but in preparation for a question. "So, Trish, how about a drink? I'm paying?"

"Oh… Ed. Look, it's late and I should get home. I have a mountain of paperwork and…"

"…No, no, it's fine, I was just saying because…"

"…I don't think it's very appropriate for two officers to go drinking together. It seems very unprofessional. Maybe in a group sometime"

"It's fine. I get it."

Trish Gladstone stubbed her cigarette out against the wall and dropped it into a bin before hurriedly making her way back inside the building. The moment the doors closed behind her Edison slapped his hand to his forehead.

"Stupid, stupid idiot," he reprimanded himself. It would be another night of anxious half-sleep for him. But first he needed to buy some cigarettes.

19.

Half way through reheating his takeaway dinner, Franklin asked himself why it always had to be like this. It wasn't that he didn't know how to cook, he'd learned from his mother at a young age, but almost always opted to settle for easy and unsatisfying meals.

If there had been someone to share his life he was certain he would put more effort in. He'd probably own cookery books and shop at farmer's markets, but the pots and pans remained unused and night after night he watched miserably as yet another meal rotated in the microwave.

When he'd finished he paused the TV and fed Felicity, who slithered wheezingly across the kitchen floor. He made himself a cup of tea and sat down in front of his laptop which was open on the coffee table.

He clicked on to Facebook, over the previous six months he had taken to social networking with cautious pleasure and had gained a handful of friends, Rowan, Edison, a few people from his university days, Alf had still not responded to his friend request and seemed unlikely to do so any time soon, but it wasn't any of them he was hoping to hear from. He was looking for a message from Verity.

Nothing. The little blue bar at the top of the screen remained lifeless. Two days without a message from her had cast Franklin adrift, she was his tether in this strange online world of angry people spoiling for a fight at the slightest provocation. Already he had experienced a fracas when he felt obliged to point out to one former housemate that no, contrary to the article he'd shared on his timeline, the government was not planning on making it illegal to say the Lord's Prayer to appease Muslim immigrants. He had been met with a chorus of angry derision from the man's friends.

To the right of the screen a rapidly updated feed informed him of what news stories were "trending" on the site. Most of the time this seemed to be what female celebrities had worn to various red carpet events but that evening an article caught his attention.

"Ellie Sutton: Controversial Journalist Criticised On Social Media For Blog Post On Bristol Murders"

Franklin begrudgingly clicked on the link but knew he would regret it. Ellie Sutton was an inflammatory journalist who kept a notorious blog in which she vented vitriol across every electronic page. Her targets ranged from fat people to poor people, from gay people to non-Christians. In fact, anyone who wasn't Ellie Sutton had at some point found themselves in the crossfire and her vast output had amassed her a small fortune.

"Why The Blackbeard Killer Is The New Face of "Great" Britain." The headline read, alongside a glamourous picture of the writer, smoky eyes half closed, red lips pouting as if to form a kiss and choppy, blonde hair caught in the breeze of a photography studio wind machine. Her expression to the reader stated: "You may hate me, but you still want me."

"The parochial city of Bristol, the birthplace of Cary Grant, Thomas Chatterton and of course, yours truly, has become the scene of some of the most sensational murders in British history in the past weeks. I thought it was about time that I check out my old stomping ground and find out just what has been going on since I left all those years ago.

"Clifton, where I was once proud to lay my hat, was my first port of call and it was disheartening to say the least to see how much things had changed. The Blair years had taken their toll on what was one of the prettiest parts of any city in the country, and, just as expected, had fallen victim to that sad scourge of multiculturalism."

Franklin sighed. He could tell already where this was heading and skipped forward a few paragraphs for the sake of his liberal sensibilities.

"A killer who is targeting the city for its past – a questionable history, it's true, but one that has served this great city well, would not have been found in the Bristol I once knew. Wave after sorrowful wave of immigrants have washed up on these shores like rats clinging to flotsam as the great ship SS European Union slowly sinks to its watery grave. Who are these people and where have they come from? Why must they come here and insist that it is us who should bend in favour of their ludicrous customs?

Britain is and always will be a Christian nation, and not long ago it was a nation where your neighbour could be trusted. You recognised them; they looked like you and your family. Where has that Britain gone? It was swallowed up years ago when we declared our borders open to every Tomasz, Fritz and Mohammed. There is no doubt in the mind of every right thinking Englishman just who this killer is who seems so insulted by a statue of an independent businessman. He is just another of the millions of foreigners who do not think the British should be allowed to own their history or culture. Just another of that ongoing failure we call multicultural "Great" Britain."

That was enough for Franklin. He closed his laptop and considered a shower to wash away his anger. If the culture of Britain that Ellie Sutton epitomized really was being eroded, Franklin could find no possible reason why that culture would ever be worth saving.

20.

It was not the first time Jessica Miller had died. Twenty years before, at the age of 45, she had collapsed due to heat stroke while holidaying in India and her heart had stopped twice in the hospital - the second time she had been technically dead for almost a full minute.

She had lived an adventurous life, traipsing across vast deserts and up colossal mountains, diving into unfathomable oceans and trekking miles across the wastelands of Antarctica. Now past retirement age she had no intention of slowing down - there was still so much of the world to see, so many corners left unexplored, so many people to meet and food to try - maybe one day, if the predictions were right and the technology was on schedule, she would be one of the lucky ones with a seat booked on a commercial flight into space. Retirement was no stumbling block for her.

Neither had been death. When her heart had began beating again and the oxygen in her blood returned to her brain, she found herself wading out from the shallows of that endless ocean of sleep not as one who had seen the light at the end of the tunnel, nor heard choirs of angels sing - she had felt nothing - not even a blackness or a void, just nothingness, a space in which even thought could not dwell. There was simply nothing at all, just an end, a complete full stop that went on forever.

Such an experience could have driven stronger women than her half insane, but Jessica Miller found solace. A sense that she had unearthed proof that life truly did not survive death and that every day, every minute, was to be treasured and celebrated. Each moment she lived after that day in India was a gift and she would live from that day on as if it were such.

Jessica had been dining with friends. She had not seen Larry and Lois Roker in over a year, but they were close enough that time proved no barrier to easy conversation. At first it had been all about work - she and Larry had both been courtroom judges - he still in the profession, she only a year out of it, and had studied alongside one another decades before. All talk had at first been about the state of the British justice system and casual gossip about various members of the bar but quickly moved on to the topic the whole city was now schooled in - The Blackbeard Killer.

"I've been saying it for years," said Larry as he uncorked another bottle of white wine, "they should just tear down that statue once and for all. It's been nothing but trouble and says only bad things about us. We're one of the most liberal cities in the country and yet we celebrate a monster in the very centre of our home."

"Here, here," Jessica raised her glass in agreement with her friend. It was getting late but another drink wouldn't hurt. Larry poured it for her. "Of course, we're all assuming that's what he wants - I can't imagine the public are being told all the facts."

Larry shook his head. "That's for damn sure. How many times has it come to sentencing and only then do we get to hear the full list of priors, it's a disgrace."

With the finishing of the fourth bottle the evening seemed to be drawing to a close. Lois Roker was unselfconsciously drifting into sleep at the table and Jessica was on the cusp between tipsiness and all out inebriation.

"Shall I call you a taxi?" Larry offered as he watched his wife stir and rise blearily to her feet.

"Thank you, but I think a walk will do me good."

Larry exchanged a concerned glance with his wife. "Are you sure that's wise... given the circumstances?"

Jessica had not wanted to ask, but as delicious as the night air may have seemed, there was the very real threat of a killer in their midst. "If you don't mind, perhaps if you could just walk me to Park Street, I could get a taxi from there."

Larry smiled warmly at her. There had been a time when she had been in love with him, when he was young and single. Now silver haired and furrowed of skin, he may have lost his youthful good looks, but those ice blue eyes still had the power to cut through to her heart. "Certainly ma'am."

The pair walked arm in arm from Clifton Village, the prosperous neighbourhood that Larry and his wife had made their home for over twenty years, and reminisced drunkenly about the good old days. The little lamplit park that led them from the village to the busy thoroughfare of Park Street was eerily empty, as much of the city was that night.

"Do you see that?" asked Larry, breaking his step and nodding down the path before them.

At first Jessica did not, but gradually, as her eyes adjusted to the bright light of a Victorian street lamp up ahead, she noticed it too. A figure standing before them, half in darkness, but wearing what was unmistakably a tricorn hat.

"Larry, it's not..." the sound of the arrow hitting her was no more than the breaking of a twig but the force it hit her with was like a punch. She looked down at her body, utterly bewildered by what had happened, to see a quivering arrow jutting from her chest. "My heart!" she shrieked as she fell to her knees. Larry slipped from her arm and spun on his feet, the last thing she saw was her friend dropping lifelessly to the floor beside her as the arrow struck his side.

21.

It was only when a notice flashed up on her TV screen informing her that she had watched five episodes back-to-back on Netflix, that Rowan realised she had not been paying any attention to the sitcom that had been merrily playing away while she tapped away at her iPad. How long had she been doing this? Lying on top of her bed, still fully clothed and following link after link through Wikipedia as she read more about Wicca than she ever thought she would care to know.

Wiccans, Druids and Pagans were all essentially the same she had learned, in that they all shared a love and worship of nature and believed in both a god and a goddess. Seasons seemed very important to them, as were the solstices - the longest day and the longest night. Many customs she had believed to be Christian, eggs at Easter, pumpkins at Halloween, virtually everything about Christmas, was a kind of cultural rebranding of ancient religions as Christianity spread across Europe. It fascinated and compelled her - the symbols which had once held an almost primal fear: the symbol of the pentacle, the goat headed man, the scratchy, etched imagery of tarot cards, now felt beguiling, mystical in a way that all religious iconography can be - it was welcoming her.

It was almost two in the morning when Rowan decided that enough was enough - her eyelids felt heavy and her concentration was drifting away from the screen and into her own messy thoughts. Just before she turned in for the night she checked the video one last time as she burrowed under the covers. She had taken to doing so every few hours, or whenever the mood compelled her.

The familiar video played at once - the dog splashing through the breakwater of a Cornish beach, its owner chirping happily to him as he tore about. She scrolled down to where Franklin had left his note to the stranger - it had been a week without a reply so the sight of fresh words on the page were an unexpected horror. She read the lines aloud and then snapped the cover over her iPad and leapt out of bed.

Her first instinct was to call Franklin but then thought better of it - if the words were true perhaps her boss' phone was being monitored. She instead dressed as quickly as she could, throwing on whatever clothes had been discarded in a messy pile and grabbed her foldaway bike from behind the door. The man standing in the hallway gave her such a fright that she almost screamed.

"Hey, Hot Chocolate," smiled Jude. "What are you doing up?" Her neighbour had just finished climbing the stairs and had paused on the landing.

"I could ask the same of you," she hissed as she tried to push past him.

"Just back from a gig," he grinned as he flashed his guitar case that was slung over his shoulder. "What's the rush, HC? Life is long…"

"It's a work thing. Need to head across town, could you get out of my way?"

"What's the magic word?"

"Piss off."

He stepped aside, "That's good enough."

As Rowan stepped from her front door, she was struck by the coldness of the night. Winter couldn't be far away and it seemed to be approaching with speed. Far away she could hear the drone of emergency sirens which she tried to put to the back of her mind as she swung her bike into shape before cycling off across the city.

Franklin was in the midst of a troubling dream. In it he was lost in the once familiar streets of Bristol - streets he had passed down a thousand times opened onto places that simply shouldn't be there, around every corner stretched a crooked road he had never seen before. In every shadow moved shapes, human, but somehow not quite - like ghosts, or aliens. All the while he was crying out for help, from Rowan, from Edison… from Alf. Thunder clapped overhead, lighting a city filled with monsters that crept just out of sight - the unquiet dead of the city… centuries of injustice from which the forgotten had returned to claim their vengeance in this strange new world that had once been his home.

The sound that broke his sleep had not been his waking scream but the banging of the downstairs door in the reception room, it sounded urgent, frenzied even. Rubbing his eyes, Franklin pushed Felicity from his chest and consulted his phone. It was 2.30 am. He dialled 9 three times on his phone and crept out of bed - all he would have to do was press call if the worst were to happen.

His fears were put to rest immediately he stepped into the reception room, there behind the glass door stood Rowan, her eyes wide in panic - he marched across the room and unlocked the door.

"I'm so sorry to wake you, I didn't know what else to do." She seemed close to tears. "Have you seen the video? The dog one?"

"Not for a few hours why?"

"Please, just look at it with me!" Rowan's breathing seemed to be getting out of control so he sat her down beside him on the sofa.

"Calm down, Rowan," he patted her kindly on the shoulder. "You're safe."

"It's not about me, Franklin. Check the video." Rowan unzipped her rucksack and passed him her iPad. "But not here, someone might be watching us."

"You're sounding a little paranoid,"

"You're not sounding paranoid enough."

"Ok." Franklin took her by the cold hand and led her upstairs to his flat. The sudden sense of safety seemed to calm her at once.

Franklin's flat was never how she'd imagined his living space to be - it was cluttered with unwashed dishes piled up around the sink and a comfy looking blanket thrown haphazardly on the sofa. A mangy looking cat paced meekly about the floor, as if hoping to find a corner in which it could curl up and die. She liked it here - she liked knowing that beneath his tailored suits, Franklin could be just as shambolic as she was. There seemed to be more beneath his suits than she had imagined too, for on the radiator beside the TV a selection of vibrantly coloured pants were drying. It was odd to imagine that her drearily uniformed friend would choose such dazzling underwear - just as it was strange to see him wearing Wallace and Gromit pyjamas.

"OK, show me what's on the video," he said as he passed her the iPad. She navigated to the YouTube page and passed it back to him.

"There will be two murders in Clifton tonight. I am the judge and shall decide who is guilty. Tell no one and remember that I am always watching you," he read aloud. "Bloody hell. Have you told anyone?"

"Nobody. I didn't even want to call you in case he really was watching."

"It was posted just over an hour ago." Franklin switched on the TV and turned it to BBC News.

"They won't say anything yet," Rowan informed him. "They'll have to inform the families and things first. Get some identification - the media won't hear until the morning once a press release is written."

"Well, first thing's first," said Franklin. "Coffee." He stepped into the small kitchen area and put the kettle on. He poured them both a mug full - black, no sugar, as they were both accustomed. They settled on the sofa where they both stared at the screen in silence as the news rolled past them in the background.

"I know," Franklin finally concluded. He tapped in a response to the last message that had been posted. "What do you want me to do now?" He pressed enter and waited, the response came sickeningly quickly.

"You will wait your turn and tell nobody. Your time will come."

"What the hell?" Franklin whispered to the screen.

"He isn't threatening you, is he?"

"No," said Franklin. "I don't think so anyway."

"It sounds like he is…"

"Can we not talk about that possibility please? I'm trying to keep a level head and that's not helping."

"Sorry," said Rowan. "You know what we have to do though, don't you?"

"Rowan, we can't call the police, he's threatened to kill one person a day if we contact them."

"If you contact them," she replied.

Franklin at first took this to mean that his friend was distancing herself from her involvement before he understood what she was really saying. "If you call the police it won't make a jot of difference to the killer - he'll know that I'm involved and it will just put you in danger… again."

Rowan tutted angrily. "Remember that day on the beach, after I'd nearly been murdered?"

Franklin turned to face her. "Yes, I think I remember that, Rowan."

"You told me that you can't stop me investigating things - that I won't stop looking for answers."

"I also said I would never let you get into that kind of trouble again."

"Whether you like it or not, I'm involved and we both need some help." Rowan reached into her jacket pocket and passed him her phone. "The killer doesn't know who I am, nobody does - so he won't be tracing my call, if that's like… even possible. Call your brother and explain everything, all of it. He doesn't have to let anyone else know, but we can feed him information and we can… do some proper investigating again and catch this bastard."

Franklin did not need to hear another word. He took the phone from Rowan's hand and dialed his brother's mobile number from memory and was surprised how quickly he answered it.

"Hello,"

"It's Franklin, we need to talk…"

"Oh no, is something wrong with Mum or Dad?"

"No, nothing like that…"

"…Then why are you calling me at this time? I'm busy."

"I need your help, Edison. I've heard from the killer again – whoever they are, they want me involved for some reason. I've known for a little while now."

"Jesus Christ, Frank, you can't keep secrets like that from me. This is a criminal investigation into multiple murders in fact…"

"…You're at a crime scene right now aren't you?"

There was a brief silence on the phone. "Is it on the news already? Did you hear people talking in the background?"

"I've heard from the killer directly and I know who he's killed. Two people, right? In Clifton?"

"Frank, how do you know this?"

"You need to take me seriously and get yourself over here… no, to somewhere else. I'll meet you at the Central Library this afternoon. Send me a text with the time you're free - you can't be seen coming here…"

"You're spooking me out Frank, can't you just say what you know over the phone?"

"It's too risky and we need to be a bit paranoid." To this Rowan nodded her ascent.

"Well, I'll tell you this much - you're right about Clifton, they were two judges, but there's one thing you're wrong about. It wasn't two murders, one of them's still alive."

22.

Rowan awoke to the sound of her mobile phone alarm and was at once thrown into a state of confusion. It was 8am but the room in which she'd been sleeping was an unfamiliar one. It was bare and unadorned, like she imagined a prison cell would be - just a single bed against a wall and a scratchy, grey carpet on the floor.

Blinking back to consciousness, she pieced together what had happened the evening before. She had stayed the night at Franklin's house, in the spare room. She must have been really tired she concluded as the full horror of the night before returned - two bodies, one alive and the killer speaking to Franklin once more. Words on a screen had never seemed so sinister, as if pure evil was emanating from its glow.

Franklin however seemed to be in fine spirits. After dressing in the clothes she had haphazardly strewn across the floor the night before, she met him in the kitchen where he was merrily whistling along to the radio.

"Good morning," he smiled as bread sizzled in a frying pan on the stove. He was already dressed in his suit as he skipped about the kitchen sipping black coffee.

"What are you so cheerful about? You don't sound like a man who was just threatened by a serial killer."

"I'm pretending that it didn't happen and focusing on the good news. Verity is coming to visit - she's going to stay here for the night!"

"Really? She's up for a second bout is she?"

"Don't be unkind, Rowan. She's coming to visit Alf but thought we could have an evening together - you know, reconnect..."

"Didn't Alf only leave home a couple of weeks ago?"

Franklin shrugged his shoulders. "I think she's concerned about him - that bus driver was killed near to his campus."

"Fair enough - but be careful, Franklin. The pair of you are quite a fertile couple, I trust you have suitable protection."

Franklin's face dropped. "Do you think that's a possibility?"

"No idea - you know her better than I do but I'm guessing she's not a complete moron. If she's staying with you, she has to be aware that it will have crossed your mind."

"Now I'm scared. And the last of my condoms are past their use by date… That's a depressing thought…"

"It certainly is, and a gross one too." said Rowan as she took the coffee Franklin handed her.

The pair ate fried bread with beans and mushrooms. It was the first breakfast she could remember enjoying in several months. Her father had always been a good cook, his breakfasts were the only thing she truly missed about living with her parents. A bowl of off-brand Sugar Puffs simply could not compete with a full English.

As they were clearing the dishes, Franklin's phone buzzed as a text message appeared. "Is that Verity?" Rowan smirked.

"No, Edison. He's just finished work and wants me to meet him at the library."

"Let's go,"

"You're not coming - I want you out of this mess as much as possible."

Rowan rolled her eyes. "It's a bit late for that, don't you think? Anyway, I don't trust either one of you to get to the bottom of this. I'm coming along."

"But…"

"…Let's go."

It wasn't just that Franklin knew not to challenge his stubborn friend, but that he knew she was right - there was no way he wanted to take whatever horrible journey he was likely to be forced through at the request of a raging psychopath. He was going to need someone there to keep him sane.

"Bye Felicia," Rowan waved to the sleeping cat on the sofa as they left.

"She's called Felicity," Franklin informed her.

"Oh Franklin, you're such a square. It's what the cool kids say…"

"Do the cool kids still say square?"

"They do now. These things are cyclical."

Peterman was due in that morning and Franklin was relieved that he didn't make an exception and arrive on time that day - he didn't want to have to explain to him why Rowan stayed the night. The pair chose to walk across the city as it was a crisp, clear morning and the library was only a short skip over to the north of the river.

In the shadow of the grand, ancient towers of the mighty cathedral stood the library, before which Edison was pacing agitatedly. It was a quiet Saturday - a gentle hangover clung to the city so that the few people that were about were buried behind sunglasses and wrapped in comforting layers. Edison looked exhausted for completely different reasons.

"Did you get any sleep?" Franklin asked his brother.

"No… and good morning to you, too," he replied. "What's she doing here?"

"She is here to help," said Rowan and Edison knew not to argue.

Inside the library there was barely a soul to be found. Most of the students who would usually fill the central hall were either still in bed, glued to a news feed about the murder the night before or had fled the city altogether out of fear. Nevertheless, Franklin thought it prudent for them to hide away in a corner of the journal section beside a tiny window that overlooked College Green. On any ordinary Saturday the expanse of grass would contain clusters of teens shrouded by clouds of cannabis smoke, but this was no ordinary Saturday.

"So what happened last night?" Franklin began. "Not the news stuff, tell us everything."

Edison glanced suspiciously over at Rowan with bloodshot eyes. "Anything I say is under the strictest confidence, right?" Both Rowan and Franklin nodded in agreement. "Okay. Well, you were right that two people were attacked last night - they were two judges, both in their seventies; a man and a woman. They had been at a dinner party - according to his wife, they had all been friends for years and he was walking her to the taxi rank. They were just leaving Clifton Village when they were attacked - a crossbow again… She was killed instantly - straight through the heart, and he, we think, was turning to run and got hit in the side - he's still alive but not by much - he suffered a huge amount

108

of blood loss but we expect he'll pull through... I've never seen anything like it, Frank, there was so much blood but it wasn't just that, it was how public it was, the viciousness, like we were being forced to be shocked by the audacity of it."

"Struck through the heart," Rowan echoed coolly.

"Well," Franklin interjected. "This is where we get involved. I received a letter a few days ago - remember that pretty writing in the skin book? It was that exact hand, directing me to a video on YouTube. The killer and I have been sort of communicating via the comment section on this... very boring video."

"A video? Why do the police know nothing about this?"

"Over twenty hours of video footage are uploaded to YouTube every sixty seconds," Rowan said. "It's actually a perfect way to contact someone as it can't be traced and the odds of someone stumbling over it accidentally are astronomical."

"I meant," Edison pressed on, "why didn't you tell the police?"

Franklin simply reached inside his jacket pocket and gave Edison the letter which was sealed inside a clear plastic bag.

"I see, another body every night... The killer's playing a very dangerous game here."

"It's like he's challenging me to tell the police, so that I'll be responsible for whoever dies next," Franklin sighed.

"You can't think like that, Frank."

"There's no other way I can think, I can dress it up as much as I want but people will die because of me if I make a mistake."

"People have died!" Edison snapped. Immediately he looked around the room to ensure it was empty before continuing in a whisper. "As soon as you hear anything, absolutely anything at all, you get back to me, you pass on everything and I promise I'll keep it to myself. I'm going to keep this letter though... see what I can find out from it."

"No one else at the station can know," Franklin pressed.

"Of course, but if things go much further, I'm going to have to speak out and the devil with what happens - the police are going to have to be the ones to catch him in the end..."

"Like you did with my sister's murderer?" Rowan hissed.

Edison hardly flinched. "That is an ongoing case, Rowan…"

"Right. Sure."

Franklin saw Edison glare at him and once again felt that painful slash of guilt. Rowan deserved to know that her father was the prime suspect in the murder of her sister, but he had absolutely no idea how to tell her.

"We will catch him," Edison reassured her, but she merely stared angrily out of the window. "I'm sorry, this is all too much for me to think about. It's been a horrible, long night and I need some sleep. Get back to me whenever you have something new… or just something less awful. See you Friday."

Once his brother had left, Franklin turned to Rowan. "Look, you can't do this every time we meet Edison. It isn't his fault - he's not even working Ruby's case."

"I know, it's just sometimes it feels as if… I mean, I like Edison I really do, it's just that… it's hard to look at him sometimes, because of what he represents. There's this awful, selfish part of me that doesn't care if this killer is caught and do you know why?"

Franklin just shook his head.

"All this news coverage was here from day one when that rich white man got murdered - nobody gave a shit about Ruby. A couple of articles in the local press and she didn't even get a mention on the national news. Every newspaper in the country will have the faces of white people on their covers this morning and everybody, everybody knows that this killer will get caught eventually… that's what being white gives you - that sense of safety, that the bad guys will get caught and sometimes… just sometimes when I feel cruel and selfish, I think yes, white people should know what it feels like to be singled out… to have the police ignore you and to have a killer run free…"

Franklin touched her shoulder. "That's not healthy, Rowan. I know you're angry - I get angry too and I wish more could be done - one day they will catch her killer, I promise you they will - just as they will catch this guy with the crossbow. Everybody should feel safe and murder… is always murder."

Rowan nodded slowly to herself. "Please don't think too badly of me, I guess it's just like the Colston statue - I see things a bit differently to you."

"I'm a straight, white man - we're the people who rule the world, what do I know about intolerance?"

"You're a ginger," she smiled and the pair laughed together.

As they were leaving the library, Rowan's phone vibrated with the arrival of a text. It was from Jude. It enticed her as much as it repelled her.

"Hey Hot Chocolate Girl. Why don't you come upstairs tonight?"

Despite her better judgment, she simply replied. "I'll be up at 8".

23

"I don't care how many times I see it," said Verity, "the sight of a D-list celebrity falling on her arse in a ball gown will never tire."

Franklin concurred by clinking their wine glasses together. The evening had been even more magical than he'd hoped for. Once she'd returned from visiting their son, Verity arrived at the door looking radiant in jeans and a shirt and bearing two bottles of red wine and a naughty smile that made her look like a teenager who'd stolen them from her father's cellar. "Wanna get loopy?"

They had spent the evening sitting side by side on the sofa, drinking and laughing at the idiocy of atrocious television. Franklin was twenty-one again - somehow dragged back through time to his university days when they were young and silly - but friendless enough to have only each other on a Saturday night.

"He's fine of course," she had said. "I'm the only one who's worried at all - I was always like that with him. It was such a huge responsibility, just him and me, that there was never a moment where I wasn't terrified that something awful would happen. I can't just turn that off, I think it's with me forever now."

"I wish I'd been there to help… I know you wanted to do it by yourself but I could at least have chipped in a bit."

Verity smiled at him. "Sometimes I wish you had been too - I think he would have liked to have had a dad around, even if he'd never have admitted it. He did ask about you a lot though. He really doesn't hate you, he just wants you to think he does."

"Well, he's doing a great job of it. How do you think you'll be when he gets a boyfriend?"

"I think I'll be fine," she said thoughtfully. "It'll be easier than if he had a girlfriend. I've always been the number one female in his life and I don't want that crown sitting on some other woman's head - this way I get to be his number one forever. I know it's childish to think like that, but it's important to me."

"I'll think I'll try and aim for fifth or sixth best man in his life. I like to set attainable goals."

"He'll warm up to you eventually. He told me about throwing up on the campus in front of you - he says you helped him out."

"I did my best, all I had were some mints."

"He was always a strange kid, even when he was really small. Other kids always notice the strange ones, it's like an odd sense they have even in primary school, they know they have to toe the line and fit in, most of them, anyway. Alf never did, or if he tried I think he knew it would never last."

"Oh no," Franklin sighed, "was he bullied?"

"Not really. Well, a little perhaps, but it was more like they just wanted to keep their distance, they didn't know what to make of him."

"I know that feeling - Edison too. We were the kids who lived in the funeral home."

"I bet," Verity nodded. "Alf was just always by himself and I used to worry so much about him because of it. I used to lie awake in bed and think maybe he was autistic or that it was something I'd done. When he came out, I was so relieved because it felt like that was it, that was the thing that had stopped him fitting in, but no it wasn't, because he was just as alone afterwards. When he was a little boy I bought him a Playstation 2 for Christmas one year, it was the first big present he'd ever got, and for his birthday I bought him a second controller to play with a friend. He never even took that controller out of the packaging because he knew it would never get used."

Franklin unexpectedly found himself blinking back tears, imagining his son as a lonely, friendless boy whose nature was simply too bizarre for the children around him. "University will change him. He'll meet people like him, I promise. Maybe he'll even calm down with the radical politics a little."
"I know, and he even had a handful of friends by the end of college. Just think of us at uni – always in on a Saturday night drinking wine while everyone was out having fun." Verity smiled and clinked her glass against his. "You've always been

very kind, Franklin. You're a decent man, it's what I've always admired most about you. Even this place - I know you wanted to escape the funeral home when you were growing up, but you came back because it was the right thing to do for your dad."

"It's nice that somebody appreciates that," Franklin smiled.

"I've missed you a lot."

Franklin bristled as his heart seemed to swell inside his chest. "I've missed you too."

"It doesn't feel like almost twenty years does it? That night on the sofa - red wine and Dale Winton's Pets Win Prizes on TV."

"Bloody hell, were we really watching that?"

"Oh yes, a labrador had just peed on the astroturf stage and we were laughing and you just kissed me out of the blue."

"It sounds so romantic when you put it like that…"

"What do you say to another bottle of wine?"

Rowan was irritated with herself for the amount of time she'd spent preparing for the evening - hair, makeup, multiple choices of outfit rated in the mirror inside her wardrobe. Why was she making such an effort for a man she thought so little of? Was she really so shallow as to go weak at the knees for a sculpted torso? She was worried that she was.

She had settled on a daffodil yellow top with matching skirt and a chunky belt around her waist. She didn't know much about fashion but Ruby had offered her tips as she grew up. She had opted out of bringing alcohol with her - that would probably end up signifying too much as far as her intentions were concerned, and would make that idiot think he stood a chance. She made sure she was exactly fifteen minutes late - she wanted him to have to wait so it at least appeared that he was little more than an afterthought. She knocked on his door.

"Hot Chocolate!" He purred as he flung open the door. He was once again wearing nothing more than a pair of boxer shorts and his stripey dressing gown.

"Hi Jude," she replied flatly. "And my name's Rowan."

He just winked in response. "Let me get you a cider," he said and she followed him into the kitchen area of his flat. It was identical to hers, save for the vaulted ceiling - it felt like an alternate universe version of her own living space, familiar yet different, sparsely decorated and not at all like the chaotic shambles she was used to.

As Jude opened a bottle of his home brew on the edge of the kitchen counter, Rowan found herself gazing lustily at his torso, tracing the line of hair from the centre of his pectoral muscles to the band of his boxer shorts, dreamily pondering about what might be held within. How long had it been since she last had sex? What was making her so attracted by this lunk-headed poseur?

"I was thinking I could play you some of my music. I'm writing this song for you - Hot Chocolate Girl, it's not quite finished but I think you'll dig it. I've written some poetry too - you make me feel inspired - more creative than I've felt in years and…"

Suddenly Rowan found herself lunging forwards and grabbing her neighbour by the curly, blonde locks around his ears, pushing an open mouthed kiss against his soft lips - partly to shut him up, but mostly by a sudden urge to consume him.

Lustily she panted into his mouth and the two fell to the floor in a heap of twisted limbs.

"You were in love with me?" Verity gasped.

"I thought you knew," said Franklin, already regretting his candour, the wine was working fast. "Just that last year but I didn't want to do anything about it because we were friends… you were my only proper friend back then, everyone else thought I was too strange - or creepy, son of an undertaker…"

"…Funeral director," Verity corrected.

"So… how about you?"

"Oh Franklin, you were my friend and I loved you as a friend."

"Ouch," Franklin winced.

"I'm sorry, I'd love to say that there was more to it than that but it was just never more than just friends…"

"Was it because of the funeral home?"

"No!"

"The red hair?"

"Of course not!"

"Am I too short?"

"Franklin, what's this about?"

He could only shrug his shoulders.

"Maybe it's different for girls," she explained, "we're conditioned not to be demanding or make the first move. We're supposed to keep ourselves under control and think rationally - I really liked you, but we compartmentalise more and I just never saw you in that way. I wish I could say I did but I'd be lying. You were very handsome - you still are, it's just that you weren't what I was looking for - I just wanted a bit of fun and I knew that with you… you would be lovely, and kind - and you really were."

"So how about now? What are you looking for now?"

"I haven't given it much thought really. There have only been a handful of men while Alf was growing up. I was always so careful to make sure I didn't upset him in any way. I wanted our home to be as stable as possible - there was a time when I could have had men come and go every other night, but I always behaved responsibly."

Franklin nodded. "This flat has hardly been a den of inequity either, I threw out the last of my condoms this afternoon as they'd expired."

"That's okay, I brought some with me."

Franklin could barely believe what he'd heard. "Sorry?"

"I didn't know if I'd want to - but I really do. How about it? One more time? See if we can feel like we're twenty again?"

Before Franklin even knew what was happening, before he even let himself believe that this moment could be true, he and Verity, the woman he had loved for as long as he had known what love truly meant, were kissing.

Rowan and Jude lay panting and naked, side-by-side on top of the bed covers. Jude pulled away his condom and held the contents aloft before their faces - a miserable looking balloon dangled before her eyes.

116

"Do you think those poor little guys feel anything?" he asked.

"I've never thought about it," she said. "They don't have brains, so, no…"

"I wonder if anyone has ever tried raising them… like pets? Would you need an aquarium or something?"

"Raising them as a pet is called pregnancy, Jude. Throw it away."

Jude sighed mournfully as he tied off the end before dumping it in his bedside bin.

"So what now?" he asked.

"If you're asking for a second go it's not going to happen, this was a one off." Rowan was certain that in her post-orgasmic chill she would have regrets or an overriding sense of guilt, but she had neither - if anything there was a sense of fulfillment, an unreachable itch had finally been scratched. Jude had been frustratingly good at sex, the kind of sex she was certain she would be incapable of turning down in the future, despite her protestations otherwise.

"You're the first black girl I've done it with," Jude declared.

"Can you just shut up please?"

"I was like, wow girl! You got the moves!"

Rowan covered her ears to block out the rest of the nonsense that came spilling from his mouth. Once it appeared that he'd grown silent, she hauled herself off of the bed and began dressing.

"So are we going to see each other tomorrow night?" Jude smirked.

"No."

"I'll take you out for a meal - somewhere fancy."

"Look, this was just a one time thing for me. It's been ages since I last did it with anyone and I just needed a little fun, d'you get that?"

"Received loud and clear Hot Chocolate. How about I pick you up at eight tomorrow and we see where this roller coaster takes us?"

"Fine," she said as she turned from him and marched out of the flat. It was only as she stomped down the stairs that she realised the hideous wreck she had driven herself into.

She had accidentally found herself a boyfriend - a boyfriend she hated.

24.

Rowan was not due to work the following morning but decided to cycle in to visit Franklin anyway - she had no desire to sit around her flat all day with her stupid neighbour just a floor above, and if nothing else, the ride might help clear her mind.

The statue of Edward Colston stood at the Stokes Croft end of St Augustine's Parade - the unofficial centre of Bristol - where little fountains and coffee shops in moveable huts did their best to hide the fact that this was little more than a gigantic roundabout. His likeness was almost hidden among trees and far from where most visitors congregated - a concession of sorts to the ever-present controversy regarding its existence. Rowan hated to look at it and despised the shortsighted appeasement from the council to those feeble-minded enough to believe it should stay. This morning however something was happening.

A young blonde man of about student age was atop a stepladder beside the statue and almost at the same height. Around him milled a large crowd that was packed in tightly to avoid the constant traffic on the roads that encircled them.

"Edward Colston," the man hollered, "was one of history's greatest monsters. We are better than this, Bristol deserves better."

Rowan stopped her bike and folded it up. Holding it under her arm she began passing through the outermost orbit of onlookers. "What's happening here?" She asked of a man beside her.

"It's a rally. They organised it on Twitter last night, I reckon they're going to tear that statue down like Saddam in Baghdad!"

This seemed unlikely to Rowan, the statue and the plinth stood at almost ten metres and was cast in bronze. Looking at the face of the figure it was hard to imagine him as a monster. He looked thoughtful, almost plaintive, as if troubled by his own past and legacy, one hand rested on his cheek thoughtfully like he was making a phone call.

"What is this statue saying to us?" The angry student on the ladder went on. "It says that we don't care about the suffering of hundreds of thousands of African men, women and children who were put into slavery and sold as commodities to American landowners. It says that we prize money over decency and put some human lives above others - had this man… this monster, enslaved white people I can promise you this statue would not be standing here today - it would never have been built in the first place!"

About half the assembled crowd - easily more than a couple of hundred - broke into applause. Rowan found herself nodding her approval.

The student went on. "What this statue represents is human suffering on an unprecedented scale, and we're paying for it now with our own blood. We can't expect our history to lay hidden forever, it will return and take its revenge as we have seen!" More applause which Rowan found herself only gingerly taking part in, she didn't quite like the implication that, whether figuratively or otherwise, the dead really had returned for vengeance.

"That's a lot of bollocks!" shrieked an indignant voice from the crowd. Following the gaze of the crowd, Rowan's eyes fell upon the red-flushed face of an elderly woman who was jabbing her finger indignantly towards the man on the stepladder. "My great grandfather helped set that statue on the very spot he stands today. Colston was a good man who made this city. Look at all those almshouses he set up for poor people in Bristol - look at all the schools! It's a bloody shame that people like you don't know their history otherwise they'd think twice about dragging his name through the dirt for the sake of a bit of attention!" It was at this outburst that the other half of the spectators broke into a round of defiant applause.

"This serial killer doesn't seem to think so!" the student rebuffed.

"So you're siding with him are you? If the killer wanted us to tear down the Clifton Suspension Bridge should we do that too? That's called bowing to terrorism!"

More cheers. Rowan couldn't help but notice that generations seemed to divide this assembly more than anything else. Hip, lefty young students up against conservative older people in cheers and jeers as the argument volleyed back and forth between the man and woman. The cheers became louder, the jeers more angered. Rowan was suddenly aware just how boxed in she was as shoulders pressed against her and the whole throng seemed to sway and jolt with every new accusation.

"Colston should be resigned to the cesspit of history and his statue ground down into dust!"

"Colston is the greatest Bristolian ever to have lived!"

Soon the crowd was not just shouting at the student and the elderly woman but breaking out into angry scuffles as the mass of irate people turned on each other. Rowan began backing away from the crowd, certain that she was witnessing the gestation of a riot - a fracture of her city caused by the mere existence of an innocuous looking statue. Breaking free from the group she saw that a line of police officers were approaching them, hoping to dispel the worst of the general disorder. She dropped her folded Brompton from under her arm and was hastily constructing it when she felt a man's grip seize her elbow. His face was a picture of pure, unbridled rage.

"No one gave a shit about Colston until people like you turned up. Why don't you fuck off back to Africa?"

Rowan yanked her arm away from him - she would have thrown a punch at his gormless face had he not already slipped away into the crowd. She felt her hands shake - a mix of fury and fright. Turning away from the statue she mounted her bike and cycled away.

It took her a while to calm down enough to stop seeing his face before her - angry and old and bitter - the face of an enraged racist. It was only when she convinced herself that he should wield no such power over her emotions, that she started to cool down.

Sundays were usually quiet at Gallow & Sons - as many people died as on any other day but the general sense of slow down every seventh day had a knock on effect to the general running of the business. Hospitals, retirement homes, even mortuaries would wait another day to release a body, and as such, Franklin and Rowan followed suit. Moreover, the process of collating information and speaking to family members could always wait until Monday; even secular people enjoyed a day of rest.

Rowan was still livid enough to be ready to blurt out the news of her racist encounter but the sight of Franklin in his office, leaning back in his chair with his feet on his desk and his arms behind his head and smiling giddily, immediately stopped her.

"Franklin. You had sex last night!"

"What? No I didn't!" he exclaimed.

"Don't lie, I can see it all over your face, you had sex with Verity, I've never seen you look so self satisfied."

"Bloody hell, is it that obvious?"

"You could see it from space!"

Franklin smirked. "Once last night and again this morning…"

"Yeah, I'm going to want you to stop now. I've heard enough. So, is she still here?"

"No. She left for Cheltenham an hour or so ago, but I'll see her the next time she's in Bristol."

"What? That's all? You have sex with the love of your life for the first time in… fifty years, and then act all cool afterwards."

Franklin just shrugged his shoulders. "What can I say, we're keeping it casual." He dropped his feet from the desk and sat upright. "I think I just needed some fireworks you know - I'd missed it more than I thought."

"Well," said Rowan as she took a seat opposite him, "I'm really pleased, it's nice that the elderly can still find happiness."

"Very funny. I suppose you've seen the news this morning?"

Rowan realised she hadn't. She usually turned it on first thing, but had elected not to that morning choosing instead to enjoy a tepid bath to ceremoniously wash away her regrettable encounter the night before. "Not another murder…"

"Mercifully no," said Franklin. "Yesterday evening the killer opened a Twitter account and has gone public with the stuff about Colston - saying the killings are revenge for Bristol's past."

"That explains the fuss at the statue,"

"I heard there was going to be a rally."

"Rally? Looked like the beginnings of a riot to me. Do they know the account is definitely him?"

Franklin shrugged. "I don't think it's been proven - but the police haven't gone public with any of the slavery stuff…"

"…People had worked that out. My friend Lise says it's common knowledge online."

"Lise Nielsen?" asked Franklin.

"Yes," Rowan had forgotten that her boss was unaware of her ongoing friendship with the sister of a man whose murder they had unearthed earlier that year. "We stay in touch… we have a lot in common."

"Well, even if people have guessed the revenge theory, the account is set up in the name of Jenkins Protheroe. According to Edison, that's not public knowledge."

"So it's him?… or her…"

"It sounds very much like it. I mean unless…"

"Unless what, Franklin?"

"I'm only asking because the police are running checks and will find out anyway, plus Edison wanted me to ask you… You didn't set up the account, did you?"

Rowan's jaw dropped. "No, Franklin. You know me better than that!"

"I know I do, I'm sorry - it's just that last time we were mixed up in a murder case you didn't always play by the rules."

"I'm not a complete cretin, I know the cost of speaking out about any of this. Anyway, I was busy last night."

Franklin raised an eyebrow. "Anything I should know about?"

"Nothing that concerns you, but since you didn't ask, I was having a bit of a liaison myself - you're not the only one who had a bit of fun last night."

Franklin scrunched his face up. "Please, I think I'd rather hear about who Alf is sleeping with - and he's my son."

Rowan decided to lead the conversation back on track. "Has Edison said anything else?"

"Not much, just that things are bedlam at the station. They don't like being shown up like this, especially as the killer is now feeding his own information to the public. It's not good for business, to use his words. He does have some other news on the matter though, news that affects both of us."

"Oh?"

"The body of Jessica Miller, the judge who was killed the night before last is going to be released soon. It looks like we'll be handling the body in preparation for her funeral."

"I see."

"The funeral could be ages off, they usually are after murders - a body is always a mine of information - but we can start the planning soon and talk to her family. Edison wants us to look out for anything unusual."

"When are we going to start?"

"I was thinking tomorrow."

Rowan agreed.

25.

Edison stubbed out the remains of his cigarette and huffed irritably into the cold Sunday evening air. Behind the low wall that surrounded the police station he could see the tops of news vans arriving and the sound of heavy equipment being transported. Why could nothing be kept secret anymore? Why did so many of his fellow officers not realize that sharing sensitive information with even their nearest and dearest had a habit of leaking out into the public sphere in record time? Just a simple tweet and the whole covert operation had become Pandora's Box and could never be locked away again.

Of course he knew precisely what the media really wanted - it wasn't looking to splash the face of Karl Kitson, the arrested man who was about to be set free, all over the front pages, he was simply the warm-up act to the big show - what they really wanted was another murder. They were feeding a greater hunger, the general public who were looking for outrage as much as they were titillation. To feign horror as they read the gory headlines from their tabloids and tablets over breakfast, to relive them in lurid detail as they claimed "Isn't it awful!" and "Something must be done!"

Then when the killer - the real killer - was caught, they would line the streets to beat on the darkened windows of the police car as it ferried him away, to throw rocks and hurl abuse, baying for his blood now that the killing of strangers was over.

It was Edison and all the other officers with no training in any specific area who had to clean up the mess - the blood that poured into the cracks of cobblestones, once the forensics team had collected all they could. To wash the streets until foam gurgled pink from it, to hose away what had once been bits of a human body, full of hope and life.

He had once seen these news vans as vultures, circling the police station looking for meat, now he saw them as the zoo keepers, throwing any scraps they could find to the hungry animals, desperate to alleviate the boredom of another day.

125

Pushing through the back entrance into the station, he met D.I. Gladstone in the corridor, peeling the plastic wrapper from a fresh pack of cigarettes.

"There you are," she said. "Kitson's being signed out. He says he doesn't want an escort but I think we should keep an eye on him as he leaves. The last thing we need is a bloodbath out there in front of the world's media."

"Something tells me that's exactly what Kitson would want - if he can't be martyred by the police, the public can do it for him." Edison replied.

"Needless to say, I won't let that happen," Trish Gladstone looked down at her cigarettes as raised voices echoed along the corridor, "I should at least monitor his leaving from inside - until he gets off the property anyway."

Trish led the way to the reception and Edison followed. Karl Kitson was being given his release forms but was refusing to sign them.

"You can't let me go!" he barked. "I did it an' I'll do it again!"

"We can't keep you any longer Mr Kitson," said Trish calmly. "There's no evidence to support your confession and frankly I don't believe any of it."

"I did it! I killed them all!"

"You must have had quite an aim Mr Kitson, to shoot two people from inside your cell. You're already in enough trouble for wasting police time, I suggest you don't bring anymore upon yourself."

Karl Kitson turned to Edison. "Are you gonna let that black bitch talk to me like that?"

Edison was about to answer but saw that Karl's attention was drawn to the waiting media circus outside.

"Are they here for me?" he asked. "Well, I'll be damned!" He needed no further persuasion, he signed his name at the bottom of the form with a surprisingly delicate signature and hastily pushed it across the desk to the woman on the other side. Wordlessly he turned from them all, cleared his throat, and pushed his way through the doors into a mass of flashing camera bulbs.

Edison felt a chill pass through him as he heard a round of cheers from the assembled crowd. This lying racist had fans. White thugs dressed in the same military style uniform that Karl Kitson favoured were here to offer their raucous support with skyward fists and angry chants. The man himself was enjoying every second of his notoriety, snarling at the cameras and flashing his middle fingers to them. He was putting on a show and the media were recording every moment of it.

"Who are those men cheering him on?" Edison asked, genuinely dumbfounded.

"He seems to have something of a following since his confession." Trish replied.

"That doesn't make any sense. Surely they should hate him - he "killed" only white people."

"Do you think they care? When an Islamic fundamentalist blows himself up and takes a load of Muslims with him, he doesn't care - he's playing the long game, just as those racists are out there. The truth doesn't matter, all that matters is that the flames of racial hatred are being stoked by someone."

"That's terrible," said Edison, his eyes transfixed by the sideshow playing out before his eyes - precisely as if Karl Kitson had just left the Big Brother house and was already planning a media campaign. "Can't we do anything to stop them?"

"Absolutely nothing," Trish replied. "Have a look online and see those people increasing in number with every day the killer goes free. It's a powder keg and they're just looking for the match to start the explosion… the war."

"What do you mean, the war?"

Trish turned to him as if he were a simple child. "The race war they've always wanted - and trust me, it's coming."

26.

Autumn had crept up on the city so suddenly that Franklin had barely noticed its approach until that afternoon. He was taking a lunchtime stroll along the harbourside and found the cobbled walkways were now strewn with brown and orange leaves, the trees overhead were bare and and a chilly fog had descended like a shroud upon the streets. He buttoned up his overcoat. It was only a week until Halloween, after which would come the brisk slide into long, dark nights and frosty mornings.

The aesthetics of the season appealed to Franklin. The muting of the colours and the mournfulness of the sky seemed to speak to him of the death he encountered every day – that all things must pass and even the year itself will wither away and die.

He took a seat by Building 30 on the Lloyd's Piazza, a large, open crescent of steps that swept before a complex of offices. Building 30 was a cylindrical structure on the edge of the harbour that sat on a raised platform accessible only by a set of stairs that were hidden from view. Franklin never minded sitting on the floor here, his back pressed against the comforting stone, away from everyone else – one of many places of solitude he had found in his city.

That afternoon the only other people present were a group of skateboarders who had taken to using the long semi-circle of seats as a sort of gangway upon which to skate. Franklin watched them, largely unimpressed, as he ate his vegetable samosa.

His phone buzzed in his pocket, a text message from Edison. "Have a look at this," it read. "On my way to have a word with this prick. Incitement to violence." Edison had included a link to a YouTube video, which Franklin followed.

On the screen appeared a young white man sitting before his webcam at a computer desk. Franklin wasn't especially good at guessing ages but he didn't look much older than Alf. On the wall over his shoulder Franklin spied a large poster, a replica of a famous wood etching of the pirate Blackbeard, with mad eyes and a beard smouldering away into smoke.

When the young man spoke he did so with a familiar twang that immediately placed him as a fellow Bristolian, a deep, somewhat clumsy patter that wasn't a million miles away from that of a pirate in an old film. The user's name was "TheRevolutionWillBeVlogged."

"A lot of people have asked me," the man began, "to say something about the three murders in Bristol over the previous weeks. So I thought I'd take this opportunity to speak directly to my followers and say what this killer means to me and the city of Bristol. First of all, let me start by saying that in no way am I justifying what he's done and I've said many times before that violence must only be a final resort when all other avenues have been exhausted. That said, I can't help but feel some sense that the wheels of justice have been set in motion by this spate of killings – a call to arms if you will."

Franklin unscrewed the lid on his bottle of water and took a swig. He was certain already that he didn't like this man.

"Those who follow me will know my thoughts on Bristol already, but for those who don't, let me begin by saying this. The city only became big and wealthy in the 18th and 19th century, thanks to merchants travelling the globe and bringing back stolen goods, pillaging entire nations for whatever scraps they could drag back to Bristol and it wasn't long before this trade became in the people themselves. Yes, Bristol made its fortune on the backs of thousands of slaves who were sold to America like commodities. Not only do we not seem to feel any shame in this, but we celebrate Edward Colston, the most notorious of all these slave traders, as our greatest son.

"Our greatest wealth is a debt owed to the world, a debt of blood that is in the veins of every Bristolian who dwells in the houses built with ill gotten money, yet there has never been any punishment for anyone involved. We built a statue for one of history's most unspeakable men and named roads and schools and theatres after him.

"Is it any wonder that this killer chooses to hide in the form of Blackbeard, the Bristolian pirate who was once the most feared of the high seas? When the merchants set sail to rob native people of their possessions, land and freedom, what were they besides pirates? When bus drivers work for a company that refused to employ black people as recently as the 60s, who treated as scum anyone who wasn't white, what more are they than pirates, robbing people of their means of income? Or judges, who consistently prove themselves to be pirates of the law by handing harsher sentences to people of colour, what are we to think of them? It's hard to look at this killer and not think that finally someone has done something."

Franklin could take no more and ended the video. It wasn't so much the vitriol that was spewing from the man, but the disheartening amount of support he seemed to have. The video had in excess of 20,000 views and a 60% approval rating. Just skimming through the comments made Franklin feel uneasy. "I hope he goes for some rich bitch in Clifton next!", "Who wants to take a bet on him nabbing a policeman!", "I know I shouldn't but I'm getting a bit of a crush on the Blackbeard!"

Franklin knew that none of this should have taken him by surprise. Wannabe revolutionaries had been co-opting historical figures throughout the ages, whether it was students who papered their walls with images of Che Guevara or protestors donning masks of Guy Fawkes, controversial figures remained forever popular with those who didn't understand history properly.

Nevertheless, it had irked Franklin more than he wanted it to and felt all the more personal knowing that it was he who had been chosen to play the pawn in whatever vast plan the killer was working on.

It had not just been the video, Franklin had noticed other signs of admiration forming across the city. Hastily scrawled graffiti of "Blackbeard" were appearing on buildings on Franklin's walk to the harbourside. Cool kids with edgy haircuts wore tee shirts with his likeness. Even the local newspaper was offering detailed biographies of the pirate alongside pieces on what the killer's end game was – questions vaguely cloaked in a kind of respect for the killer, or at least for his audacity.

His phone buzzed again. Rowan was calling him. "Afternoon," he said.

"Hi, I've just had a call from Harmony Miller, she's the daughter of the judge who was murdered. She says we can meet her this afternoon, providing you can make it."

Franklin winced as he imagined Harmony watching the YouTube video with its broad support of her mother's gruesome murder. "Yes, I can fit her in between picking up a couple of bodies from the hospital and collecting ashes from the crematorium. Are you coming as well?"

"Of course I am, Franklin," she replied. "A killer has involved you and you think I'm going to let you do any of this alone? I'm with you whether you like it or not." Franklin smiled at the phone. "Besides, if we have any chance of catching him, you're going to need my intellect … we can't leave it to Edison to sort this out."

Franklin agreed and the pair concluded their conversation. As he made his way back to the funeral home through the quiet, misty streets of the city he had always adored, a strange mood descended on him. He knew there was a serial killer in Bristol, but he hadn't until that moment appreciated how volatile the situation was. Something was happening just as surely as when Guy Fawkes and his gang were stocking the basement of parliament with kegs of gunpowder. All that it needed was a spark and the whole thing would go up.

27.

"He has about 15,000 followers," Rowan informed Franklin as she consulted her phone from the passenger seat. "That's actually not very many in relative terms but it's probably going to go up if he keeps posting attention grabbing videos like the last one."

She was assessing the profile of the angry young man who had posted the YouTube video. In many ways the internet felt like a volatile foreign nation to Franklin, always outraged about something, merciless and cruel and likely to switch loyalties with the change of the wind. One day it had seemed to be all about Facebook and Twitter, things he'd only just managed to fathom, the next it was Periscope and Snapchat and once again he was lost in confusion.

"Do you think he's dangerous?" Franklin asked her.

"Not really. Remember, a lot of people hate-follow other people. Just because he has 15,000 followers it doesn't mean they all agree with him. Some people just like getting enraged."

"Even so, it's quite disconcerting."

"I wouldn't worry, ideas are only dangerous if someone is listening, my bet is that this idiot will get bored as soon as people stop paying him attention."

Franklin nodded. He wanted to believe she was right but couldn't shake the worry that she wasn't.

"His profile doesn't give much away. He's liked a bunch of videos on how vaccines are going to make us all autistic and lots of conspiracy stuff from mainstream media... stuff about chemicals in aeroplane jet fuel causing mind control... No one will pay attention to someone so clearly unhinged."

"That's what they said about Charles Manson," said Franklin as he turned off the road from Clifton Down.

"Who's Charles Manson?" Franklin was about to berate Rowan for her youthful naivete when the phone rang in her hand. "Crap," she said mostly to herself. It was Jude. She switched it to silent mode.

"Can I ask who that was?"

"You can ask all you want but I'm saying nothing," she replied. "Just stupid personal stuff I don't want to have to deal with right now."

"I see."

"The thing is," said Rowan, evidently wishing to change the subject, "we seem to be forgetting the most important clue in all of this... How it all began with the skin book."

Franklin nodded. "I've been thinking the same thing. That seems to have gone cold, but as no body has been found it stands to reason, I suppose."

The car pulled into the driveway of a spacious mid terrace postwar house in the wealthy Westbury area on the outskirts of the city. The front garden was paved with potted creepers scaling the red brick façade of the home.

"Are you ready?" Franklin asked.

"Not really, but I never am."

They were met at the door by a middle aged woman named Harmony Miller, the only child of Jessica Miller, the judge who had been murdered in Clifton Village. Her clothes were neat and formal but everything else, from her unwashed hair to her blood shot eyes, screamed of a woman trying to hold it together.

"Ms Miller, first may I begin by saying how deeply sorry I am for your loss," Franklin opened.

The woman just swallowed hard and ushered them through a hall lined with watercolours of English landscapes and into a bright, modern kitchen that overlooked a lawn where a small child and a mature woman were playing football.

Harmony puffed on an electronic cigarette and sipped a mug of tea. "Thank you for making time for me at such late notice," she wispered.

"Not at all," Franklin replied, softly.

Rowan sat on a tall chair before a Formica worktop and opened her iPad to begin taking notes.

"As you can imagine, these past few days haven't been easy. For the sake of Jackson... my son, I've kept quiet about much of what's happened. He's only six, he barely understands the concept of death as it is, murder is something altogether very different."

"Of course," said Franklin. "Today we shall only be going though some of the formalities regarding the service and…"

"…Who could be so wicked?" Harmony asked as she gazed through the window at her son, who was laughing in the way only a child could. "My mother wasn't a racist. She was a member of a board that promoted law studies for young women and minority groups… she had a peerless record for colourblind sentencing… she didn't see the world that way, it wasn't her nature."

"I'm afraid none of us can have any idea what the motive for these murders is, but he will be caught, I promise you." Franklin said.

Harmony was not listening, or was rather lost to her self. "All that stuff she went through just to get a good education as a woman, all those years of tireless work, and it was all for nothing. Nobody will remember any of that now, will they? She'll just be that judge who was killed with a crossbow." She wiped a tear from her face. "I'm sorry I…I"

With that the woman opened the door to the garden and stepped out into the sunlight. Rowan and Franklin watched in silence as she walked to her son and the older woman. The woman offered her a hug; her son offered her a large sycamore leaf he had found on the lawn. The older woman returned to the kitchen.

"I'm sorry about that," she said warmly. "This is rather a raw time, as I'm sure you can imagine. My Name's Lois Roker, the wife of Larry, the other judge who was attacked that night."

"Oh, Ms Roker," said Franklin, "I'm dreadfully sorry. May I introduce myself, I'm Franklin Gallow and this is my assistant Rowan Kaplan. May I ask how your husband is?"

"He's awake. He's taking food again and his memory seems to be drifting back, with time we should be able to piece together precisely what happened that night."

To Rowan, the woman, who was clearly well into her mid seventies, was the kind she had always hoped to become as she aged, sensible jeans and dyed strawberry blonde hair with an immaculately tailored jacket over a chunky knitted jumper. Had she lived in another time this woman would have been flying solo across the Atlantic, she thought.

"I know it's terrible to say such things," Lois continued, "but I can't help but feel guilt about the whole thing. Larry's in hospital but he will recover, but poor Jess, she had a daughter and a grandson and so much more to live for. Her family grew up with us, we love Harmony and Jackson as if they were our own and I just know that Larry and I would rather it had been us."

"You can't think like that, Ms Roker." Franklin offered. "The only guilty party is the murderer and he will not be free for much longer."

Lois Roker looked at the ceiling and shook her head. "One thing my husband has learned through his career as a judge is to never underestimate the stupidity of the police. That's why I'm not just going to stand idly by as this lunatic wipes half the city out. That's why I encouraged Harmony to ask for you in particular, Mr Gallow."

Franklin and Rowan exchanged worried glances. "Sorry?" he asked.

"Everybody knows that it was you who caught that killer last spring, the Danish boy and the woman in the harbour. The police want to claim that, they always do, but everyone knows who really solved the case."

Franklin looked over at Rowan who had her head down over her iPad. "Actually, it was a bit more complicated than that."

"Don't be coy, Mr Gallow. My husband is privy to a lot more information than you may be aware of. It was he who sentenced him to life."

Rowan felt compelled to speak. "The Home Secretary has said he should be given a whole-life sentence, never to be released."

Lois Roker nodded appreciatively. "In a way I suppose that's even worse than hanging."

"But, Ms Roker," said Franklin.

"Lois, if you will."

"Lois, I really don't know how we can be of any assistance to you. We only specialise in funerals, we aren't detectives."

"Please," Lois seemed on the brink of pleading with him, "just come and meet my husband in the hospital. We've discussed this already and have always gone with our instinct when it has come to things like this. If you see anything or can provide us with any information, we'lll see you are handsomely rewarded by whatever means."

"I couldn't ever accept money, Lois. We simply run a funeral home… but," he passed a glance towards Rowan, who simply nodded. "Very well, but I can't promise anything. We shall meet your husband."

The woman smiled. "Thank you, this will mean so much to us and I knew that if I didn't ask I'd go to my grave wondering if I should have."

"We'll do our best," Rowan added. "The pair of us are a kind of team."

"Oh yes, of course, then you are welcome to come along too. Now, Harmony knows who you are and I suspect believes that I will ask of you what I have, but she doesn't need to know any of the gory details and of course anything you uncover must be addressed to the police. Until that time may I just say thank you, on behalf of all of us, my husband and me and Harmony and Jackson." With that the woman returned to the garden.

"What the hell are we getting ourselves into, Rowan?"

"It can't be any worse than the mess we're in already. The killer's already singled you out and we're involved in one way or another – at least this way we'll be giving ourselves an advantage."

"This isn't a game, Rowan. Please don't treat it like it is."

"No it isn't a game… not for us anyway, we're like those little targets at a funfair that someone gets to shoot at. He's the one playing the game, at least this way we have a fighting chance if… you know, he does come after you in the end."

Franklin clambered onto a stall beside Rowan. "Dear God. Why is this happening yet again? Can't a man just enjoy a peaceful life among his corpses?"

"That'll always be the dream, Franklin," she smiled and nudged him in the shoulder.

Harmony broke off her conversation with Lois and began slowly making her way up the path to the kitchen. "I'm dreadfully sorry about that it's just that I get so angry."

"It's completely understandable, Ms Miller."

"When they catch him," she said, "and they will catch him, I want to look him in the face and for him to see not a shred of fear, grief, or even rage… I just want him to see utter disgust. I'm looking forward to that day."

"I think the whole city is thinking the same thing, Ms Miller."

"Are they though?" she asked. "Spend a few minutes online and you'll see a bunch of people who think he's some kind of folk hero."

Rowan and Franklin could only nod in silent agreement.

"Well, I think I'm ready," she declared. "Let's sort out this grim business, I can at least offer my mother a funeral to be proud of."

Rowan began to type as she described just what she wanted.

28.

Rowan didn't quite know how he'd managed it, but on Saturday evening she found herself on a date with Jude. It wasn't that she'd wanted to go, just that Jude had an almost supernatural ability to grind her down through sheer persistence. One morning she'd woken up beside him and in a half dazed state had agreed to go out for a drink – not a date, a drink. Yet actually walking through the streets of Bristol with him she realised the difference was not clear cut.

Perhaps it was because she was faintly nauseated by him when they were doing anything other than having sex, or perhaps it was just being seen with this hipster made her feel embarrassed, the pair had next to nothing in common and Rowan had been more than happy to keep things strictly between the sheets.

"Where should we go, Hot Chocolate?" he asked as he attempted to hold her hand.

"Stop calling me that," she snapped as she yanked her arm away from him. "It's gross and a little bit racist."

"Hey, I'm no racist. I love women all the colours of the rainbow. I even wrote a song about…"

"…Just shut up for a bit, Jude," she would have found it harder to resist the urge to whack him in the face were his face not so handsome.

The pair were descending Christmas Steps, a pleasant and narrow walkway that wove at a perilous incline between crooked little boutique shops that leered above them, twinkling warmly in the glow of ornate streetlamps. The passageway took its name not from the yuletide celebration but from a corruption of a darker source. The street had once been a haunt of 18th century robbers who would slash at the heels of passersby with a blade, sending them tumbling backwards down the precarious steps, where they could be ransacked of all possessions. In those days it was called Knifesmith's Steps.

It was clear that Christmas itself was still a way off as in every warped and ancient window was a reminder Halloween was less than a week away. Carved pumpkins were in abundance, as were artificial cobwebs and plastic spiders – the orange and black of the Halloween aesthetic adorned every display along down the passage.

"Everyone thinks the killer's waiting for Halloween," Jude said.

"Really? Who's everyone?"

"Think about it. Everybody's in costume, it's the perfect chance. Half the city's probably going to be dressed up as Blackbeard anyway, so he can sneak about wherever he wants."

"No one's going to dress up like a serial killer are they?" Rowan knew it was a stupid question.

"Of course they are. It's perfect. Yeah, it's poor taste but how many people did you see dressed up like Jimmy Savile last year?"

"None, thank Christ."

"I guess you don't go to the same sort of parties as me then."

Jude almost certainly went to parties where people played acoustic instruments all night and smoked cannabis from hookah pipes as they discussed art house films none of them had actually seen. Rowan could imagine them, rich kids with no actual problems who thought an asymmetrical haircut and a banjo masked their privilege.

"I don't think I'd want to go to those sorts of parties."

"Relax, it's just harmless fun," he chirped.

"I work in a funeral home, Jude. I see things a bit differently."

"And I never forget just how badass that is!"

The pair made it to the bottom of Christmas Steps and turned into St Augustine's Parade where they immediately met with a small demonstration beside the huge statue of Edward Colston. They numbered no more than a dozen, their faces ablaze in the glow of electric lanterns as they sung "We Shall Overcome."

"Protestors really need to learn some new songs," remarked Jude. "Maybe I should write one for them."

Rowan ignored him and found herself being beckoned by one of the demonstrators who asked: "Would you like to sign our petition to have the statue taken down?"

Rowan nodded. "Of course." She took the clipboard from the young woman and was pleased to see more than ten pages of signatures already. She added her name and passed it over to Jude who did likewise.

Before she left she turned skywards to face the statue of Colston. Contemplatively he stared into nothingness above her, oblivious to the chasm his presence was causing, she handed the clipboard back and make her way across the road with Jude.

"It won't do anything, I'm sure," he said, "but you've gotta let your voice be heard."

"I sometimes think if they took him down and melted him and changed the names of all the schools and streets named after him, well… people would be outraged for a week and then they'd just forget."

"Do you think that'd be enough to stop the killer?"

Rowan just shrugged her shoulders. "No one seems to know what he wants and his Twitter's gone silent, but maybe we're all focusing on the wrong thing. It isn't about Colston, well, not just about him. It's everything that went unpunished that he's avenging."

"Let's just get a pint at the Hatchet," she said, hoping her companion might be more bearable with some alcohol in him.

The Hatchet was known locally for two things, it was the oldest pub in Bristol, and its door was once bound by the tanned skins of convicted criminals, legend had it that beneath the layers of paint their leathered flesh could still be found. It attracted an unusual clientele of assorted rockers, goths and counter cultural types, alongside a handful of gays, lesbians and gender nonconformists, owing to it being situated in the heart of the city's LGBT quarter.

Rowan ordered a couple of pints at the bar and took a seat across from Jude at a dark wood table.

"So, is this where you usually come?" he asked as his eyes wandered around the room.

"Are you asking if I come here often?"

Jude offered a half giggle, which made him look suddenly boyish and infantile, barely old enough to be drinking at all. "I mean... they don't really seem like your crowd."

The music was loud and the screech from the vocalist was of indiscernible lyrics. It had not occurred to her that Jude felt as out of place here as she would at one of his parties. She found herself warm to that, just a little. "It's a nice place," she said. "Bit loud on Saturdays."

Jude nodded and gulped his pint. By his third cider he was looking considerably more at home, though markedly slurred and unbalanced.

"The thing is," he droned, with an arm outstretched along the back of the bench on which he sat, "we're the first generation who can live without the social divisions, men, women, black white, gay, straight, nobody cares anymore. That's the revolution and nobody's even talking about it because nobody listens to us, but we're just getting on with stuff and being cool and creative and making art and music and just being like, 'Hey, come and hang with us.'"

Rowan checked her watch and wondered how long she could politely stand this. Jude wasn't a terrible person, just an astoundingly naïve one.

"Those things, racism... sexism... homophobia... they're part of our parents' generation, and their parents. We'll be the first to be truly, like, free, you know?"

"No I don't," Rowan didn't mean to snap, but the words tumbled out of her in a flurry of frustration. "All those things are still rife. What do you know about any of that? I don't think I need a straight, white man telling me that the war is over and prejudice is a thing of the past. Tell me Jude, what's your story? Because even though you're living in a hovel on the bad side of town, you could cut glass with that accent. You may've decided that being poor is in this year, or that it gives you some kind of credibility as an artist, but it's a load of crap – you're a posh boy who thought he'd be a tourist until daddy's money ran out."

Rowan didn't quite know where those words had come from, something akin to them had been fermenting in her mind all evening, but suddenly they came frothing angrily from her mouth.

Despite the loud music the moment of silence between them before Jude spoke felt harrowing. He just looked down at his empty glass and said, "Yes, I'm a posh boy, so what? What do you want me to do about it? I got lucky having rich parents who sent me to whatever expensive school would get me out of their lives for most of my childhood. Yeah I'm a man and I'm white and straight, mostly, but you don't know anything about me, or my dad, or my family – or anything I've overcome. I live in the rough part of town because it's all I can afford, and for your information I don't rely on a penny from my family and I never will. I barely even know them and if you met them you'd understand why."

"Jude, I'm sorry," and Rowan truly meant it.

"Don't bother. I don't want your pity," he looked up at Rowan with big, sad eyes. "I really thought better of you."

Desperately trying to salvage the night she offered, "Do you want another pint? I'm buying."

"No, I'm going home." Jude stood up from the table and moved uneasily through the door and Rowan followed him into the street.

"Jude? You're quite drunk, you shouldn't go home alone – it's not safe."

He shrugged his shoulders. "I don't care."

"Well you should, there's a madman in the city murdering people at night," she followed him up the narrow, piss soaked steps onto Park Street where they found themselves lost among a hen party singing a Tom Jones song. They waited for them to pass.

"You don't know anything!" he blurted to her. "I have a heart that can be broken!"

"Oh God," Rowan breathed as she looked around, embarrassed. "You're really drunk. Were you drinking before you came out tonight?"

"Not enough to dull the pain!" he wailed.

She had met Jude at her flat but he'd just returned home from what he enigmatically described as "a gig." He could have been drinking all afternoon for all she knew.

"Look, we're going back to the same place anyway, do you want to go halves on a taxi?"

Jude paused on a bridge against some railings. Before them was a massive Banksy mural of a naked man hanging from a window. For a moment she thought he was going to be sick over the side, but instead seemed to regain his composure. "Can we go home and have sex?" he asked in a childlike whine.

"Oh Jude, absolutely not."

He nodded. "That's fair, I suppose."

Rowan saw his eyes pass from hers and over her shoulder. With an almost imperceptible change of expression he turned his back to her.

"Jude?"

"Look, I've got to get going. Don't follow me, it's for the best alright? I can make my own way home." Then, with a clumsy jog, he took off down the hill, his shoulder brushing along the edge of a building until he rounded a corner and was out of sight.

Rowan looked about exasperatedly for a taxi. Two police officers walking their beat were slowly making their way towards her – the streets had been full of them for the past fortnight. It was then that she understood what had just happened.

Jude had run away from them, not her.

29.

Rowan was not feeling her best the next morning, but a strong coffee and a long shower soon washed away her troubled night. She hadn't slept well; guilt never sat comfortably with Rowan and her outburst at the Hatchet had left her with a sense of shame – why did she struggle with keeping her mouth shut and her thoughts in check? But it wasn't just the guilt that troubled her in the early hours, it had been the myriad of questions she had of Jude; her sort-of boyfriend who she knew nothing about save for the fact that he had secrets.

She met Franklin outside of the Bristol Royal Infirmary at ten o'clock as they had planned, the walk through the city managed to lift what remained of her hangover. As always, he was on time and waiting patiently for her at the entrance of the vast building.

"I can't stand hospitals," she informed him as they made their way to the ward that was caring for Larry Roker.

"I don't think anyone's fond of them," said Franklin.

"It's not just the sick people, it's the sterility, and the silence, all those nurses in crisp uniforms."

"It smells like the funeral home, really. I think they might use a similar bleach to us," whispered Franklin. "Have you ever stayed overnight in a hospital before?'

"No, never even broken a bone before. Even in the spring when that bastard tried to kill me all they did was give me a checkup and then sent me on my way. How about you?"

"Once, when I was a kid. Edison was always daring me to do stupid stunts and he somehow got me to jump out of my bedroom window with a bed sheet – we thought it would work like a parachute. Broke my ankle and my coccyx."

"Ouch, that sounds painful."

"It was, but it was almost worth it for the amount of trouble Edison got into. D' you know it still makes him feel awful when I remind him of it? Those childhood memories can be incredibly potent"

"I don't think I'll ever understand how your relationship with him works."

"To be honest, neither will I. Brothers can be weird – I think that day a big wedge was driven between us and we just sort of grew apart."

Lois Roker was seated on a bench outside the door to the ward. She wore a tartan jacket with a brooch in the shape of a lion's head, which she had coupled with a pair of formal black trousers, tucked into knee high leather boots. She stood up as soon as she saw them approach.

"Thank you for coming," she said. "It means so much to both of us, more than you can imagine." She pushed her way through the doors into the ward and spoke to a receptionist at the desk. "We are here to see Lawrence Roker."

The young woman smiled. "I'm sorry but patients are only allowed to receive one visitor at a time today."

"That is a shame," said Lois coolly, "I'm afraid you'll have to change that rule as I have two friends with me and I shall be taking them to see my husband."

The receptionist knew better than to argue with this woman as she only had to look at her to know what a formidable opponent she would be. Lois Roker was not a woman to be bargained with. Lois Roker always got her way. Rowan could only look on in silent adoration.

It was only then that she realised how much trepidation she felt about this encounter. What would he look like, would he show signs of the violence that had been inflicted on him?

She need not have worried as she was relieved to find the patient propped up on pillows on top of the bed playing a game on his tablet. "Visitors!" he beamed.

He was nearing eighty but could pass for considerably younger, with impeccably parted grey hair and a surprisingly smooth face for a man of his years. He wore a pair of striped pyjamas and thick, woolen socks.

"I have heard a great deal about you, Mr Gallow and must say I am something of an admirer. You have a fascinating profession, very noble."

"Thank you," Franklin replied.

"I have read about your work on the case earlier this year. I think it was quite evident that the police wouldn't have had a hope of catching that monster had it not been for you."

"Well, I believe Rowan was responsible for much of it, probably more than me. She has a keen eye for these things."

Larry turned to her with a smile. "Aah, the suspicious eye of the youthful. Don't ever lose that."

Rowan smiled back at him. This man was delightful.

"Have you spoken to the police yet?" Franklin asked.

"Of course, they were here when I regained consciousness. They put me under to remove part of the arrow, went in right through my thigh and out the other side. A few inches over and it would've sliced right through my unmentionables."

Rowan was impressed by his casual cheerfulness. Perhaps, she thought, at his age such encounters with violent death could more easily be brushed away.

"How are you feeling now?" Franklin asked.

Larry shrugged his shoulders. "It hasn't been the greatest experience of my life but it could have been so much worse... Oh dear, poor, sweet Jess. "

Lois took a seat on the bed beside her husband and held his hand. "Go on, tell them what happened. They need to know everything."

"How well do you remember the evening?" asked Franklin.

"It's all crystal clear. There's not a moment that isn't burnt into my mind. We'd been having a little get-together at our place, just a couple of friends were invited but Jess was the only one who could make it. We were drinking some bottles of the Cabernet I'd been saving, it was delicious but rather stronger than any of us were used to, and around about midnight things were getting a little slurred and Lois was... well, you were falling asleep at the table."

Lois shook her head. "It's the little things that stick with you, like how I never got to say a proper goodbye to her that evening."

"Anyway, I was to walk with her to Park Street, why we didn't just get a taxi I'll never understand. From Clifton Village we went across the little park in Victoria Square.

146

About halfway along there's a little old streetlamp, it's very pretty, like something from Narnia, but it was there that the man was waiting, I have no idea how he knew we were coming that way or even if we had been his target, but there he was, dressed like a pirate with a ludicrous wild beard and huge overcoat. We both froze when we saw him because we knew precisely what this meant. I've never seen evil before, not true evil. Over the years I've encountered some of the worst people in our city but none of them were this malicious. The evil was emanating from him, like a force of some kind, just pure hatred. Jess got hit first and I just panicked when I saw her go down. To my shame I turned and ran and that's when I got hit and just collapsed."

Lois held her head in her hands. She must have heard this story before but with each retelling it couldn't have been any easier.

"I don't remember losing consciousness. I think I was kind of drifting in and out for some time, but I remember being found – a couple of students were on their way home and I heard them running towards me. That was long after the pirate had left and he'd... you know?"

Franklin shook his head. "What?"

"They haven't released that to the public," Lois informed her husband.

"I see," he replied. "I watched him take out a little saw and he... he cut Jess' hand off right in front of me."

Franklin and Rowan both gasped in unison.

Larry stared into the distance as the scene played out in his mind; his eyes were soon swimming with tears. "So when I say I have seen true evil, I mean it."

"I do believe you may be right," Franklin agreed. "There's just one thing, that I'm sure the police must be looking into. You don't think you were targeted by the killer? You think you and Jessica were just in the wrong place that night, is that so?"

"Yes," Larry nodded.

"I'm sure that's true, but what if it wasn't random? How many people knew you were having this little get-together, apart from the other people that had been invited?"

Larry shook his head slowly. "Unless you think it could have been one of our neighbours? Or that someone was watching the house?"

Lois visibly shuddered at the thought.

"I'm sure it's nothing," Franklin was quick to reassure. "You must remember that I'm no expert, all I can offer you is my thoughts, and of course the promise that Jess will be looked after well leading up to the service."

Larry squeezed his wife's hand. "Thank you Mr Gallow, we appreciate that."

As Franklin and Rowan were leaving, both shaken by the distressing encounter, Rowan asked her boss, "Do you believe in evil?"

Franklin was momentarily stumped by the question. "What do you mean?"

"I mean actual evil, something that exists, like Larry said… like a force."

He thought about it for some time. "I believe there are certainly evil people in the world, and the things they do are evil, but no, evil doesn't actually exist, it's just our interpretation of it. It's our mind trying to distinguish between good and bad behaviour. Why do you ask?"

"It's nothing really, just something I've been thinking of for a while. I've been getting a bit interested in energies. You know, in nature and things like that."

"Do you mean Paganism?"

Rowan nodded slowly. "Does that sound mad to you? It kind of sounds weird when you say it."

"All religions sound barmy to an atheist, but good luck with it, it seems rather harmless compared to other beliefs – just lots of dancing naked in the moonlight and singing songs to rivers and stuff."

Rowan laughed. "I don't know, I'll see where it goes. It's just sometimes it feels as if there has to be a bit more to life than what we see and maybe there really are things beyond our control… like some huge force, and that evil really does exist not just as an idea, but as real as everything else on earth."

"Intriguing," was Franklin's only response.

"Whoever the pirate is, I can't help thinking we are confronting something massive and terrifying. Something so vicious we'll never fully understand it."

"That's one thing," said Franklin, "that we can both agree on."

The pair left the hospital and went their separate ways.

30.

It had been many years since Edison had been on the beat and though many of his fellow officers complained about their new duties, he found it agreeable

"The thing is," Colin, his partner on the late night shift moaned, "people want to see the police out and about, but do you know how often we actually witness a crime?"

Edison shook his head, distracted by the chaos around him.

"Once every ten years," Colin confirmed.

Colin was more than two decades his junior yet already had about him a sense of weariness. Edison's idealistic notions had put up a much greater fight before surrendering to the bleak realities of police work. Colin Harlow had seemingly already given up.

"It's bollocks really isn't it?" he went on. "I could be inside right now in the warm with a pasty and chips, they've got us out here just for show like a pair of animals in the zoo."

Edison disliked Colin but couldn't even muster the strength to do that with much intensity. Colin was given to complaining about everything from the food in the station cafeteria to the ungrateful public who gave him none of the respect he felt he deserved. Edison had long given up moaning about such things, at work at least. For him his shifts were a careful balancing act between ability and ineptitude, doing everything he could to appear as if he was doing nothing at all, treading water in such a manner as to attract neither censure, or worse, promotion.

He'd never aspired to lofty heights in his career and was simply content to ride out his days until retirement with as little fuss as possible. What reason was there to want more? He had already achieved his sole aim in life – to escape the confines of the funeral home and the predestined job he had been assigned at birth.

"Check out the baps on the one over there," Colin whispered sleazily into his ear. "Eight o' clock, looks like she should be on the front of a ship."

Colin chuckled to himself, Edison refused to react and checked his watch. It was midnight; he had five more hours of this.

It was an ordinary Monday night yet the city seemed to be lost in madness. With the passing of a weekend without a murder the drinkers seemed to have decided the streets were once again safe and had ventured out in their thousands making up for lost time. The scene was that of bedlam, impossibly young looking students spilling out of bars and nightclubs, toppling into discarded food and puddles of vomit. Streams of urine flowed from alleyways and all about came the persistent screams of revellers, lost to shame through drink.

A fortnight ago, this year's intake of students had been quite different. Blinking into the fresh dawn of their new lives the kids had stepped nervously out into the night and immediately resorted to what they had known – gathering around park benches with bottles of cheap cider. It had taken two weeks for them to discover that the city was as much theirs as anyone's and held limitless possibilities of how to puke away their moderate student loans.

It would all calm down soon, Edison was certain. Once the strain of independent living took hold and those loans weren't looking quite so ample the city would go back to normal, but for the time being, chaos ruled Bristol after dark.

"See," Colin grumbled, as a young woman fell into the road at St Augustine's Parade and had to be hauled from the path of oncoming traffic by a group of no-less intoxicated friends. "We're trying to help people who don't want to help themselves."

St Augustine's Parade was the epicentre of Bristol nightlife at that hour. The hardcore clubbers wouldn't emerge until later, but the more casual barflies gathered in throngs about burger and kebab joints to line their queasy stomachs.

"We're maintaining order." Edison said. "Why d'you think an officer only sees a crime once a decade? It's because just being here stops the worst of it from happening."

Colin shrugged but otherwise left the comment unacknowledged.

Edison spied a small gathering of people in the centre of the parade – an island surrounded by roads in all directions that stretched from the waterfront to the statue of Edward Colston. A couple of dozen people were laughing and pointing, but their numbers were increasing as more drunks stumbled over to see what the commotion was. The pair made their way across the road.

Edison was hardly surprised to see Karl Kitson standing before the crowd. He was flanked on either side by skin-headed men who were attired, as he was, in bomber jackets and camouflaged combats. This was clearly trouble.

"You shout all you want love, but you know I'm sayin' the truth!" Karl grinned at a young blonde woman who was screaming into his face.

The other men were handing out leaflets to onlookers, most of whom were gleefully tearing them to shreds and scattering them on the wind.

"Shit, this is trouble." Edison warned Colin.

"Isn't he that thug who confessed to the killings?"

"Yes he is, seems he'll do anything for attention."

Whether Karl Kitson recognised Edison or not he wasn't letting on as he handed him a leaflet with a hollow smile. "Evenin' officer."

The blonde woman was still screaming at him from the assembled crowd. "You're what's wrong with this country. You're the one who should go back to where he came from!" Colin tried half-heartedly to calm her while Edison read the home-printed leaflet.

"TAKE BACK ARE CITY!" bellowed the black on white text. "FIGHT FOR RIHGTS FOR WHITES! COME TO ARE DEMOSTARTION SUNDAY NOVEMBER 2 AND RECLAIM ARE STREETS!" Beneath the text in gigantic typeface was a little cartoon monkey with a cross through it. When Edison looked up from the leaflet he found he was quickly becoming swamped by a surge of outraged onlookers who had flowed across the parade once it had become clear what the commotion was about.

Colin, who was frantically trying to act as a one-man buffer between Karl and the angry tide called out to Edison, "Help me! They're gonna knock his block off!"

Edison elbowed his way through the front of the crowd, yelling into the walkie-talkie on his jacket. "We're about to have a riot on our hands if we're not careful. Request for backup."

Karl Kitson stood undaunted, his face one of practiced ease. "Everythin' alright officer?"

"You know damn well it isn't, Mr Kitson. I'm going to have to ask you to move on, you're causing a breach of the peace."

"Am I really?" Karl deadpanned. "Last time I checked I was well within my rights to stand on the streets of me own city."

"This is an incitement to violence."

"I'm not askin' for anyone to get 'it, am I?"

The crowd was inching closer and they were breaking into chants of "Racist scum! Out! Out! Out!" The presence of two police officers seemed to be more of a challenge than a deterrent. Karl Kitson was right. He was not inciting violence against anyone but himself – he was inviting it.

The man knew the law well, and instead of spitting racial slurs to the crowd he stood his ground with a smug silence that seemed to draw even more anger from his onlookers. His henchmen followed suit and stopped handing out leaflets – all they needed to do now was wait for the violence to begin.

Edison was taken aback by this strategy. His training in the de-escalation of confrontation had never mentioned what to do if someone was inviting violence on themself; Karl Kitson wanted to be attacked to portray his detractors as savage beasts.

Moreover, Edison wasn't sure what role he should play in this. Was it possible, or even legal to arrest a man for silence? A smug smile certainly wasn't a crime, but at what point did provocation become incitement? He was relieved to see a police van had pulled up across the parade from which the requested back up were sprinting towards the untidy melee.

153

Karl's henchmen whipped out their phone cameras and began recording the action. The only thing better than their leader being beaten to pulp would be footage of him being dragged away by police. That was the way martyrs were made.

With the approach of the officers Edison eased his way against the crowd until he was out of the scrum. He knew this was probably not the wisest course of action but Trish had mentioned she was working late, so he phoned her. She answered on the second ring.

"Gallow?" was her blunt reception.

" Hi… Look, I know you said you're working tonight and… Well, I…"

"…Spit it out Ed, I'm busy. What's that? It sounds like you're in a nightclub."

"No, no. There's just a bit of a commotion on St Augustine's Parade. Karl Kitson has been handing out leaflets and they're… pretty incendiary"

Trish sighed on the line. "When you say, incendiary, are they likely to actually combust?"

Edison understood immediately that she was mocking him. "No, but he's dangerous. He knows more, I'm certain of it. He didn't tell us everything when we interviewed him."

"When I interviewed him," she corrected. "He told us nothing because he knows nothing. Now please, why did you phone when you know I'm busy? Some little spat among drunks has nothing to do with me."

"I know that, it's just, you should look at him, hell, I want to smash his face in. That man knows more than he's letting on, trust me, he's trouble."

"I don't doubt that for a second, but Ed, listen to me, you need to stop those lefties from ripping him limb from limb, as much as I'd like to see that happen, I can't imagine it would look good if the police just stood by and let it. You do your work and I'll do mine – trust me on this, there are bigger forces at play here than you may have reckoned on. I'm playing a long game. Now get back to work and leave me in peace."

With that she was gone but her words still echoed in his head. It really made no sense that she had been so eager to let Kitson free after he'd confessed to murder. He might not have been the killer but he was full of secrets – a little shake and they would all have come tumbling out.

Why had she wanted him to go free? What was her plan?

31.

For Vanessa Tilbury, death had come to feel like a friend.

With each year came the passing of more friends, who would be solemnly removed from her address book with the swipe of a pen. She was the last of them, the old guard who'd grown up in the city back when good breeding had meant something. Death would come to claim her and would be met with nothing but weary relief, a dreamless sleep which would go on forever.

On the last night of her life she had watched a somewhat stagnant production of Doctor Faustus from her box high above the stalls in the Colston Theatre. She had never much cared for Marlowe, nor for tragic histories in general, but had come to enjoy being alone in her box, hidden from view in a secluded cell over the heads of the masses who found it perfectly reasonable to attend the theatre in jeans and jumpers. Not so for Vanessa Tilbury, who wore her finest gowns and rows of pearls for such occasions.

She was one of the last of the Bristol greats, the founding families of this once glorious city. From Clifton they had amassed their fortunes, each generation building upon the last; crafting great houses along the edge of the gorge, surveying the city from on high like the true owners of the land they believed themselves to be.

Those were the days; that was her time. When people knew their place and knew their manners. Hers was a life to be lived grandly, respected as a superior. She had watched as piece by piece the city divided and the old families died away, their homes taken by lottery winners and Russian oligarchs. Clifton Village, once a village within a city for promenading, for parasols in summer and readings at the Assembly Rooms in winter, was now little more than a playground for rowdy students who drank and swore and spat, who filled those magnificent houses with the smell of hashish and unwashed bed sheets. When death came for Vanessa Tilbury it would find no sorrow.

When the play was over and the final curtain call was done, Vanessa slipped through the lobby unnoticed by the class of people who would have once been virtually owned by her father. She then suffered the indignity of waiting for a taxi in a queue of noisy simpletons who were shamelessly discussing the cheapest places in the city to buy drinks and shouting noisily into their phones. When a taxi stopped for her, the driver was brown – they all were nowadays.

She was deposited at the driveway of her magnificent 18th century mansion on the outskirts of Bristol. Through the huge bay windows of the ancient edifice she could see the chandeliers twinkling enticingly as she imagined the simple joys awaiting her inside.

No longer in possession of any staff, she would have to make her cocoa herself. Perhaps she would listen to some music on the radio, she might even pour herself a glass of vintage brandy with which to take the pills that soothed the various ailments that beset her 92 year old body. Perhaps she would dream that night of better times and happier days when she was young and her family name had meant something.

All of the descendents of Edward Colston were treated as monsters now. For centuries they had toiled away, building schools and almshouses for the poor, cutting swathes across the oceans and exploring uncharted lands and yet all her famous ascendant was remembered for was a few African savages who had been civillised by their years on Christian plantations.

She unlocked the door with the turn of a key and, as it swung open, instantly felt the hit. It would not have been her first heart attack for she had survived two of them, but a familiar pain struck her chest nonetheless. It had happened so suddenly that she barely had time to register the pain and to find with horror that the point of an arrow was protruding between her breasts, blood spluttering from the wound like an old bathtub with antique plumbing.

It was then that she was struck from behind, a whack to the back of her head that sent her stumbling face first onto the marble floor. It was with fascinated horror that she watched the blood puddle out beneath her and felt another presence tower overhead.

So this was how death would come for her, not in her sleep and not as a welcome friend, but by the hand of an unknown assailant. The last thing she heard was the door behind her close and for the briefest moment it was just her and her killer in the house together.

And then she died.

32.

"What's got into you Franklin? You don't look like a man who's about to collect a body."

Franklin was impatiently waiting in the parlour of the funeral home with his receptionist, Meredy. "Oh, just had a good night's sleep last night."

Meredy eyed him suspiciously before returning to the crossword on her desk. His receptionist had been a loyal addition to Gallow & Sons for the best part of two decades. Plump and maternal, she had a near miraculous way of soothing distraught and grief stricken clients be they on the phone or in person. Without her, Franklin was certain the whole business would have crumbled around his feet many years before.

When Rowan appeared behind the glass panel to the reception with her Brompton bike tucked neatly under her arm, Franklin excitedly opened the door for her and exclaimed: "Are you ready to go out?"

"Hang on, I've only just arrived, let me at least drop my bike off," she said as she stepped into the room and said good morning to Meredy. "I thought we were supposed to be collecting Jessica Miller's body today? Why do you look like you're off to get an award?"

"Good night sleep, if you can believe it." Meredy said, not looking up from her puzzle.

Rowan shoved her way past Peterman, the other funeral director at Gallow & Sons. She had never taken to the burly, aged and often drunk man who only kept his job as a favour to Franklin's father. The feeling was certainly mutual and the pair had resorted to barely acknowledging the others existence.

"So what time's the been coming in?" asked Peterman.

Franklin sighed gruffly. "Don't call them beens Peterman, and you're not doing this service so bugger off."

"But it's a famous one, innit? Can't help but be a bit interested, all the country wants to know what's going on."

"You're not involved Peterman," said Franklin. "This is between us two."

Peterman simply grumbled to himself and returned to his office in the back of the building.

"Keep an eye on him, will you?" Franklin asked Meredy. "I think he's getting worse, or more drunk or something."

"He stares at my chest like he's reading a newspaper article off of it," said Rowan.

"Mine too," Meredy added. "How bad is it supposed to get before your dad lets him go?"

"I have no idea. They were in some half-baked society together at some point – the Masons or something of the ilk."

"Your dad's a Mason?" asked Rowan.

"Not quite, it's a society for Bristol businessmen – and I do mean only men. I think they're supposed to stay loyal to each other or some such tripe. Anyway, are you ready to head out?"

Rowan shrugged her shoulders. "As much as I'll ever be, but aren't we heading out a bit early if we're collecting her at noon?"

"I'll explain on the way," said Franklin.

They took the van from the collection of vehicles the funeral home had at its disposal. The van was inconspicuous for a reason – bulky enough to carry two large bodies in the back but anonymous enough to hide from prying eyes, with no windows or markings to suggest what might be inside. The van was meant to slip in and out of hospitals and mortuaries, retirement homes and prisons without its presence registering by those going about their business. The van was their covert vehicle.

"So I give up. How come you're so chipper today? Even Peterman didn't seem to grind you down as much as usual."

Franklin smiled as he pulled onto North Street. "I got a text message late last night."

"Oh no," Rowan gulped, "from the killer?"

"No, nothing like that, it was from Alf, inviting me over!" Franklin reached into his jacket pocket and handed her his phone.

Rowan opened up the page of messages and read the only one from Alf aloud. "Have got ticktets to my show next week. Do you want 1? Drop by if you do. Afl." Rowan reread the message. "He spelled tickets wrong – and his own name."

"I saw that too, but it was late. He was probably tired."

"Or drunk. I hope you're not reading too much into this."

"What d'you mean?" Franklin immediately looked somewhat squashed.

"Sorry, it's just that it doesn't quite sound like a declaration of peace between you two. It's just an invitation to his art show – and it's not even his art show. They put one on every autumn for the new students to show off their work – that way when they all leave and take up jobs stacking shelves in a supermarket for the rest of their lives, they can feel that their BA in art history was worthwhile."

Franklin shook his head. "Why must you be the relentless voice of reason in my life? Can't I have a little fantasy every so often?"

Rowan hoped she hadn't hurt him too much but his measured, weary response suggested that he knew she was speaking the truth. "I just don't want you to land with too hard a thud – you've only met Alf a handful of times and every time he's been a bit of a prick to you, just don't get your hopes up too high."

"Well, it's a bit late for that, we're on our way to his halls."

Rowan just offered her friend a bemused smile. "I tried, don't say I didn't try."

The van bounced over road humps as it drew into the university campus. The grey stone building loomed like a fortress against a gunmetal sky. Rounding a corner Franklin drove into a small car park and applied the brake. "Do you want to wait for me here or come inside?"

"Oh, I'm coming with you," she said. "If you're going to make a fool of yourself, I can at least try and save you from total public humiliation."

Franklin ignored her and hopped out of the van. Rowan followed across the car park and through the double doors that lead into the reception hall – a pristine space with a shiny floor and a sweeping staircase that led past an ostentatious chandelier.

"Swanky," was Rowan's summary.

"It's very different to my old uni," said Franklin as he made his way up the staircase with Rowan in tow. "Mine was an old polytechnic that looked like a giant breeze block that had fallen out of the sky, it had tiny windows and…"

"…Please stop," Rowan interrupted. "There's nothing more tedious than people going on about their university days. It really isn't that impressive."

"You're just a little ray of sunshine today, aren't you?" said Franklin as the pair walked along a lengthy corridor until Franklin found the door he was in search of. He knocked upon it, when there was no answer, he knocked again.

An impossibly youthful looking Asian teenager, with scruffy hair and sleepy eyes, opened the door. "Are you here about the TV?" he asked blearily. "We got a license for it last week, it just hasn't come through yet."

"No nothing like that, I'm here to see Alf. I'm his… dad."

"No way, the undertaker? That is gangster man, I remember you from the day Alf moved in." Franklin saw the young man reach forward with what he assumed would be a handshake but was instead a fist outstretched before him. Franklin stared at it dumbly until Rowan bumped her own fist against it.

"That's how it's done, grandpa," she said.

"I'm Ajay," said the man. "D'ya wanna come in? I think Alf's still in bed. Had a bit of a night last night."

"Yes please, I'm Franklin and this is Rowan."

"Hey," said Ajay.

"Hey," said Rowan.

All three made their way into a large living room, with an open kitchen tacked onto a far wall. Three teenagers, two girls and a boy, were slumped on a sofa eating bowls of cereal before a TV that was showing children's cartoons. A fourth student was sitting in a canoe on the floor.

"Shit, Dec, put that away! It's Alf's dad." Ajay demanded, it was then that Franklin noticed that the boy was smoking a hefty looking joint. Wearily he stubbed it out in an ashtray.

"Don't worry about me," Franklin smiled in what he imagined was his most casual tone, "I'm not a regular dad – I was young once." The moment these words left his mouth he wanted to bludgeon himself about the head with them – there was nothing less cool than someone's dad trying to act cool. He could feel Rowan's mortified eyes burning into him without even looking at her. An embarrassed silence fell upon the room, which Franklin felt compelled to break. "I like your canoe."

"W-what?" the stoned boy within it offered.

"It's my canoe, actually," said Ajay, "and it's a kayak." The thick cloud of embarrassment had not shifted so Ajay tried instead to call out to Alf. "Wake up! Your dad's here!"

Franklin heard the clamour of motion from somewhere in the hallway and a door open, he swallowed nervously and Alf made his appearance. He was wearing nothing but a pair of boxer shorts and a tee shirt that read: "Milk is Murder." He rubbed his eyes and tried to focus. "What are you doing here? Is Mum alright?"

"Your mother's fine." The sight of his estranged son, bedraggled and clearly hungover on a Monday morning caused an unexpected reaction in Franklin. "Isn't it a bit early on in your year to be cutting lectures?"

"Umm… isn't it a bit late in my life to act like it's any of your business?" Alf spat back. "Anyway, I have Monday and Wednesdays off."

"You texted me last night, you said you had some tickets," said Franklin, trying to steer the conversation back to less dangerous waters.

"Did I? How much gin did I drink last night?"

"A lot," said one of the girls from the sofa. "You were going on about Palestine again."

Alf winced as memories flooded back from the night before. "Oops, sorry."

Suddenly the boy on the floor cut into the conversation. "No way… I just realised that kayak spelled backwards is kayak." All eyes in the room turned to the strange, stoned creature.

"Racecar is the same backwards too," said Rowan, intrigued by this odd specimen of student life.

The boy simply stared, lost in the mystery of palindromes. "Wow… words…"

"So," Franklin went on, "the tickets, I don't know if you still feel like it."

Alf stepped out of the hallway and returned with a handful of glossy cards. "Here, they gave us loads so it's no big deal." He handed one to Franklin who read the title aloud.

"Provocations: The Art of Now."

"Here, you can have one too." He handed one to Rowan who took it sheepishly, acutely aware of how much it would depreciate its value in Franklin's eyes.

"I'm going back to bed," said Alf. "Bye Franklin, bye Rowan. See you whenever."

With that they were once again abandoned in a room full of strangers. "We'd best get going," he announced to the room, though nobody seemed to react much to their departure, save for Ajay who walked them to the front door.

"Mr... Duke?" he said.

"It's Mr Gallow, well, Franklin."

"Don't give up on Alf. I know he's a bit hard to like sometimes but he does talk about you a lot. I don't think he means to be so difficult. I've got some weird stuff with my dad too and it isn't easy. Give it time and make sure you go to his show – I've seen what he's been working on and... it's important."

Franklin stood in the doorway completely taken aback by this unexpected moment. "Thank you, Ajay. I will."

With that Ajay nodded and held out his fist to Franklin, who bumped his own against it and left triumphant that something that morning had gone as he'd hoped.

33.

"It's like unwrapping the grimmest Christmas present," said Rowan as she stared at the body that lay before her on the metal table zipped up in a surgical bag like a shroud.

She and Franklin had applied their gloves and slipped into their wipe-proof overalls. They had been provided with very few details about the condition they were likely to find Jessica Miller's body in, and had seen only her face for identification purposes so far. They were taking no chances, so beneath the table Franklin had attached the sloped sluicing tray to trap blood runoff and the edges of the steel frame had been raised to prevent the escape of whatever unpleasant surprises awaited them. Rowan had learned from experience that it varied from one pathologist to the next as to how neatly a body would be stitched up after a post mortem.

"Well, there's no point in waiting any longer," said Franklin. "Merry Christmas." With that he unzipped the bag and revealed the corpse within.

Jessica Miller was in far better condition than they had feared. In her time at Gallow & Sons Rowan had seen some awful sights, mangled bodies held together by little more than sinew and skin, bodies that had been burned and crushed, sliced in half and mangled beyond recognition but what had stayed with her the longest was the smell. It was the smell of human decay, of bodies left in abandoned flats in the heat of summer, or bloated by water for unknown stretches of time. It was a smell that permeated her skin and felt as if it would never leave, that haunted her long after the bodies had gone.

Jessica Miller, however, smelled only of industrial cleaning fluids, bleach and chlorine. The skin on her face lay loose and pale. Her hair, once a short stylish bob, was now a shaggy mess of grey, washed through with puddle water. Whatever blood she had once had either run out or congealed within her.

"That's what did her in," said Franklin as he nodded to a dark hole at the left of her bare chest, an impossibly small gap beyond which lay only merciful darkness. "It was quite a shot."

"It would have been quick, at least."

"I think so. There's very little bloodstain on the skin around the wound – that suggests that her heart stopped almost immediately. That, I suppose is a small solace."

No matter how many corpses she saw, it was always the nakedness of those returned from the pathologist that most unsettled her. It wasn't just the haphazard stitches running across exposed skin, but the strangeness of seeing a body at its most vulnerable and private.

"And that is what he took," she said, gesturing towards the stump at the end of the right arm. Just below the wrist, jagged flaps of skin exposed white and shattered bone surrounded by cross-sectioned muscle and tendons. "Why do you think he did that?"

Franklin drew in a breath. "I think I know. Remember the first man on the bridge, the businessman?"

"Spencer Nordstrom," Rowan replied.

"He was shot through the eye with an arrow, and that bus driver, Edison said he had a tooth removed."

Rowan nodded slowly. Somewhere in the midst of memory came the phrase which she spoke aloud. "An eye for an eye, a tooth for a tooth."

"Exactly. The Bible's own take on vengeance. But that's not the end of the quote, it's something like an eye for an eye, a tooth for a tooth, a hand for a hand, a foot for a foot."

Rowan shivered at the revelation. "Jesus Christ," she whispered.

"It makes sense doesn't it? If this whole thing is about taking revenge on the city then the Bible seems as likely a place as any to draw inspiration."

"So do you think this is a religious thing? The killer's a Christian?"

"Perhaps, but even I know the quote – it's an Old Testament thing so we could just as easily be talking about Judaism. But to be honest, it could just be that he wants to add a little style, to remind us that this is for a purpose. I think it's from Exodus if I remember rightly."

166

"Wait, how d'you know your Bible so well?" Rowan asked. "I thought you were supposed to be an atheist?"

"I've read the Bible," he responded, "why do you think I'm an atheist?"

Rowan took this as the joke it was intended to be but could not bring herself to smile over the corpse of a murdered woman. "Sometimes it's even harder when you know who they were," she said, almost lost in thought. "To know what she was like and who loved her, to know how she died."

"I think it's important to know that they're not just bodies, to never forget that they were once just as alive as you or me."

"I forget that about the living sometimes. A few weeks back I had this feeling that came out of nowhere, I was on a bus and suddenly I realised that everyone around me sitting in silence was living a life inside their head that was just as real as my own."

Franklin looked passively at the broken body. "I suppose that's what a murderer will never understand. In order to kill someone you can't believe they are just as alive as you otherwise you'd never be able to do it. To kill someone is to rob them of absolutely everything they have."

A silence fell between them, which settled like a frost. Rowan felt the need to break it. "We're getting maudlin again. It's not healthy for either of us."

"You're right, I suggest we go to the office for a bit – I have a Bible in there among my books for service readings. I want to look up that quote, it goes on a little bit from what I remember."

Rowan agreed and zipped the bag back up around Jessica Miller. After he'd tapped the electronic code into the door, she followed Franklin from the death chamber into his little office that overlooked the garden, now strewn with autumn leaves.

"It's here somewhere," he said once he'd discarded his gloves into a wastepaper bin. "Got it."

Rowan watched as he leafed through the pages in search of the passage in question. As she was oft to do, she pondered the terrifying truth of life that so frequently dragged her from her sleep in the middle of the night. Human beings are so fragile. Their bodies are so feeble and so easily damaged, vulnerable to so many things, every moment in need of a breath and the pump of a heart, of food and water, bones break, blood leaks, flesh burns. She was snapped from her musing only when Franklin declared he had found what he was looking for.

"Here it is, I knew there was more to it. If any harm follows, then you shall give life for life, eye for eye, tooth for tooth, hand for hand, foot for foot, burn for burn, wound for wound, stripe for stripe." He snapped the book shut. "Seems like a pretty nasty call for vengeance to me."

"What are we supposed to make of that?"

"Buggered if I know," said Franklin, "but I wouldn't be surprised if a body is found without a foot sometime in the future."

"So more bodies then. How many? Four?"

Franklin looked over the quote again. "A foot, a burn, a wound, a stripe."

"What's a stripe?"

"It can mean a lot of things, but maybe like a lash of a whip or perhaps a strip of something."

"Like skin?" asked Rowan.

Franklin nodded. "Like skin. The book he sent me."

Rowan pushed the memory of that dreadful item from her head. "Who in the world was that, and why has nobody found them yet? You don't think anyone could survive having that much skin taken from them, do you? Imagine if the killer did that to himself, he seems crazy enough."

"Not a chance. We kind of think that skin is just there to keep our insides from falling out, but it's there to regulate our whole body. Even if you survived stripping away that much skin – and that was a lot of skin, enough to bind the front and back of a book, infection would take you down in hours. Not to mention that without pores you would die of heat exhaustion as you wouldn't be able to sweat, your organs would be overwhelmed by water and they'd essentially break apart and…"

"…I get it, Franklin, thank you. You need skin to live, it was just a thought anyway."

"Sorry," he said, "it isn't the most pleasant thing to imagine."

"I suppose the important thing is that it sounds like there's going to be three more murders before this killer is through." Rowan threw her hands to her face. "How did we get mixed up in a murder case again?"

"We didn't choose this, Rowan. The killer chose me. I suppose that's the most frightening bit – whatever he's planned, I seem to play some role in it somehow, I just don't yet have any idea what that might be."

They returned to the death chamber and between them wheeled Jessica Miller's body over to the refrigerated unit fixed to the wall. After sliding her inside and locking the steel door, they slipped out of their paper overalls which were discarded into plastic bags and thrown into a medical waste bin. For Rowan, stepping back into her regular work wear was the first stage in casting off the sense of gloom and melancholy.

"Are you going to call the police?" she asked.

"Of course, well, I'll call Edison. He'll know what to do. I don't think the police want us prying into their duties more than we have already. Besides they've probably figured it out already anyway; they seem to be keeping a lot of stuff out of the press."

"I wouldn't bank on them sorting anything out by themselves if last time was anything to go by."

"That was very different and you know exactly why."

Rowan nodded. Franklin consulted his watch.

"Hey," he said, "it's pretty much five o'clock, how about I let Meredy go home early and you and I go for a pint. I don't know about you but I need a drink to clear my head."

Rowan smiled at her friend. "That sounds perfect to me."

34.

Evenings by herself were a precious time for Rowan. When she was younger they were little more than a buffer between the end of school and sleep, during which time she would slump on the sofa and let whatever nonsense her parents were watching on TV wash over her like a tide.

Everything changed after Ruby died. Evenings with her parents ached with her absence. The armchair where she sat with her legs draped over the side was now like a black hole, sucking all joy from the room as they all pretended not to notice. The chair still bore her shape as a constant reminder of what they had lost. Rowan had taken to early nights.

It was a habit she had kept in her new home. Her evenings now mostly consisted of being propped up in bed with a book or her iPad with a mug of tea resting enticingly beside her. That evening she was studying a battered old paperback she had found in a charity shop on the subject of Wicca.

She didn't read the book hungrily, for she was not one to fool herself. She knew her exploration into Paganism came not from any sort of faith in the god of nature, or of the cycle of the seasons, but from a need to find something, anything, from which to find solace. She yearned for the comfort and structure of belief, a promise that something could survive long after the body had died.

Her mind was distracted. Overhead she could hear Jude pacing back and forth across his flat, she thought he sounded ill at ease and distracted somehow. She looked over to the crack in her ceiling and almost hoped it would start to leak again, just to give her an excuse to go upstairs and speak to him, to say sorry, if there was anything to apologise for.

She hadn't spoken to him since the night of their semi-date and had avoided him by listening for his departing footsteps out of fear of meeting him on the landing. Several days had passed, with that strange night playing on her mind, yet she had resisted the impulse to ask what it had been about.

She told herself his pacing was enough of an intrusion to justify a complaint and cast her duvet aside. She dressed quickly and casually and made her way upstairs with her somewhat pitiful excuse at the ready. She knocked on the door and waited.

"Just a minute," came the response and Rowan leaned in to the door to hear Jude scurrying about his flat.

When he opened the door he was wearing nothing but a towel around his waist, which annoyed Rowan immensely. It was simply unfair for a man who looked like him to wear so little so much of the time – how was she to have a rational conversation with him?

"Oh, it's just you," were his devastating first words.

"Sorry?"

"No, I mean… I thought it might have been someone else."

"It's almost eleven, do you often have people drop by unannounced in the middle of the night?"

Jude stepped aside to let Rowan in. "No, it's just I sell a bit of weed on the side sometimes and people get desperate."

Rowan nodded but felt her gut twist. She had spent the weekend telling herself that Jude had slipped away from the police due to some low-level drug dealing, but clearly he felt no need to hide this detail from her, so whatever the reason it had to be something more serious.

"I heard you walking around upstairs and I'm trying to sleep," she said.

"Sorry Chocolate. When I'm writing I need to be free, you know. It won't come unless I'm up on my feet."

Rowan nodded and Jude tossed aside a pile of unwashed clothes that had been piled on the sofa. His flat was as unkempt as usual with dirty dishes piled around the sink and discarded balls of paper strewn about the floor.

"Sit," he said, though not unkindly.

Rowan sat and Jude fell on the sofa beside her, his towel gaping open around his thighs. She tried not to look. "It wasn't just the noise I came up for, I just thought I'd see how you were, you know, after the other night."

Jude shrugged his bare shoulders and tossed his mane of blonde hair. "I barely remember it to be honest. Everyone gets a bit pissed now and then."

"Right, it's just that I felt a bit bad for going off on one and wanted to check that everything was… ok."

Jude stared into her eyes. "I don't know what you mean. I thought we had a nice night, I just had a few too many before we met – I met up with someone beforehand, you know, a work thing with a client. Hit the bottle too fast, you know how it is."

That seemed to be explanation enough for Jude but for Rowan it seemed to only open up further questions but she decided that it wasn't the time to seek answers.

"I don't think I've ever asked you before, but what do you actually do?"

He laughed to himself. "You know me, Chocolate, I'm a poet, a musician, a dreamer. I go wherever inspiration takes me."

"Yes, but what do you actually do for a living? Is it drugs, if it is I don't mind… I mean, it's none of my business."

"I'm not a dealer if that's what you mean, not proper stuff anyway. I'm just a rung on the ladder of the great pot-exchange. Buy it low, sell it high – quite a little capitalist really, my father would be so proud."

"So your parents, do they help you out?"

Jude picked up his guitar and began strumming. Rowan was in no mood to be silenced so pushed her hand against the strings. "I'm serious, Jude. I know nothing about you and we're supposed to be… whatever we are."

"I'm living a life less ordinary. I get by doing what I can where I can, it doesn't make me rich but it makes me feel alive. I've never understood why, when we are given such short lives, but like, limitless possibilities of how to spend our time here on earth, everyone goes and does the exact same thing. Go to school, go to university, get a job, get married, get a mortgage, get some decking and a widescreen TV. It's a waste of a life… wow." Jude was evidently impressed as he immediately scribbled down the highlights of his speech on a notepad.

"Some people like direction," said Rowan. "Otherwise it's like going into the wilderness without a map. There's nothing wrong with that kind of life."

"Sure, but how many people want to live that life, and how many people just think they have to?"

Rowan sighed. "I don't know. A couple of days ago I went with my boss to this university campus up in Fishponds. There were a bunch of kids just sitting having breakfast, all hungover and a bit stoned and they were all slopping about the living room and I just thought how it could have been me, you know? I kind of wanted that for me, like maybe I've missed out."

Jude shook his head slowly. "That's what society has made you think, Chocolate. You don't have to do anything but live an extraordinary life."

Rowan didn't know how she had found herself in this conversation. Perhaps it was the closeness of him sitting next to her with his arm across the back of the sofa and the faintest smell of fresh sweat emanating from him, but she found herself mesmerized by his ease. "I think I want an ordinary life but will never have one."

"Don't say that, you're far too interesting to…"

"…My sister was murdered."

Jude's body jolted as if he'd been electrocuted. "What?"

"My sister, Ruby. She was murdered two and a half years ago."

"Shit. Rowan, I'm so sorry."

She had never had these words come so easily to her and when she spoke is was as simple as breathing. "She was a singer. She was in a few bands but she could never find one to fit her, no matter how talented the musicians were it didn't matter, she was always the best. When she sang it was like time stopped and the walls fell away and this spotlight fell on her and everything else was just darkness. She was going to be a star, it was her destiny, or so we all thought. She was in a studio not that far from here on the night it happened. She was there with her boyfriend and they were recording a few videos for YouTube in the hope

 that someone would notice her. When they finished she said she was going home, but she didn't. She went towards

173

Gloucester Road – seven cameras picked her up on the way. She walked almost two miles in the opposite direction from home. I was out with friends that night and the first I heard anything was when my mum sent a text message asking if I knew where Ruby was. They found her a little after two in the morning. She'd been left in one of those abandoned warehouses; they only found her because they heard her phone ringing – there was almost a hundred missed calls from Mum. Ruby had been stabbed in the neck and chest nineteen times, the police said it had been some kind of frenzy. I've read that when someone's killed like that it's from true hatred, so it stands to reason it was someone who once cared about her."

"Wait, are you saying they don't know who killed her?" Jude asked softly.

"They have no idea. I think the trail has gone cold as we never hear anything about the investigation. They say they never close murder cases until they're solved, but when all roads lead to nothing, I think they just let them fall away after a while."

Jude just pulled her into his chest and she allowed a tear to roll down her cheek. He embraced her tightly and Rowan found herself kissing him. This was not the passionate desire she had known from him but a soft, gentle, loving kiss. She brushed her hand along his cheek and he closed his warm arms around her. When she pulled away from him, he wiped away her tear.

"D' you know Jude," she smiled. "You're not too bad when you aren't being a total wanker."

"Thanks. I think."

"What are you doing tonight?"

She felt him shrug his shoulders. "I was thinking that maybe you and I could watch some Netflix together in your flat."

"I think I'd like that."

"And I could always like, stay the night if you wanted me to."

"Yes please," she said and kissed him again.

35.

Franklin studied the emblem on the wall as Herbert Herman applied a hot towel to his face. He'd seen the symbol many times before but had never thought to ask about it. It was no larger than an ashtray, a small circle emblazoned in gilt with the image of two unicorns facing one another as if ready to engage in battle. It had always seemed familiar to Franklin, though he was never quite sure why.

"I assume you'll be wanting the usual?" asked Mr Herman, Franklin's barber, whom he visited every morning before a service, for what was undoubtedly the closest shave in the city and to have his already neat hair carefully trimmed.

"Please, Herb."

"I don't suppose this funeral is that poor woman who was killed last week is it?" Mr Herman said as he lathered shaving cream around Franklin's jaw.

"You know I can't tell you even if it is." He replied.

"It's all anyone's talking about, of course, even when they catch him we'll hear of nothing else for months. It's all just so ghastly, and to have it so close to home, here in Clifton, well, it's unspeakable."

Franklin tried to answer but Mr Herman was already gliding over his face with a cutthroat razor. It was a pleasantly old fashioned experience which Franklin believed set the tone for the rest of the day.

"If you ask me, hanging's too good for him. They should chop him up and feed him to the animals in the zoo."

Of course, with old fashioned aesthetics came old fashioned values, which jarred with Franklin's liberal views, but he could certainly concede that if the only way to stop this monster was to kill him, he wouldn't be shedding any tears over it.

When the barber had finished he held up a mirror and Franklin nodded agreeably at the result. He paid his bill and left in his Smart car for Gallow & Sons where he found Rowan waiting for him in the driveway.

Her short ringlets had been clipped back with little dark slides and she wore a cream blouse under a black waistcoat with a matching skirt. "Morning Franklin," she smiled wanly as he stepped from his car.

"Is Ms Miller in the hearse?"

"She is, the day labourers put her in just before you arrived. They're getting the wreath ready."

It was an unseasonably warm autumn day with clear skies and radiant sun, which still held the trace of midsummer. Franklin dressed in his standard funeral attire, suit, hat and tails and inspected himself in his bedroom mirror. Service wear was all about layers, from vest to shirt to waistcoat to overcoat and the stifling heat of summer was mercifully behind him. There was something about autumnal funerals that bore the melancholy of death – the withering of the seasons, the passage of time and the end of all things. Today would go well, he told himself.

He rejoined Rowan by the hearse, which was waiting in the garage. The day labourers, the workers who were called in just for services, had arranged a dazzling array of flowers that cascaded like water over the casket. Franklin nodded his thanks to the men, who were to follow him and Rowan in the procession across Bristol.

"Shall we get going?" asked Rowan, as she consulted her watch.

"Give it a couple of minutes," replied Franklin as the pair climbed into either side of the hearse. Franklin knew from experience the time it took to cross the city, a hearse was not like any other vehicle, cars moved respectively from its path, just its presence was enough to slow traffic to a maudlin, predictable pace. He aimed to arrive at their destination at the exact minute he was expected.

"This is my first murder service," said Rowan, "I mean proper murder where everyone knows that it's a murder. I mean…."

"Don't think of it as any different to the others. Don't let it get under your skin either. Remember that if you were there, you would have done something to prevent it, but you weren't and neither was I, and nothing can be done about it now."

"I'll be fine, I promise. It just feels a little different, you know. I know what it's like from the other side."

Franklin nodded sympathetically. "So the best thing we can do is give Jessica Miller the send off she would have wanted and to make it as easy for her friends and family as we can."

"I know, and the hardest work for us is done already. I'm glad we won't be attending this service."

"So am I." Franklin watched the digital clock click over to three minutes past eleven and started the engine. "Here we go. Good luck."

Two cars followed the hearse. The arrangement had been that this procession was likely to be lengthy and slow moving, but until they reached the home of Harmony Miller at Westbury-on-Trym, it was much like any other ride across the city. Pulling into the gravel drive of the house, Rowan placed her top hat on her head and positioned it correctly in the rearview mirror. She stepped from the car and rang the doorbell.

Harmony was waiting at the door with Lois beside her. Both were dressed in long, dark dresses with an identical expression of mournful contemplation. On seeing the hearse and the flower laden casket Harmony looked for the briefest moment as if her expression might crack, instead she shook her head and composed herself, pulling herself back from the brink of tears.

Lois held her hand and led her to the car. In the doorway appeared a younger man who Franklin recognised from pictures as Lois and Larry's son, Andrew, and after him came Larry himself. The older man was seated in a wheelchair but was recovering well enough for his son to help him to his feet, taking hold of him one side as Rowan took the other as they guided him into the back of the car.

More and more cars joined the procession, which eventually numbered about twenty, passing the Downs and along the Portway under the mighty suspension bridge and back out of the city towards the largest crematorium in the county.

The mourners regrouped in the car park and Franklin and Rowan stood with bowed heads as the casket was drawn from the back of the hearse and carried to the huge double doors that opened into the belly of this vast chamber of sorrow. Six men, one of whom was Andrew Roker, hoisted the oak coffin onto their shoulders as the doors swung open to reveal the vast cavern within lit with candles along the aisles. The music began and the pallbearers took their cue.

Harmony followed closely behind the body of her mother, flanked on either side by Lois, who dabbed delicately at her eye, and Larry, who teetered precariously, though nobly, upon his injured leg.

Then came the assorted mourners of whom Franklin knew nothing. They had gathered in their hundreds, some having waited for the arrival of the ceremonial cortege, some still arriving. The organ played Amazing Grace until all the congregation had gathered within and the doors were closed. The final chapter of Jessica Miller's life was about to end.

"I know we hear that song all the time," said Rowan as the pair returned to wait in the hearse. "But it still moves me."

"I know what you mean. They're classics for a reason."

The service was expected to be a lengthy one, taking up the best part of an hour. Jessica Miller had evidently lived a busy, eventful life and there was much ground to cover, once Franklin and Rowan had overcome the profound sense of melancholy they began to relax.

"Do you want to play a round of I spy?" Franklin suggested.

"Not really, sitting in total silence is more interesting than playing I spy."

"That's probably true, it is a uniquely boring game."

Rowan looked across the car park to the doors of the crematorium. "I hope they're coping in there."

Franklin nodded. "It can't be easy."

"It isn't. When I was at Ruby's service I just wanted it to end, it was so awful. I became convinced that this was somehow all a joke and any moment Ruby was going to bounce out of her coffin and we would all laugh at her marvellous prank, but it just kept on going on and on and I started to believe that it was really happening. I'm still not convinced that any of it was real."

Franklin patted her shoulder gently in a paternal manner. "How about we play just one round, this talking thing doesn't seem like it's helping much."

"Fine," Rowan chuckled.

When the service was over the mourners came blinking into the sun with tearful eyes. Franklin and Rowan stepped from the hearse and waited to offer their condolences if approached, but to otherwise stand by in silence.

Lamentations in the crowd were few, but they were harrowing. The sheer weight of the horror had overwhelmed some of them who had formed a discreet huddle alongside a small memorial garden, Franklin was certain Harmony was among them.

"Thank you Mr Gallow," said a thin voice. He turned to see Lois standing before him with Larry at her side. "Thank you Ms Kaplan. That was a beautiful service you arranged, Jessica would be very proud."

"Thank you. Once again may I offer my deepest sympathy."

"Larry and I were just wondering…" she ventured, leaning inwards. "If you've thought of anything, anything at all that was amiss. Just the slightest clue or something you noticed that perhaps the police haven't told Harmony."

Franklin swallowed hard. The guilt of having to withhold information, of the skin book and having contact with the killer, several times in fact, was wrenching at him. "I'm so sorry but I've found nothing I'm afraid."

Lois and Larry just nodded sadly.

"They owe it to her," Larry said as he gestured towards Harmony who was in a vice-like embrace with a friend, "the police do. They can't let this go unpunished, they have to catch him. Poor Jackson, he's so young and still doesn't know what happened. He's with a babysitter and is spending the day blissfully unaware. He's asked about his grandmother and we just don't know what to say to him."

Lois scrawled her email on a piece of lavender coloured notepaper which she handed to Rowan with a smile. "Just in case anything occurs to you, this way Harmony won't have to know anything that will upset her."

179

The pair returned to the crowd of mourners. "We can't do anything more for Jessica Miller but we can do something for Harmony and Jackson. We're gonna catch that bastard."

36.

When Franklin returned from the crematorium it was turning dark and he was looking forward to changing out of his suit and into a pair of pyjamas. He and Rowan had been invited to the wake in Harmony's home and accepted with the manners with which it had been extended. They had stayed for what they mutually agreed was a reasonable amount of time and then slipped away unnoticed once the family and friends began tearful reminiscences.

After he pulled into the garage of Gallow & Sons, Franklin retrieved the brass urn from the back of the car and paused briefly to contemplate the weirdness of death. Ten days ago Jessica Miller had been preparing for a dinner with friends, expecting a lovely night of good food and expensive wine; she probably took a bottle round herself. There could have been no way of knowing that ten days from that night would find her charred remains in an urn in the hands of a stranger. Life was so very strange and death only ever one wrong turn away.

Murders were rare and mercifully so. Franklin had only ever dealt with a dozen or so in his career of almost twenty years. Often the distance between the crime and the funeral were torturous in length; so often a body was the greatest repository of information an investigation would access, but for Jessica Miller there was to be no such wait.

Her body had already yielded its greatest secrets, for the investigators knew precisely who had killed her – a madman who dressed as the pirate Blackbeard and killed vengefully across the city. She would be allowed some peace in death, and Franklin hoped he had played his part in that.

An Indian takeaway with a bottle of cider and a few episodes of Neighbours on his TiVo were his plans for what he imagined would be a tranquil evening, which was why the sight of the woman standing by the door to the reception made his heart sink.

"Excuse me," he asked the silhouette, "can I help you?"

The woman stepped into a pool of light cast by the security lamp on the edge of the garage. "Franklin Gallow, I've been expecting you." The woman was instantly recognisable but Franklin could not place where from. She wore thick foundation and blood red lipstick and her sandy blonde hair had been cut into a shaggy bob.

"I've been meaning to contact you for a while, Franklin, let me introduce myself, I'm Ellie Sutton, a journalist for the Star. Perhaps you've read my column or maybe my blog?"

That was it. She was that dreadful woman who wrote incendiary articles aimed at maximizing outrage, targeting minority groups and poor people and every word she typed sent Twitter into a storm of protest. She was the mouth-for-hire who was routinely wheeled out on breakfast TV to say something vile about immigrants and rile half the nation into a frenzy of rage while swelling her bank balance. To Franklin, she was the journalistic equivalent of a hand grenade.

"That's a marvellous suit, Mr Gallow. I saw your pictures online and people told me you were handsome, but I had no idea until I saw you in person."

"Excuse me," Franklin was in no mood for this nonsense, "I've had a busy day and just want some peace."

"I'm not sure if you've heard of me, but I write the number one opinion column in the UK and my readers would love to hear first hand how you solved those murders in the spring… and of course, your opinion on the Crossbow Killer." She took a step closer to him and Franklin felt his skin crawl. "I'm a great admirer of your work, Frank. Perhaps you could invite me inside for a chat."

"I don't know what you're talking about Ms Sutton, I've no more insight into the murders than you have. Now could you please leave me alone!"

She took another step closer, her heels crunching gravel, "I would reward you, handsomely of course, I'm sure you'd be more than able to sort out this riddle and my readers would love to hear from you. Did you know that two-thirds of my readers are women? I'm sure I could arrange to have a few photographs taken in that sexy suit to."

"I have absolutely no intention of giving you an interview, so please leave my property before I call the police"

Ellie Sutton smiled. "Do you mean your brother, Edison? I've done my homework Frank; I know all about you."

Franklin snorted a laugh, "Isn't your column more interested in which celebrities have put on weight or how Muslims want to ban Peppa Pig?"

"I'm branching out, I go after the big stories Frank and these murders are the biggest story right now. Everyone wants to read about them, it's only fair that I dip my toe in."

"Congratulations," Franklin huffed as he pushed past her, "I'm sure you'll be the next Truman Capote."

"I'm going to be writing about it whether you want to be involved or not, wouldn't you prefer it if…"

"…I'd prefer it if you slunk off back to whatever pit you emerged from. Write what you will but I'll have no part in it." Franklin unlocked the door to the reception and stepped inside. He felt an enormous sense of pleasure in letting the door slam back at her while she was still talking. It was only as he was ascending the stairs to his flat that he noticed his fingers were trembling with rage at the loathsome woman who represented everything he despised.

She thundered on the door behind him and called out through the class panel. "I don't need you anyway, you…fucking ginger!"

He decided not to ring for an Indian takeaway for fear that he'd have another encounter with her when he went to pay for his food, instead he settled for a cheese omelette and a glass of neat gin.

When an hour had passed and his anger had only got stronger, he decided to call Rowan.

"Hello? What's up?" she asked.

"Have you ever heard of a journalist called Ellie Sutton?"

"Oh yes. I had a run in with her a few weeks back, she's loving this, I keep on seeing her around the city."

Franklin was concerned. "D' you think she knows who you are?"

"She does, she knows a lot. Why are you asking about some nasty hack from the gutter press?"

"I just had an unfortunate encounter with her on my door step, she wanted an interview with the great undertaker investigator."

"I can't say I'm surprised, she's been working double shifts on this story. Her blog's being updated almost hourly."

"Seems that my secret was far from safe, which is pretty worrying as it means that our killer wasn't someone with special knowledge as far as my involvement was concerned. It's disturbing that she knows who you are, how do you think she found that out?"

"Not a clue, but I wouldn't put it past the police to have a leak somewhere on their team. What did you do? You didn't say anything to her did you?'

"Of course not Rowan, d'you think I'm mad? I slammed the door in her face… she called me a ginger."

Rowan laughed. "I've been called worse. In fact, I've been called exactly the same, if you rearrange the letters."

It took a while for Franklin to understand what she meant. "Rowan? Has someone called you that before?"

"Don't say it, Franklin…" she warned.

"I would never…"

"…I don't think white people are even allowed to think that word anymore."

"It has been unthought." Franklin smiled.

"Well, it could be trouble if she writes about you, but what good would that do? Her readers are vultures looking for fresh meat. She's not telling them anything besides a funeral director helped solve a murder six months ago, she's got nothing new without an interview."

"Thanks. That's actually very reassuring to hear."

"I'll keep an eye out for her. Not sure how much of her blog I can stomach though so you might be on your own with that one."

The thought of having to trawl through Ellie Sutton's vitriol made Franklin's stomach heave. "I will if I have to. I'll see what Edison knows about any police leak as well, the last thing we need is your name getting into circulation too"

They said their goodbyes and Franklin was soon sprawled out on the sofa with his cat purring on his chest as a string of Neighbours episodes queued up on his TV. His laptop informed him that he had a new email which he clicked on obligingly.

Just as he'd hoped, it was from Nell, the Scottish woman who ran a funeral home in Edinburgh. The pair had been batting back flirtatious messages like tennis balls for weeks now.

"Hi Franklin. Just wanted to see how things went with the service today. Had a horrid one myself – 22 year old who came off his motorbike."

Franklin turned on his messenger and gave a little hiccup of joy when he saw she was online.

"Hi Nell. Day could have been worse. Not too bad for a murder." Franklin considered adding a smiley face at the end but decided against it as it might come across as a little glib given the circumstances.

A little icon appeared on the screen informing Franklin that Nell had received the message and was replying. Her icon was the flag of St Andrews with the word "Yes" emblazoned on it. Franklin had decided a while back that he would not take Nell's support for Scottish independence as a slight against the English.

"Evening Handsome. Nice to see you online. Got the house to myself for a change!" Nell had included a smiley face, which made Franklin regret his choice.

"Any chance of a chat tonight? I could call you on the phone or we could go on Skype. It's been so long and I'd love to finally see you."

"Not tonight, sorry. I look a mess, just chilling out with wine and a movie."

"I don't mind."

"Well, I do."

Franklin watched the screen as the little icon flashed out and a textbox appeared informing him that she had gone offline. Franklin huffed and contemplated his frustration. His mind began to wander. Who was this woman who wanted to keep their conversation solely confined to words on a screen after all these months? What, if anything, did he know about her?

37

Halloween fell on a Friday and was expected to be a night of unbridled mayhem, the likes of which the city had seldom seen. Whatever fear had seized Bristol in the previous weeks and driven its residents behind locked doors had grown smaller in menace – not even a killer could keep a city under self-imposed curfew for long. Eventually even the worst terrors must be put aside in the pursuit of pleasure.

Year upon year Franklin had watched with confused bemusement as Halloween escalated in both size and devotion. At the tail end of September orange and black filled the shelves of supermarkets alongside plastic ghosts and putridly coloured sweets. "I don't understand it," Franklin told Rowan as they crossed the road to the Tobacco Factory, "is it supposed to be a good thing? Are we embracing death or something?"

"It is what it is, Franklin."

The Tobacco Factory was a popular bar and restaurant beneath a theatre, famed for its avant-garde take on Shakespeare. The interior mixed industrial against creative, with provocative art displayed on bare brick walls beneath a bare, unfinished ceiling of exposed pipes and heating vents. For many years, Franklin and his brother Edison had met here every Friday, as a kind of tradition to ensure they saw each other once a week – regardless of how irritating they found each other's company. Rowan had taken to occasionally joining them, particularly when she felt compelled to talk over matters with Edison.

Franklin found his brother seated at a table in the far corner. The bar was filled with people, mostly dressed in suitably blood soaked attire. For every zombie there was a vampire, for every werewolf there was a woman dressed in little more than her underwear and a pair of rabbit ears. Franklin tried not to stare.

"Welcome to the madhouse," said Edison.

Rowan and Franklin took seats across from him he'd already bought his round, a bitter for himself, Ashton Press cider for Franklin and a large glass of red wine for Rowan.

"What time are you on duty tonight?" Franklin asked.

"Nine o'clock. I'm not looking forward to it much. Tonight's the night the whole city loses its mind and everyone gets as drunk as humanly possibly."

"Isn't that every weekend?"

"Trust me, it's going to be much worse. I'm just staying for the one drink – I'm going to need a clear head to get through this night."

"I think it's fun," Rowan commented as she peered around the room. "It's a celebration of the dark side of things. It feels kind of healthy to me."

"It's another bloody American import is what it is," Edison grumbled. "Can't bloody escape it. We'll be doing Thanksgiving soon, and the Fourth of July."

"What does Dad make of it?" Franklin asked. Their father had an abiding, yet inexplicable, love of all things American, from its politics to its landscape, from its TV to its annual customs. He had even gone so far as to name his sons after two of the most renowned men in its history – Thomas Edison and Benjamin Franklin.

"No bloody idea. He never bothered with it when we were kids, nobody did back then."

"Nobody ever comes to the home," said Franklin, "I was watching earlier as the trick-or-treaters were going along the street. They stopped off at every house along the way but wouldn't come near my door. Make believe horror is one thing but an actual real life funeral home is not the kind of scary they're looking for."

"You're lucky then. They were at my door every five minutes – sanctioned begging is what it is." Edison grumbled.

Franklin wished he could partake in the fun of the evening. There was an air of good-natured morbidity that appealed to his sense of the macabre, a flirtation with the inevitability of death that touched only slightly on his everyday life of confronting it full in the face. It appealed to him in the same way it appealed to children, bats and ghosts, witches and skeletons were so different from the everyday terrors of adult life; a brown envelope from the tax department falling on the doormat; finding a suspicious growth on a testicle in the shower; the sudden horror of realizing that half his life could easily have been spent already. Was it any wonder that adults had taken to this celebration of the terrors of the night?

"It'll be a night of havoc," Edison warned grimly.

"How d'you mean?"

Edison drained his pint miserably. "Nobody's saying anything, not really, but we're all thinking it. There's a killer in the city who seems to have a fondness for dressing up. Seems as good a night as any to get dressed up and go out killing."

Franklin looked at Rowan. "I must admit that it's crossed my mind, I'm guessing that you would've said something if you'd had any warnings."

Edison shrugged his shoulders. "What good would it do if we did? These kids aren't going to pay any attention, it's all a joke tonight. They want us to take care of them but they won't do the sensible thing and stay inside. We're having a hard enough time just teaching them not to go wandering off by themselves and to stay in well lit areas. If we issued a warning it would just be another scary story for them to not take seriously. I mean, look over there…" Edison gestured towards the door where a young man had just pushed his way inside. He was dressed in a long overcoat and a pirate's tricorn hat matched with a huge fake beard to ensure there was no doubt who he was supposed to be. "It's all a bloody joke for them."

"Who would do that?" Rowan asked, incredulously.

"Dithering idiots," Edison replied.

"No, I mean, yes, it's poor taste, but isn't it also dangerous? I'd be scared of a mob beating me up."

"I wouldn't bet on it," Edison said, "If you look online half the city seems to think he's some kind of hero."

"It's not half the city, we're not that bad." Franklin added, defensively.

"You have a much better opinion of this generation of than me, Frank. It's hard getting them to take anything seriously at all."

"Sorry?" Rowan interrupted.

"Present company excepted, of course."

"Don't try blaming my generation for this, we aren't responsible for any of this crap – we didn't build that terrible statue and we are the ones who want it taken down."

Franklin felt compelled to prevent this squabble from escalating. "Can we please not turn this into a generational thing? It really isn't helpful."

"I'm getting a drink," Rowan huffed, "same again?"

Franklin nodded, Edison declined. On her way to the bar, Rowan stopped to confront the man dressed as Blackbeard. "That's disgusting," she told him, as far as Franklin could ascertain through lip reading. "People have died." The man and his gaggle of friends just laughed at her.

"What's the point of saying anything?" she complained as she returned to the table. "You can't force somebody to care about other people."

Edison steered the conversation back on track. "You may be pleased to hear that we were aware of the eye-for-an-eye thing. We've known for a bit really, ever since the bus driver had his tooth removed. It was clear that was done to send a message but we've been holding that information back. Believe it or not, people want to confess to these crimes, well, one person does anyway, and we can prove he's lying if he knows nothing about the motive."

"Someone's confessed?" Rowan was astonished.

"It's nothing really. He's some scumbag white supremacist looking for a bit of notoriety. He's the one behind this demonstration on Sunday – Take Back Our Streets. Rights for whites and all of that stuff. He couldn't fire an arrow to save his life and whoever the killer is must be some kind of expert marksman. To take someone's eye out with an arrow isn't easy."

"I bet," Franklin nodded. "Have you tried looking around archery clubs or places like that?"

"Yes, Franklin, believe it or not we do actually know what we're doing down at the station. They know nothing and are none too pleased to have their clubs come under scrutiny."

'What's happening with this demonstration then, on Sunday?" asked Rowan. "Can't you do anything to stop it – breach of the peace or something?"

Edison shrugged his shoulders. "That's what I want to happen but the investigating officer wants to see it go ahead – even wants that racist bastard free and out on the streets for some reason."

Franklin and Rowan exchanged glances. "Isn't that a touch suspicious?" he said. "Considering he's confessed to the crimes, shouldn't you keep him under surveillance anyway?"

"Come on now, Frank. You can't just blame the police every time."

"You can't possibly be accusing Trish, she might not be great at her job but she's no killer."

Rowan just shrugged. "I don't know, but if I was going out and killing people, I'd want to make sure there was someone else out there who I could blame it on."

For the briefest moment it appeared that Edison was contemplating this possibility. He shook the thought away. "That's absurd, and offensive... but, it is a bit strange. Trish is usually much more on the ball and she keeps on talking about how I should trust her and that everything is under control, she does like to play with her cards close to her chest." Edison stared dreamily into space as he thought about the infuriating officer, of whom he knew next to nothing. "I'd better get going, it's going to be a long night. I'm being partnered with some infant called Colin who does nothing but complain."

"Oh really?" Franklin smiled. "Imagine having to spend time with someone like that?"

Edison seemed not to understand the implication and simply took a long draw on his vape pen. "Have a good night. Happy Halloween."

As soon as he'd left, Rowan and Franklin were lost in speculation.

"What do you think he meant about that woman, Trish?" Rowan asked.

"I don't know, but he's not letting on all that he could. Perhaps he doesn't want to confess that the police are clueless, or that he thinks the case is being mismanaged."

"I wish he could have stayed for a few more drinks, he's much more free with the information when he's drunk."

"I know," Franklin agreed. "But it may be that he's completely out of the loop. If he doesn't know any more than we do, there's only so much information we can get from him. Then there's the very real possibility that the entire police force is in the dark. D'you know how rare serial killers are? Do you know how rare it is for them to go uncaught? There's a reason why we all know who Jack the Ripper is and that's because he escaped punishment, that's almost unheard of. The reason why this killer hasn't been caught might just be because he's too good, he knows what he's doing and it took a long, long time to plan."

Rowan took a sip of her wine and looked around the room at the costumed strangers, their true identities hidden beneath masks and fancy dress. The killer no doubt had a job and friends, maybe even a partner to come home to after another night of killing, all the while hiding who he really was.

Franklin watched the strangers with a sudden sense of impending doom he could not shake. It wasn't so much a fear of these unknown, disguised people, but a sudden overwhelming regret that he hadn't told his brother to be careful that night.

38

When Rowan stepped off the bus into the stinging night air, she found Lise already waiting for her outside the old cinema on Whiteladies Road.

She had kept her plans discretely to herself, fully aware just how cynical Franklin would have been had she made her intentions clear. Even in moments where she found the most clarity she was unsure of exactly how she expected this night to pan out.

"Sorry, am I late?" she began. "I had a drink with my boss and the time might have got away from me."

"It's fine, I'm a little early," replied Lise. The teenage girl slipped a metallic hipflask from the pocket of her woollen overcoat and swigged liberally from it. "Do you want some? Just a bit of gin."

Rowan eyed the flask suspiciously, fully aware as the legal adult she should probably say something responsible but instead took a gulp of it herself. As she handed it back she noticed the engraved lettering, which spelled "Henrik".

"Henrik always liked an affectation," Lise informed her, "I don't know if he ever used it for anything but water but he always liked to carry it with him. I found it amongst his things, his girlfriend got it engraved for him. I don't usually drink, I promise, it just seemed like tonight might be a night I could use a little extra courage."

Rowan nodded her understanding. "I'm a little bit nervous too. I think I want you to be wrong, but if you're right – I want to see that bastard taken down."

"If I'm right, I will destroy him," Lise said coldly.

Merrymakers roamed the streets, mostly students who filled the thoroughfare of Whiteladies Road every weekend but on that evening had done so dressed in full Halloween costume. Lise's eyes followed a group of girls who could not have been much older than her who were dressed as the cast of Orange is the New Black. Rowan saw in her friend a kind of longing for an ordinary life that she knew only too well.

"I was thinking about this area," said Lise.

"What about it?"

"D'you think it's safe? Whiteladies Road and Blackboy Hill, it's the kind of place I'd imagine Crossbow would want to strike if he's trying to prove a point."

"We're safe," replied Rowan, who had studied the history of the streets following the conversation they had shared the last time they were here. "They were pubs in the olden days, it's just a coincidence that it sounds kind of racist. The white lady was a ghost I think and the black boy was Charles II. They called him the black boy because he had very dark hair."

"That's assuming that the killer knows his history. I think most people just assume it's something to do with slavery."

"I think one thing that's certain is that this killer has been doing his homework. Trust me, we're safe – well, as safe as we are anywhere. Anyway, shall we go in?"

Lise nodded and followed Rowan through the rotating doors and into the lobby of the cinema. Rowan saw her friend reach for her wallet. "It's free," she informed her.

"That's very interesting," she replied, "this psychic, Tegwyn Jones? It seems that he's aiming for something else then. Get people in for the shows and soon he'll be on sellout tours and have his own series on ITV2"

"Please try to keep an open mind. Last time I was here it felt really special… it felt real."

"If it's real he'll have proof. If he is a liar, I shall have the proof."

They crept through the lobby and down a corridor where a door had been propped open with a fire extinguisher and the same elderly woman who had met Rowan previously welcomed them to what she referred to as "church."

The auditorium was about twice as full as it had been the last time. No doubt the dual prospect of Halloween and an unidentified serial killer had drawn in a larger crowd. The woman escorted them to a pair of seats a couple of rows back from a stage that had been fashioned on the spot where the screen would once have hung.

"Here," whispered Lise as she handed Rowan a compact video camera, the likes of which she'd not seen for many years. "It's better for low lighting than a phone camera and doesn't jump around as much, I want as many people to see this as possible. If I stand up, start recording but don't let anyone else see it."

Rowan flipped open the control panel and quickly familiarized herself with the workings of the machine. A sign in the lobby had informed them no recording equipment was allowed, but she was fully aware that her friend was on a mission that was far greater than any trifling rules.

When Tegwyn Jones took to the stage, a few minutes past the time he due to begin, it was without even a whisper of fanfare. He just stepped out into a pool of light and those who noticed the arrival of this diminutive man offered only the meekest of applause.

"Good evening, friends," he began. His microphone screeched so he took a step away from the amp at the front of the stage. Just questioning his veracity had made the man seem amateurish in Rowan's eyes. Stripped of the wonder of his supernatural powers, she saw the man as smaller, older, and more intimidated by the audience, she could not help but feel a little sting of pity for him and the trap he may be stepping into.

"Oh what a treat to see so many of you here tonight. And look, it's my favourite girls! Edna, how are you, love? How's your hip?" The man eased into his role like a studied pro, his affable campness sat well with his audience which comprised mostly of elderly woman. "Do you know, I was just saying backstage that I always look forward to my Bristol congregation, not just because you're all so lovely, but this old cinema is full of stories, just full of them! Some nights it feels that the spirits are queuing up along the street to speak to their loved ones, and tonight – Halloween, of course, I can feel them closer than ever. What's that? I've got one right here…"

Rowan watched as the man strolled about the stage, tuning into whatever lay in the great beyond as if hunting down the source of a smell. Beside her Lise sat with her arms folded tight across her chest.

"I've got someone's dad here," the medium announced, "says his name is… it begins with a "J," anyone?"

A few hands drifted upwards. In the corner of her eye, Rowan spied Lise swig deeply from her brother's hipflask.

"He's saying it was his heart that took him, oh he's a dear old boy, and he says it took him ever so fast." About half the hands in the auditorium dropped. "He says he had a little girl and when she was tiny he bounced her on his knee like she was riding a pony…"

"…Dad!" shrieked a voice from the audience, Rowan swivelled her head to see a grey haired woman rise slowly to her feet. "Daddy!"

"Oh, he was your daddy, was he?" asked Tegwyn. "What's your name, petal?"

"Angela," the woman sobbed.

"That's right, he's telling me that now, Angela. Like the angels where he is now. Did you know that at night he still comes to tuck you in? Even after all these years you're still his little girl and he likes to sit at the bottom of the bed and tell you stories." The woman's bottom lip was trembling but she seemed about to speak, nevertheless Tegwyn continued on a different tangent. "I'm looking for a Louise," he announced.

The elderly woman looked around her, at first unaware what had happened, until a friend tugged at her side and gestured for her to sit down.

"Louise. She's here looking for her daughter who died earlier this year, are you out there, sweetheart? Your daughter was called Dylan, is that right?"

Rowan watched in horror as a woman, no older than her early forties, rose from her seat. "That's me," she said. The woman who had escorted them to their seats was immediately upon her with another microphone.

"Oh yours was a sad, sad story, but Dylan's with me right now. She was fifteen, is that right?"

The woman simply nodded as tears streamed down her cheeks.

"What's that Louise?"

"Yes, fifteen," she wept.

Gasps came from the audience, Lise locked eyes with Rowan and shook her head dismissively.

"She says she's sorry for that night, she didn't mean to cause you so much pain, but she says she's happy now. It was the bullying at school, you see, it just overwhelmed her and one day she'd just had enough. She never wanted to hurt you but she just couldn't go on living anymore."

"I love you, Dylan!" the woman all but screamed. "I love you and I miss you everyday!"

"Now, I've got someone else here," Tegwyn continued as the woman fell into her seat. "I'm looking for a Sophia, is there a Sophia here?"

A slap to the shoulder from Lise woke Rowan from her trance. Her friend rose to her feet and Rowan fumbled with the video camera which she had discretely hidden beneath her arm.

"I am Sophia," she said and the usherette approached at once with the spare microphone.

"Oh Sophia, what a beautiful little princess you are. Your mother is so proud of you. Her name was Loren, is that right?"

"Yes, my mother was called Loren," said Lise into the microphone.

"What a lovely, Scandinavian name! She's here with me onstage right now and she wants you to know that when the car crashed it was over in a flash and she was on the other side before she even knew what happened. She wished she could have been around to watch you grow but she's been checking in with you all the time. She's so proud of the young woman you've become and..."

"...This is horseshit!" Lise roared into the microphone. Stunned shrieks issued from the audience like a wave. "This man is a charlatan. Two days ago I posted on the Facebook page for Bridges to Another World using an alias and a fake account. I said I was called Sophia and my mother, Loren had been killed in a car crash five years ago and how I was so hoping I would be able to contact her here tonight. It was all bollocks, just like this whole farce is, and you should be ashamed of yourself for lying to these desperate people."

Tegwyn Jones was white with terror. He raised his microphone to his mouth but could manage nothing beyond, "You sneaky little bitch."

"My name is Lise Nielsen, and you, Tegwyn Jones, are nothing but scum!" with that Lise let her microphone drop to the floor and marched down the aisle. Rowan took to her feet and scurried after her.

Pushing out into the street, a rush of adrenaline coursed through Rowan's veins like a drug. It had all happened so fast, yet so perfectly.

"Did you get it?" gasped Lise.

"I did, I think. You were... fantastic. I never knew you could be like that."

"Nobody fucks around with the dead or grieving and gets away with it, not if I have anything to say about it."

Rowan stared at her friend with a mixture of awe and fear. She hadn't known the little girl who'd worn her hair in plaits only a few months earlier had such fire inside her.

"I gotta go," she said. "Text me when you get home so I know you're safe." Lise took the camera and gave Rowan a kiss on the cheek and slipped away into the Friday night crowd on Whiteladies Road.

Rowan shook from her head thoughts of the despair that must now be filling the auditorium behind her. It was sad, of course, but the truth often was. The thought that Ruby had not been on the stage that night was a gloomy one, but so had been the thought that her sister was forever near but always out of reach. Much better she decided was what Lise had already concluded; the truth was what she needed more than anything else. Whatever truth there was to be found, it was not here in Tegwyn Jones' ministry.

39

Colin Harlow thought death would wait a long time to find him. At only twenty-three he was certain the reaper was decades away. He'd been content to live a structured life, to enter the police force, to rise through the ranks. It had been a small dream but one that had given him a huge source of pride.

Catching sight of himself in the uniform still startled him, as if it was unreal that he'd become the man he'd always wanted to be, as if destined for this all along. Destined to be a policeman, certainly not destined to die young.

Colin had been partnered with an older man named Edison Gallow for their beat around the city. He found his partner to be both boring and frightening, as he did not talk much and mostly seemed to just grumble or bark at him when he made a mistake. But a night walking the town still felt exciting to him, to be in among the drunks and unpredictable types who couldn't look after themselves. He represented order and justice, there to protect the good people from the bad.

That's how it had been that evening – at first, at least. Like most of the duties he was assigned, they initially seemed promising, as if he would finally see some action, but it very soon became evident that they were simply walking laps of the city centre in an endless cycle, seeing nothing but mounting piles of vomit with every pass. Rather than chasing criminals, Colin would sit in cars and measure their speed, or give presentations on drugs to bored school children. Many times Colin fought the urge to confess to himself that this job had not been what he'd hoped for. Perhaps in time he'd end up like Edison Gallow, maybe that's what years in the force did to a man.

Halloween had been far less eventful than he'd hoped. The preparations for this night had started a week earlier, with meetings in the station, meetings with local hospitals, meetings with the council. Nobody had known what to expect but they knew that it would likely be a night like no other, however, when the date finally arrived, it seemed that the drinkers themselves were unprepared.

They had peaked earlier than usual, falling down drunk in the streets through an inability to pace themselves for a a full night. The city was littered with discarded wigs and broken heels while masks and plastic pumpkins rolled idly on the breeze. Occasionally a drunken reveller would squeeze his behind thinking that he too was in costume; Colin was quick to laugh this off but Edison vented his fury in no uncertain terms. This night was to be taken seriously.

But it wasn't serious, not really. Just any other night, only a shade louder. Certainly not a night on which to die.

Just after four in the morning he and Edison rounded a corner into Queen Square, a picturesque park in the city centre bordered on all sides by charming doll's house buildings in pastel colours with mighty trees here and there. By night it was lit by ornate brass street lamps which played upon fallen leaves that crunched beneath their boots as they walked the path leading to a statue of a man on a horse in the centre of the square.

"Colin, wait." Edison held his hand up to Colin's chest to stop him from walking further. "Up ahead."

Along the path, no more than ten metres away stood a man. A bulk of a figure swamped by a huge overcoat, his face was buried beneath a forest of beard and on his head he wore a hat that met in three corners.

"Ed, it's just another one of those people in costume, we've seen loads of them."

"Hello?" Edison called out to the man, but he did not respond. "Sir, please speak."

The man took a single step forward and suddenly a little spark ignited before his face, he had struck a match.

"See, he's just having a fag." Colin tried to sound calm but he did not like the look of this man at all. It was then that the match seemed to explode and the small flame engulfed something in the pirate's hand. By the time Colin realised that the man had set fire to an arrow, an arrow drenched in flammable liquid which he was positioning into his crossbow, it was far too late. He had managed a half turn when the

199

arrow struck him. It passed through his neck and knocked him backwards against a tree, pinning him against the trunk.

Edison shrieked and attempted to pull the arrow from Colin's throat, but the fire and the searing heat was now almost to the quill.

Death came quickly for Colin. As his life ebbed away he watched through the flames as the pirate turned and walked briskly away. That was all the life he had been allotted. Tonight truly was a night unlike any other, for Halloween night was the night Colin Harlow died.

40

When the call came in the early hours, Franklin had almost been expecting it. It certainly wasn't uncommon for people to contact him in the middle of the night – sometimes mortuaries became overcrowded and needed bodies collected at unsociable hours, but before he had even answered the call, he knew something was amiss.

Ever since Edison had left the Tobacco Factory, Franklin had a troubled mind. At first he'd put it down to the strangeness of Halloween and the macabre foreboding of the city, but no, it was something deeper, more acute.

It was the feeling that the killer was drawing closer to him, that he'd become a strand in a vast web. That nobody understood this complex game or the role they played in it, except for the killer.

His sleep had been shallow and his dreams vivid. Something was going to happen that night, he was sure of it. The killer had been quiet for too long and Franklin was certain is was not because he was finished.

"Hello?" he answered.

"Mr Gallow, this is Trish Gladstone of Bristol Police, I'm investigating the recent murders in the city," said a woman's voice on the line.

"I know who you are. Is Edison alright?"

"He's fine, he's with me at the station. There's been an incident… an unfortunate incident in Queen Square that's resulted in the death of one of our officers. Edison has requested that I ask you come to the police station to meet him. He was a witness and as you can imagine is rather shaken up."

Franklin was already out of bed and dressing with his free hand. "What happened? Is he injured?"

"He's as well as can be expected, I promise, but he's going to need a little time to recover and should probably have some company today. He mentioned having parents in Bath but he didn't want to contact them so early in the morning."

"I'll tell them, leave it to me," said Franklin as he picked up his keys and bounded down the stairs and out the door."

He hung up without saying goodbye and leapt into his Smart car. Dawn had broken overhead to give a murky glow to a dirty sky of heavy cloud. He checked his watch - half past five - and considered for a moment whether or not to call Rowan. There was no immediate cause to alarm her but if anyone was able to provide calm to the confusion he felt, it would be her. He elected not to as he pulled out of the drive. This morning was a matter for Edison and him and this was no time to allow his panicked mind to get the better of him, he had to look after his brother.

Franklin found himself cursing the killer loudly as he drove frantically across town. The last of the night's revellers were making their way home, costumes in tatters, makeup rolling down cheeks. He wondered how fast word spread across the city and if any of them knew already. He presumed the police would have told most of the drinkers to go home. He imagined the worst of them outside the cordon that had no doubt been placed around Queen Square, jostling each other for a better look at where a man had just died. He shook the image from his head.

He was relieved to see Edison standing outside the station building, leaning on a handrail on the wheelchair ramp and staring blankly ahead as he puffed on his vape pen.

"Edison," called Franklin. "What happened?"

Franklin was not expecting what happened next. Edison snapped from his daze and almost jogged down the slope towards him and threw his arms around his brother's shoulders. "Thank Christ you're here," he gasped. "Thanks so much for coming."

Franklin couldn't remember the last time his brother had hugged him and had certainly never known an embrace like this. This was not the touch of a man expressing his affection for his younger sibling, but the urgent, desperate need to reach out to a loved one from a man who had seen a collegue die in front of him mere hours ago.

"I'm so sorry, Ed. What happened?"

"It was horrible," he said as he broke off the hug. "I've seen bodies before, of course I have, but I've never seen somebody die."

The door to the station opened and a petite Asian woman in her mid thirties stepped out into the morning light. "I'm Trish Gladstone, we spoke on the phone I'm investigating the…"

"…Yes I know that, Trish. What's been going on?"

"He killed Colin Harlow, that kid I was walking the beat with," said Edison. "Shot him right through the neck with fire."

"Shot him with fire?' Franklin asked.

"It seems that an arrow was fired into Colin Harlow's neck, I'm sure death was very quick." Trish said dispassionately. "At the moment we're treating it as a lone incident as there's no reason to suspect it's related to the earlier murders."

"What?" Franklin asked, incredulously. "He killed someone with an arrow."

"He was dressed as Blackbeard the pirate," Edison added.

Trish stood unmoved. "That may be the case but a great deal of people seemed to think it was fun to dress as Blackbeard last night. As yet we aren't drawing any conclusions."

Franklin shook his head, utterly bewildered. "But it was Queen Square."

"I fail to see what that has to do with anything," she replied.

"Really? You're investigating a case where a killer is taking revenge on the city for its past and nobody has thought to break the spine on a book of Bristol history? Queen Square was where there was a massive riot in the 1830s, the police were sent in on horseback and a bunch of people died protesting for their right to vote."

Trish seemed unconvinced by this revelation. "Bristol is an old city, I'm sure that anywhere you go you can find something terrible that happened in the past."

"What's going on here?" Franklin asked.

"I think it's sensible that we don't jump to conclusions until we've developed a full picture of events, I would like to remind you that you are not investigating this case and should leave your speculation to the professionals."

"Bollocks to the professionals," Franklin snapped, "I'm involved already, it was me that bloody horrible book was sent to, you can't keep me out of this."

Trish remained undaunted, "I see, you're the undertaker." She turned and pushed her way through the doors and back into the building.

"What the hell is going on? Is she for real?"

Edison puffed on his vape pen. "I told you something was up with her. There's got to be a reason why she's underplaying all of this."

"It sounds like she's pulling strings to make it easier for the killer to get away with it."

"I don't know," Edison wondered as he stared at the door, "she only has so much control over what's happening, she'll be overruled eventually, maybe even taken off the case if she refuses to be realistic."

"Good. I should hope so too." Franklin sighed. "So, what happened? I mean, if you want to talk about it."

"I think I do, I've already given my statement, they like you to do that as soon as possible. It's amazing how quickly your memory gets clouded – memories are weird, we think that we're replaying them in our heads, but what we're really doing is reconstructing them. Each time we change little details and then remember them like that, and the more times we do it, the more muddled they become. We learned that in our training."

"Did you see the killer?"

"I did and it was just, so strange. We'd seen so many people dressed like that, but this guy, he was just so very obviously different. Everyone else had cheap looking hats or costumes they had made themselves, plastic beards and toy crossbows, but this man, it was clear that this was the real stuff, not just the costume, but the hate was real. You could practically smell it coming off him; he was just so vicious. I never really liked the kid, I found him difficult to be around, but that was no way to die. It just happened so quickly, one minute he was there, just talking, and the next he was pinned to a tree with fire coming out of his mouth as he screamed."

This description of an agonizing death and the casual way in which Edison expressed it, made Franklin instinctively reach for his neck and imagine the horror of having it pierced with a flaming arrow, to scream and feel it fill his mouth, to breathe and have fire swell his lungs.

"It could have been me," said Edison, thoughtfully. "D'you think that's what he wanted? D'you think he knew I was your brother?"

"Of course not," but he really had no further words of comfort. Of course it was possible the killer might try to make a victim of somebody close to home, but until his plan was clearer, who knew what he was hoping to achieve or what role Franklin would play. Besides, with an aim that precise, he was certain that if the killer wanted Edison dead, he would be dead.

The door to the station opened again and Trish stepped casually out onto the wheelchair ramp. "Edison, you are to have two weeks mandatory compassionate leave – paid in full, of course, after which time you'll see a psychologist who will ascertain your fitness to return. I've also contacted the mayor and informed him of all the developments this morning and suggested that the city implement a voluntary curfew at midnight."

"What does a voluntary curfew mean?" Franklin asked.

"It means precisely what it sounds like. We can't force people to stay in their homes at night, but we can strongly recommend that businesses don't open late into the morning. So far all the murders appear to have happened after midnight, so it seems reasonable that we don't provide the killer with further victims."

"So you're just expecting businesses to do the right thing and lose out on thousands of pounds of revenue?" Franklin said.

"It's all we can do, I'm afraid."

"What about this demonstration on Sunday? This reclaim the streets thing from those racists, is that still going ahead?"

Trish's face was inscrutable. "An organization has been granted the right to assemble on St Augustine's Parade tomorrow afternoon, that is correct, yes. There will be a strong police presence to keep order. The right to protest is one of our most important liberties."

"I know that," Franklin barked, irritably, "but surely an exception has to be made in this instance – this is going to be like throwing water onto a chip pan fire. The whole city will be in danger of riot."

"Then it shall be the duty of the police to ensure that no such thing occurs. Now if you don't mind, could we please both stick to our professions."

With that she was gone.

"She's gonna keep me in work, if that's what she means," said Franklin. "There won't be anyone left alive in the city if she gets her way."

"I don't think it's possible to cancel the demonstration, they were really determined that it had to be this Sunday."

Franklin pondered that Sunday and its importance. There was something about that date that lodged uncomfortably in his memory. He pulled out his phone and drew up a Wikipedia page.

"I knew it," he told his brother, "the second of November is Edward Colston's birthday."

41

Rowan thundered on the door of Gallow & Sons while wondering why Franklin had not yet come to answer it. Shortly after he'd sent her a confused text message in the small hours, she had replied with a frantic phone call.

She'd pieced together the relevant information between her brief conversation with Franklin and the news reporting on the television. A murder in Queen Square, home to Bristol's grandest people and scene of one of the bloodiest confrontations in the history of the city. Over hurried mouthfuls of cornflakes she'd watched with fascinated horror until the unwelcome face of Ellie Sutton appeared on the screen.

"One of the first at the scene," the reporter informed the viewers, at which point Rowan narrowed her eyes and turned off her TV.

The streets were abandoned with most of the detritus from a night of debauchery swept away. She cycled across the city in record time, making sure to steer clear of Queen Square as if it were the site of a massive atomic fallout.

"Morning," Franklin said half heartedly as he opened the door. He was wearing a suit he had no doubt fallen asleep in.

"What the hell's going on?" she demanded as she pushed her way inside.

Franklin explained again the events of the previous night, only this time in far greater detail.

"Is Edison here?"

Franklin nodded. "He's in the spare room – his old bedroom."

"How's he doing?"

"Better than you might imagine but I think a lot of that is bravado – the rest of it's probably shock. It might take a while for it to truly hit home what happened to him."

Rowan nodded. Many people had said the same to her, that eventually she would be haunted by what happened to her in that car. Six months on and she'd so far escaped the worst of those horrors. "Is he asleep?"

"I think so. I told him he should stay here for a while, until the press has died down a bit. One of his neighbours called and said there's a bit of a media circus outside his house. Bunch of animals."

"Don't remind me. That Sutton woman is already doing the rounds on TV."

"He says he's going back to work," Franklin sighed.

"D'you think that's wise?"

"What?" Edison's voice came from the stairwell beyond the reception. "I think I know what's best for me." He appeared before them, fully dressed, with a cup of coffee and looking significantly more rested than Franklin.

"Edison," Rowan began. "I'm so sorry."

The man simply shrugged. "What can be done about it? Not much if I just sit around hiding here all day."

"You can't be thinking of going back today?" asked Franklin incredulously.

"I am going back today. There's nobody on the force who's better equipped. I've seen the killer and know what he can do. There's not a chance in hell that I'm going to leave it to the rest of them, especially when Trish is there directing the whole thing."

"The detective," Rowan said, mostly to herself, "what can you do about her?"

Edison paused for a moment, evidently not having thought this far ahead. "I can at least keep an eye on her, see what she's up to, she's a strange woman but she isn't a stupid one, she must have a plan, I just have to figure out what it is."

Rowan nodded her approval. She'd never especially liked Edison, finding him rather too prickly and grumpy for her liking, but she'd never doubted his integrity. "I think moving on is the only thing you can do. It seems callous sometimes but the day after I got attacked, I went to the cinema with Lise and then out for drinks."

"Precisely," Edison concurred.

"We'll discuss this when I get back," Franklin huffed. "Rowan and I are supposed to be going over to Westbury, we're taking Jessica Miller's ashes to her daughter."

There was brief silence as an unspoken chill fell upon the room. The bodies the killer had left in his wake were everywhere.

"Then go," Edison replied, "I need more coffee anyway."

With the sense that he was being forced from his own home, Franklin took the Smart car from the garage and Rowan climbed in beside him with Jessica's ashes held firmly on her lap.

"This is appalling," he said sadly as they pulled out onto North Street, "it's like the killer's everywhere"

"You haven't heard from him in ages," Rowan tried to reassure him. "Maybe your role in this is over, perhaps he just wanted you to go to the media or something, make it a bigger story."

Franklin tried to agree but both seemed to silently acknowledge that was almost certainly not the case.

As they pulled into the gravel drive of Harmony Miller's home, Franklin's phone began to ring. He parked the car and answered it.

Rowan half listened to the conversation and inspected the urn of ashes in her hands. It was a simple cylinder, the type that most families seemed to favour, with a metal lining from which ashes could be easily scattered. An entire life and an entire human body reduced to dust.

"Well," said Franklin once he'd hung up. "Looks like we've another body to collect – natural causes, I promise. That was the nurse of a woman up in Clifton who died last night, wants to know if we can take her once the forms are filled out."

Rowan nodded as she stepped from the car. She never liked to admit it, not even to herself, but there were times when the endless conveyor belt of bodies disturbed her mind.

As if reading her thoughts, Franklin offered a kindly smile. "I'll put you onto a bit of admin for a while if you want, Peterman can deal with the bodies for a change."

Rowan just nodded before pressing the bell to the house. Harmony Miller opened the door.

"Ms Kaplan, good morning. Mr Gallow." The woman looked tired and in the background Rowan could hear the news coverage of the latest murder. "It's never going to end is it?"

When her eyes fell on the urn she burst into tears and from behind her came a loving embrace from Lois. "Harmony, get some sleep," she whispered, "I'll deal with this"

Lois Roker was as immaculately put together as ever with a tweed suit jacket over a cream blouse. "I'm so sorry. We honestly thought she was getting better after the funeral but this murder... that policeman. My goodness, it was like it happened all over again."

"It's quite understandable, Lois. Truly it is." Franklin said.

"Bodies are filling the streets, it feels like the world is ending," Lois said to herself.

The woman took the urn and softly stroked it. "Dear, sweet Jess," she sighed.

"I hope this isn't the end of it, but I realise you may have done all you can, the police will pull out all the stops now that he's killed one of their own. I just hope that if anything good can come of that poor man's death it will be that whoever was responsible will be put away for ever. Killed with fire... sweet lord, the inhumanity."

Rowan and Franklin took their leave and drove off towards Clifton where another body awaited them.

"Is there anything else we can do?" Rowan ventured. "I hate seeing anyone like that, I know what it feels like when the ashes come home – that's the real ending."

"I know, but she's right. Maybe the police will double their efforts now he's gone after an officer. I mean, to kill someone so publicly, right in front of a witness like that, it's audacious but it's also incredibly stupid. Nobody can get away with that for long. He's getting braver, but he's also getting messy."

"And the location can't have been by mistake," Rowan added.

"I was reading about the Queen Square riots last night. Did you ever do them at school?"

"A little I think, local history was never my strong point."

Franklin cleared his throat and began his tale. "It was 1831. The whole city was incredibly corrupt with massive taxes on the poor and less than one in ten people eligible to vote. So a protest was held after a reform bill failed in the House of Lords. A magistrate was chased by a mob to a house on Queen Square and over three days 500 men rioted in the square, windows were smashed and houses were burned until the police were sent in on horseback, some of them holding swords. Four people died and eighty odd were injured. Another four men were hanged for supposedly organizing the protest."

"The same old story then, people fighting for their rights are stopped by a rich minority who want to maintain control."

"A tale as old as time," said Franklin, dryly.

"I'm guessing that nobody else was ever brought to justice – the police I mean?"

"No,"

"Well then, it sounds like we know our killer's motive."

As they entered Clifton Village, Rowan read the address of the old mansion house they were visiting that Franklin had hastily scrawled into his notebook. The building was a fortress of Bath stone, with a massive family crest over the door and Roman pillars lining the façade.

"Bloody hell," Rowan gasped. "Rich people really do build the ugliest homes."

Franklin agreed. He'd never found much good taste in flaunting one's wealth over the common man. He pulled up in front of the entrance and the pair stepped out.

The first thing they noticed was that the door was slightly ajar, Franklin stepped closer to the entrance but Rowan found herself fixed to the spot, intuiting something peculiar about the scene.

"I suppose people have been coming and going all day," said Franklin as he pressed the doorbell, which rang hollow from within. "Hello?" he called through the gap.

"Franklin, who was it that called you?"

"It was her nurse."

"What did she sound like?"

Franklin raised an eyebrow judgmentally. "He sounded perfectly normal."

"Yes, but when he called, did it display the number on your phone or did it say withheld?"

"Withheld, I think…" Franklin understood her tone. He pushed open the door gently and it swung inwards on its hinges.

Beyond was white marble flooring upon which an enormous amount of thick and blackened blood had been strewn. Streaks of it lead up the hallway towards the foot of a staircase where the body of an elderly woman was propped, her throat slashed, her peach gown scarlet with dried rivers of blood.

On her lap sat her foot, still nestled within a stiletto shoe.

The vile tableaux was visible only for a moment before the door swung closed on a draft, but it was long enough for them to see everything.

42

The room in which Franklin was being interviewed was so stark and miserable that he could easily have found himself confessing to the murders himself just to escape its confines.

He had been brought here along with Rowan soon after the police had arrived at the house in Clifton, and had been asked to give a full statement as soon as possible. It had only been 45 minutes, but for Franklin, who was reliving the horror in intricate detail over and over again, the end could not come soon enough.

He should have been better at this than he was. Surely few people were more equipped to discover a body than someone who lives and works among them everyday, but the impact of that bloody corpse had been such an unexpected horror that the shock felt like a jolt of electricity that left him frightened and confused.

Across the table sat a woman who was becoming tediously familiar to Franklin, D.I. Trish Gladstone and beside her, a younger, somewhat naïve looking male colleague. She sipped on a mug of coffee that had not yet left her hand. The mug before Franklin remained untouched.

"There seems to be a great deal we know about the woman already," Trish said as she scrolled nonchalantly through the notes she'd been handed. "Her name was Vanessa Tilbury, 92 years of age. Lived all her life in the house where you found her…"

"…A slave house," Franklin interrupted.

"Sorry?"

"Those houses, all those old families with money from the past, they all had links to slavery."

Trish sighed and nodded her head. "She more than most as she was a direct descendant of Colston himself."

"How did she die?"

"A crossbow. The arrow was left at the scene, it's being dusted for prints but I can't imagine anyone would be foolish enough not to wear gloves."

"She looked like she'd been out for the evening, she was in some kind of fancy ball gown."

Trish locked eyes with his. "You are very observant, Mr Gallow, she had been attending a play at the Colston Theatre – she had a box in the wings apparently."

Franklin pondered this evidence. It seemed Vanessa Tilbury could not have made herself a more tempting target for the killer.

"But if he's attacked somebody in their own home, there has to be more evidence. He must have taken some time to hack her foot off and put her on show like that at the bottom of the stairs."

Trish casually pushed the pause button on the cassette recorder that sat on the table between them. "Mr Gallow, I can assure you we'll be taking that into consideration. Of course, there is yet to be any proof that this murder is connected with the others"

"What? Are you joking?"

"Copycat killings are very common. When there are high profile murders it's only to be expected that others will take advantage, do away with their rich, old family member in the style they've read about and pocket the inheritance."

Had he not been so horrified, Franklin would have laughed. "You can't be thinking like this! No wonder you stopped the tape, what's wrong with you?"

Trish simply started the tape again and proceeded undaunted. "Mr Gallow, what with your brother last night and the book showing up at your door earlier in the month, not to mention that you've apparently been in direct contact with the killer, I do find it very strange that you keep appearing in the midst of all of this."

It took a while for her words to sink in. "What are you insinuating? That I have something to do with it?"

Trish sat motionless; her colleague beside her offered a perplexed sideways glance. "I'm simply pointing out that other people could find it rather strange that out of all the people in this city, it is you who seems to be at the centre of this case time and time again. Where exactly were you last night, Mr Gallow?"

Franklin chose to ignore the question. "D'you think I chose to be the object of this killer's attention? He involved me, he wants me along for the ride for some reason. How long ago was Vanessa Tilbury murdered? The blood around her was black and oxidized – it takes quite a while for that to happen and her skin was loose and white – that means that all the liquids in her body had drained or pooled in her lower extremities. I see this stuff everyday and I know what I'm looking at when I see a corpse and that woman was murdered days ago. The killer must have grown frustrated that nobody had found her and that's why he called me; he wants the bodies found, that's part of it. It's like some big, bloody performance art."

"That's all fascinating," said Trish, flatly, "but I'd rather leave it to the pathologist to come to a conclusion. In the meantime, somebody will be around later to drop off your phone, and aside from that, you are free to go. Thank you for your cooperation." Trish Gladstone verbally marked the tape and ended the recording.

For the briefest moment, the young man beside her allowed his eyes to flicker across to Franklin's, his expression was one of utter bewilderment as to what he had just witnessed.

Upon leaving the tiny, dark interview room, he discovered Edison sitting on a low, uncomfortable looking bench outside the door. "What are you doing here?" asked Franklin.

"Someone told me you found a body."

"No I mean what are you doing at work at all? They gave you mandatory leave."

"We've been through this already, I'm not sitting around all day it's a waste of my time. If I'm gonna catch this bastard I'd best get to work."

"That's a very noble work ethic Edison, but I don't think it's a very good idea."

"You just found a body, Franklin, will you be taking two weeks off work?"

Franklin shrugged. "I think you've got me there."

"We're the Gallow brothers, we grew up around corpses, and it takes a lot more than most to traumatise us!"

215

Franklin smiled at his brother, feeling a welcome closeness to him. Throughout their troubled relationship, he had never considered them to be the Gallow Brothers, and they were unlike any other brothers because of it. They had each seen their first corpse as young children, and had been gradually eased into the horrors that can be inflicted upon a human body as they grew older. That peculiar set of circumstances should have been a much firmer glue to bond them than it had been.

"I've got something to show you," Edison announced. "I've done a little snooping this afternoon and… it's a bit strange, and certainly suspicious."

"Oh?"

"Follow me," he said and led the way from the corridor into a large, open plan office with desks scattered at uneven angles as if in a school classroom. Fevered activity gripped the office with officers scampering back and forth with arms full of paperwork while others entered text into outdated computers.

"This way," Edison declared.

Franklin was concerned that his being there would look as alien as a giraffe being led through the office – the only person without a uniform, whose face was becoming an increasingly regular sight around the station, but he followed Edison nonetheless.

Trish Gladstone's office was not part of the open plan labyrinth they had made their way through, but a glass-fronted room built into the far wall which overlooked the River Avon from four floors up. It was small but impeccably neat when compared to the workspaces of the other officers, which were overflowing with the detritus of too much paperwork.

"I don't think we should be doing this," Franklin cautioned as his brother slid the door open.

"Of course we shouldn't," Edison replied, "which is why you should keep an eye open to see if Trish is coming."

"Wait, what? She'll see us. This whole room is made of glass."

Edison wordlessly dropped into Trish's orthopedic chair and moved the mouse beside her computer. The screensaver flicked off and was replaced by an open email that was in the process of being finalized. "This is it, this is the proof we need," he declared.

"What are you talking about?" Franklin could not bear to take his eyes from the far wall beyond the office.

"She's writing stuff to somebody." He began to read from the screen aloud. "Here's the latest that we know just to keep you in the loop. As always, you never heard this from me. A further body was found this afternoon, just about to interview the man who found it. Religious connection to the killings, eye for an eye, tooth for a tooth (bus driver's tooth missing at scene of crime), hand for hand (the judge in Clifton had her hand cut off), Foot for foot (rich bitch in Clifton had her foot removed, burn for burn (police officer in Queen's Square killed with burning arrow.)"

"I don't understand," said Franklin. "Who's she writing this to?"

"I don't recognise the email address, she's feeding information to the public."

"Rowan and I had our suspicions about that, but why would she?"

Edison reread the words on the screen, his mind ticking over. "Hysteria," he concluded.

"What? She's hysterical? That's a little sexist if you ask me,"

"Shut up and listen, Frank. For some reason she's trying to raise the temperature until we reach boiling point. She's building it and building it until it explodes, everything she's done up 'til this point is to escalate things, to deflect attention and drive the public into hysteria."

"The protest tomorrow." Franklin gasped.

Edison read further. "Witness to the murder of Colin Harlow, another police officer named Edison Gallow."

"What can we do? Do you have anyone we can tell?"

"We need to know who she's spilling the beans to – and why. We need proof." Edison erased his name from the email on the screen. "Goodbye Edison Gallow, your new name is Edward Gallway. That way all we need to do is search all the media outlets for that name tomorrow."

Franklin offered his brother a cautious smile. "That's quite brilliant, Ed, let's just hope it works."

"We've got the Sunday papers tomorrow, not to mention all the weekend updates of the news blogs."

"Do you think you'll get in trouble for this?"

Edison shook his head confidently. "Not anywhere near as much as she will."

"D'you know, Ed, you're not too bad at this when you put your mind to it."

Edison arched his eyebrows. "Thank you, I think. Now all we need to know is where this information is going to end up – if I was trying to write something to rile an entire city to the brink of madness, I think I'd want to find the most inflammatory reporter."

Franklin nodded slowly. "I know exactly who I'd go for."

43.

TV felt like a wasteland to Rowan. Her reliable diet of old faithfuls felt as if they'd lost their shine when their trivia brushed abrasively against the memory of an old woman sat at the bottom of her staircase with her severed foot resting on her lap. The horrors of discovering a body echoed through her head and the simple distraction of trash television was not going to help.

She could hear Jude pacing around his flat overhead, so she consulted her watch and decided to go upstairs and see what his plans for Saturday night entailed. When she knocked on his door she heard him hastily end the phone call he was conducting on the other side of it.

"Hot Chocolate," he beamed at the sight of her. As always he wore nothing but boxer shorts and a loose dressing gown, his mane of yellow locks shaggily falling about his head.

"Hi. I was just wondering if, well… Take me out, I need to escape my head for a few hours."

Jude smiled. "D'you mind me asking what's brought this on?"

Rowan shook her head. "D'you mind me asking who was on the phone?"

Jude winked at her and chuckled. "Good call, H.C. I'll be down in half an hour, I know just where we can go."

In an instant Rowan felt the dark clouds lifting, the simple routine of preparing for a night in the city unleashed a kind of practiced giddiness as she rifled through her wardrobe, singing along to the radio, content in the knowledge that across Bristol, thousands of women were enacting this very same ritual.

She poured herself a large glass of white wine, which she gulped at greedily between bouts of makeup application. Her acts of ablution fell just under the wire of the allocated time and soon Jude was knocking on her door.

The sight of him almost made her laugh in his face. He wore a red velvet waistcoat over a chequered shirt with dark, formal trousers and matching shoes. His hair was tied back and mostly hidden underneath a bowler hat.

"Bloody hell, Jude, you've really out-hipstered yourself."

"It's for a reason, you'll see," he smiled.

"Are we going somewhere really wanky? Should I change into something more annoying?"

"You look great," he said as he glanced over her.

Her combination of a sleeveless top, which exposed only modest amounts of cleavage, and stonewashed jeans had been a classic of hers for many years. The kind of unshowy simplicity she had stolen from her older sister. "Keep it simple," Ruby had told her, "except for your belt; go big and go bling."

Their walk into town took them via St Augustine's Parade, where the statue of Edward Colston, a day shy of his 378th birthday, loomed menacingly over a semi-circle of police officers who would be standing guard throughout the night. Rowan noticed Jude eyeing them cautiously, and his arm, which was locked into hers, guided them through a wide path around them.

"Where are we going?" asked Rowan, as they passed into a flood of Saturday night revellers, none of whom seemed the slightest bit concerned for the non-mandatory curfew the city had placed on itself. "Just a little while further, we're almost there."

"But this is the student's quarter, they're just a bunch of freshers at this time of year," she announced.

"Don't worry, I'm taking you to a different kind of night on the town."

The pair strolled under the arches that lined the waterfront stretch of bars and nightclubs, a sheltered terrace of old boat-building warehouses that had been converted to accommodate the industry that had replaced the seafaring past – intoxication.

Jude pushed open the door to a long, glass fronted bar which was heaving with people, all seemingly dressed from the same prototype. The men wore hats and black skinny jeans, American bowling shoes and braces, the women, old-fashioned cocktail dresses and flowers in their tightly bound hair. Rowan at once felt underdressed.

"I didn't know you were taking me to bar for arseholes."

"Just wait until the music starts, that'll change your mind." Jude nodded to a small stage at the far end of the bar where a large band was struggling to fit itself on. Their instruments were not those Rowan was familiar with – a double bass, a couple of trombones, even a clarinet. The lone woman in the band, who was dressed not unlike Rosie the Riveter, sat behind a curious assortment of drums.

"What can I get you?" Jude asked.

"A pint of lager, anything strong." Her eyes wandered to a table where a young couple were drinking dark cocktails from what looked like jam jars, it made Rowan more irritated than she knew it should. "Get me a shot of vodka too," she added.

She found a table for two, and when Jude returned with the drinks, the music kicked in. It was incredibly loud and unlike anything she'd ever heard played live. The cacophony at first seemed like a kind of madness, until she realised the rhythm was simply repeating so fast that it sounded as if the entire band had thrown their instruments down a stairwell.

The patrons themselves seemed to react in a very different way. A shriek of joy, louder even than the music, erupted as people leapt to their feet. "What the hell's going on?" Rowan marvelled.

All about her tables and chairs were being pushed against walls as a dance floor was instantly created. Suddenly it was filled by gyrating bodies, not just dancing but throwing each other around the room. Women were being hoisted over shoulders, dresses were flaring out around tight pirouettes as knickers were flashed with abandon.

"Is this swing dancing?" Rowan called over the music.

"Sort of, it's Bristol's only Lindy hop club."

"What?"

"It's a kind of dance, from America, it was big in the '40s."

Rowan's natural instinct to find her generation's tendency to revere only the old and obscure was at odds with the wonder she felt on seeing the dancers. One girl seemed to cartwheel as she was flung over her partner's head; another slipped between a man's thighs and twisted as she slid on her heels.

221

"They're good," she gasped, "they're really good."

"They come here every Saturday night, so they should be."

As Rowan watched, her analytical mind found sense within the seeming chaos of their movements. The dancers were in pairs and clung almost erotically close to one another between moves, after which they would swing away in carefully choreographed twists and lifts before falling into each other's bodies on the return.

"So?" asked Jude who was beating out the rhythm on the table with his fingers. "Want to give it a go?"

Rowan looked down at his hand which he held out for her. "We'll look like fools, I don't know what I'm doing."

"Neither do I, not really anyway. Who cares?"

Rowan looked around the bar and beyond, where a line of intrigued passersby had stopped to gawp at the curious sight beyond the glass wall. Why should she care how she looked, she told herself, for she really did want to try it.

She knocked back her pint, which she chased with a shot of vodka. "Let's do this," she said as she took his hand and stood up.

At once they both seemed lost, trying to find a rhythm which they could dance to, like surfers in shallows, waiting to time their move with the next rising wave. At first they did little more than jiggle, but it wasn't long until something in the music seemed to make sense, it passed in a series of eights, before repeating, which Rowan found herself counting off in her head, and then something strange, almost miraculous, happened. Suddenly she had fallen under a kind of spell and was dancing.

She wasn't dancing well, but neither was Jude, they trampled on each other's toes and often backed into other dancers, but the fundamentals were there, and seemed to come as naturally as if this music and this movement had always been inside them.

She tried a twist, to which Jude obliged. She tried kicking out her legs in time with his. Her heart thundered in her chest with a sensation she'd not encountered in such a long time, something was taking over her body, a feeling that had been absent for years. What it was, she could scarcely remember.

"You ready?" Jude shouted.

She nodded as she felt his hands on either side of her waist, they squatted, and as she rose, she felt her feet lift from the ground. Up and up he raised her as she passed high above his head, her arms outstretched as if praising the sky. She heard her gasp in her ears and for a second she felt suspended, weightless in the air staring upwards to beads of sweat that had settled on the ceiling. It was in that moment that she remembered this sensation; this was what joy felt like. This what had been missing from her life since Ruby had been murdered, a kind of hole she tried to fill with religion or morbidity, pushing her parents away from her, eating bad food and drinking too much. This was joy, and it seemed to fill every cell in her body. The armour she had built around herself seemed to crack just a little, and she remembered what being Rowan Kaplan once felt like.

The evening passed in a flash and by the time the bell for last orders rang Rowan was drenched with sweat, a baptism in euphoria. The long windows were steamed with streaks of condensation and slowly the patrons were filing from the doors.

"Jude," she gasped, "how did you know that was what I needed?'

He just shrugged his shoulders. "Everyone needs a Lindy hop from time to time."

Barely able to conceal her grin, Rowan clung hungrily to Jude's arm as the pair walked back across the city.

"Fancy stopping off for another pint?" he offered.

"Why not, it's my round."

"It's a little out of our way, but it's worth it, I want to show you something."

The pub he had in mind was part way up one of the steepest streets of the city, St Michael's Hill, a long, wide road that stretched over the brow on which Park Street sat.

Jude stopped outside a charmingly antiquated little building with hanging baskets and old-fashioned lamps on plinths. Rowan must have passed it many times but had never spotted it, or at least, had never acknowledged its name.

"The Colston Arms?" Rowan asked. "Why would you take me here?"

"It's a nice pub," Jude replied.

"I'm sure it is, but look at the name. I don't go anywhere named after that bastard!"

"That's why we're here. I wanted to tell you a little bit about this place."

"Jude, I promise you, I'm not interested. I've had such a great night and I don't want you spoiling it by… being weird again."

"Rowan, did you know that during the Second World War Bristol was host to thousands of American soldiers? Most of them were black."

"Yes," Rowan lied, for she had never heard such a thing.

"Well, America had a segregated army, the couldn't mix together over there, but here, they could go wherever they pleased. This made the Yanks really angry, so they gave orders that Bristol should segregate and that businesses should not let them drink together."

"What happened?" Rowan found herself asking.

"Bristol said no. The orders were ignored. At first most places did as they were told, but slowly it was overturned, one business at a time. And d'you know the first pub in the city to say no, the one which organised a boycott of all businesses that practiced segregation?"

Rowan found herself looking at the sign over the door with a sense of admiration. "The Colston Arms?"

"Exactly," Jude nodded. "It's just a name, and this pub has its own history now, one that it should be proud of. That's what this city needs to learn – there's a different story of Bristol, and Colston plays no role in it. He's dead and gone, and even if a few buildings or streets have his name, we've moved on to become good people."

"But what about the statue?"

"Oh that statue can go melt itself," Jude spat. "It's horrid."

Without a thought Rowan found herself kissing him, with a sense that this idiotic man, who barely wore clothes, and had a dubious private life, was actually far deeper and more sensible than she had imagined. It wasn't just his body or his looks that attracted her, there was something about him that was making her lose her senses. Was this what falling in love was like? If it was, it felt wonderful.

"Do you fancy that pint?" he asked as their lips broke from each other.

"I'd love one," she smiled.

44.

When Edison awoke his first sensation was that of dread. It was not a dread of the upcoming demonstration, but more a generalised insecurity about what he might have to do that morning. He had never been one for confrontation and the prospect of having to defy a senior officer filled him with anxiety.

Puffing on his vaporiser pen, he opened his laptop and searched for Ellie Sutton's blog. Not a day passed without one of her venomous outpourings, and Edison was certain she would not miss the morning before the protest to vent her hateful spleen. He was not wrong.

"DEATH BY FIRE! THE HORRIFYING DETAILS OF POLICE SLAYING!" read the headline beside a dead-eyed headshot of the journalist herself. "As I have been saying for some time, it seems that the murderer known as the Crossbow Killer has had to step his game up to maintain the public's attention. In these days of Twitter and £3 cups of coffee, even the most evil among us cannot assume they hold the attention of the public unless they increase their brutality, brutality that should put to rest the idea that the liberals and the PC-loving have not bleeding hearts, but hearts as hard as granite. This killer, who has become a hero for many of the softheaded lefties who are littered about "Great" Britain, has shown the kind of merciless savagery usually reserved for the streets of some godforsaken Middle Eastern city. His latest act of barbarism was perpetrated on a young police officer. A source has revealed that Colin Harlow was killed by a flaming arrow to the throat, an act even more bloodthirsty as it was performed in full view of his partner on the beat, Edward Galway…"

Edison snapped his laptop shut and jumped out of bed. His clock informed him that there were still two hours before his pre-demonstration meeting, more than enough time to report D.I. Gladstone and have the protest cancelled. He raced through his shower and hastily brushed his teeth before throwing on his clothes and running out the door.

226

His first instinct had been to go to the police station. Even if all he could do was throw open the door and shout that a traitor had been leaking information to a journalist, who had in turn been stoking flames within an already angry and terrified city, but the sight of hundreds of police officers lining the streets of St Augustine's Parade in preparation for the day, made him think twice. Instead he turned his car towards Redcliffe and the small terrace house in which his superior officer lived.

Number 8. He was sure he'd remembered it right. He was good at retaining numbers and addresses; he had always thought of it as one of his few specialised talents. The house was three storey's, but narrow, and painted fuchsia pink, at odds with the other houses in the street who's facades were all in contrasting hues – a strange tradition of Bristol which turned many of it's terraces into something akin to brightly coloured sweets. He rang the doorbell, and when there was no answer, beat upon it until she came to the door.

"Edison, what the hell are you doing here, how d'you even know where I live?" She was dressed in loose tracksuit bottoms and a cardigan over a t-shirt emblazoned with the face of Janis Joplin.

"I know what you're doing. You're leaking information to Ellie Sutton."

Trish's face was immediately seized by panic. "What? No I'm not! How dare you?"

"I read your email. You had it open on your computer."

"You did what?" she roared. "I heard this is what you do, you turn on your own, like you did last spring."

"This isn't about me, I just want to know why you did it."

Trish looked feverishly about the street beyond Edison. "Does anyone know you're here?"

"No, I wanted to hear from you first."

"I don't have to tell you anything, in fact, I could report you."

Edison shook his head cautiously, this was becoming every bit as hostile as he'd feared it would. "What you've done is worthy of disciplinary action, even a dismissal."

"Look, just come inside and we'll discuss this properly." She stepped aside to let him enter.

The narrow corridor led to a living room, far smaller than Edison imagined it would be. On the TV a video game had been paused, and on the coffee table between a pair of sofas, sat a controller beside a half eaten bowl of cornflakes.

"Sit down," she commanded.

Edison did as he was told and fell onto a black, faux leather sofa while Trish took the other. "You know I have to tell someone about this, don't you."

Trish sighed. "I suppose I always knew what would happen if I was found out, it's for a greater good though."

"Don't get me wrong, I'm not mad, I know precisely what I've been doing. It's called a long game and I've been playing it for some time. It might not catch a killer but it will suck the worst venom out of the city."

Edison was confused, she seemed to not be talking any sense. "I don't understand, you've turned Bristol into a pressure cooker, thanks to that god-awful journalist."

"I'm no fan of that disgusting creature either, but sometimes you have to take strange bedfellows when you realise you both want the same result."

"Which is?" Edison asked.

"To get Bristol into a state of panic, to split the city in half over a statue of a long dead man. I'd feed her information, she'd write something foul and incendiary and the people would do the rest. If you get them to pick sides on something as divisive as civic pride, it doesn't take much to turn a street demonstration into an all out riot. Ellie Sutton wants the same, the more hysteria she promotes the more hits her blog gets, but me, my motives were much purer."

"You want to cause a riot?"

"1980," she said coolly, "The St Pauls Riots. People were sick of the police raiding the Black and White Café on Grosvenor Road, they knew they were being targeted for being black, so what did they do? They fought back. It may have been the raids on the café that caused the spark, but the tension had been mounting for years – racial tension across the city, especially when it came to the police."

Edison was stunned. "You're trying to cause another race riot? Dozens of people got hurt in St Pauls."

"But stuff changed afterwards. The streets were safer and minorities were empowered by knowing they didn't have to be pushed around by the police, that they could stand up and defend themselves. That's what changed."

"You're insane."

She simply smiled. "Not even close, I couldn't have come to this conclusion in any more of a rational way. I don't want people to get hurt, I don't want to see the police mobbed, but I do have a very clear end goal. I want to see Karl Kitson and his mob of angry, white supremacists locked away. D'you know he and his cronies have been arrested more than a dozen times? We've given him slaps on the wrist and cautions, but nothing he's ever done has been enough to get him in serious trouble. He's slippery, so I knew what I had to do, orchestrate a scenario that would force him into violent action. To get him to incite racial hatred, to say something, just a word beyond what the law permits, hell, punch some poor black man in the face if that's what it takes to get him off the streets and locked away."

Edison pondered her words for some time. Few people wanted that vile thug, Karl Kitson, locked away more than he did, he would not even be able to contact the outside world to portray himself as a martyr. A stern judge could sentence him to decades if they were clever with the wording of incitement to racial hatred.

"You don't know what it's like," Trish went on, "you can never know. You're a white man who doesn't get how it feels to have an animal like that free to walk the streets."

"No, I don't, but you're supposed to be catching a serial killer. Blackbeard's still out there and you've been orchestrating some pathetic revenge to get your nemesis locked away."

"I've been doing what I went into the police force to do – keep the city safe from scum like Karl Kitson."

Edison's held his head in his hands. "I don't know if you understand what you've done. This protest could be a bloodbath, a massacre. Yes, you'll probably get your man, but at what cost?"

Trish merely shrugged. "I suppose my white whale has been a white supremacist, but can you blame me?"

"I can," Edison announced as he stood up, "I do. Now, I have to go and file a report and then attend this protest and try to prevent it from destroying the city."

"Well, if you're going to the station, you might as well take me along to hand myself in. Not much point fighting it now."

Trish stood up beside him. Her face showed no sign of regret or remorse. She had done everything she'd needed to do, and if she was a casualty, then so be it. Her plan, after all, had worked.

45

"You're late," Franklin chided gently as Rowan approached him.

"Sorry, I had a busy morning."

"I see," Franklin raised an eyebrow suspiciously. "And that little spring in your step?"

Rowan shrugged. "Let's just say I had a good evening."

"Say no more," said Franklin as he pushed open the glass door that led into the gallery, "but… is this about a boy?"

"It might be," Rowan beamed, barely able to control the grin that was spreading across her face.

"Whoever he is, I trust you found a good one. I'm pleased for you."

Rowan felt herself blush as she stepped through the doorway and into the white space beyond.

Franklin approached a table by the entrance where a surly looking young man was lazily rearranging piles of pamphlets. "Here are our tickets," Franklin informed the youth.

"Don't bother," he sighed. "Bugger all people've turned up anyway, same as every year. I don't know why they bother really."

Franklin nodded and turned away from the table with Rowan. "Nice to see the tuition fees I'm spending on Alf are paying for such enthusiasm."

The gallery was a privately owned studio just off of Millennium Square, which ordinarily housed a constantly rotating menu of works by local artists, but once a year was hired by the university campus to showcase the contributions from the new students. This was where Alf and his fellow creatives could demonstrate their talents to a public who would meet them with nothing less than apathy.

"I thought they'd have champagne," Rowan huffed.

"I don't think it's that kind of a gallery opening," Franklin replied. He read aloud from the pamphlet he'd taken from the table. "This year's exhibition is meditations on the theme of "Agent Provocateur. In this time of instant internet outrage and constant violent and sexual imagery, what does it mean to provoke a reaction? We asked our students to answer through art what provocation means to them. Is it the power to shock? To start a revolution? Or simply to hold a mirror up to the challenges of the world in which we live."

"Holy crap, this is going to be annoying," was Rowan's reply. "I guess First World Problems was too on the nose when they were thinking of titles for the show."

Franklin looked up from the pamphlet to a piece of sculpture in the centre of the room. Before him stood a shop window mannequin of a young girl, naked, but draped in a dirty cloth. She wore a black hood over her face and was perched atop a cardboard box, from which wires protruded up to her fingertips. In one hand she held a china doll, in the other a cheerful, red helium balloon on a ribbon. The exhibit immediately and intentionally repulsed Franklin.

"Those Abu Ghraib photographs were a gift to unimaginative artists," said Rowan. "How long d'you think they're going to keep dining out on them?"

"Don't be unkind," tried Franklin, "I'm sure whoever made this spent a lot of time and thought on it." He didn't look at her but could feel her eyes burn into him.

"See, maybe I just don't get art."

"It's just… challenging," said Franklin, pragmatically.

"I don't mean this. I don't think I really get any art. I mean, I get why people think it's important and some people certainly think it's worth money, but even the stuff that's famous for being good has never really spoken to me. Does that make me a philistine?"

"It does a bit," he replied. "Maybe it's just the gallery setting that puts you off. Loads of things are art that you enjoy, music, films, even TV."

"Oh I see, so the stuff you put in a gallery is whatever art's left over when all the fun is taken out?"

Franklin stifled a laugh. "I'm just trying to keep an open mind, that's all."

Rowan was quiet for a while as she studied a crude painting of the Little Mermaid, her cloaca agape and running with what she assumed was menstrual blood. "D'you think the killer thinks he's an artist?"

Franklin pondered the question. "Perhaps, I've certainly thought that before. There's a certain finesse – stylised violence to attract the maximum attention. I wouldn't be surprised if when he gets caught he claims it was a kind of performance art piece."

"The skin book," Rowan said to herself. "Are you worried about today?"

Franklin looked at her. "No, should I be?"

"It's Colston's birthday, if I was a killer with a grudge against his legacy, I'd pick today for the grand show."

"Are you worried?"

"Of course I am, but murder probably doesn't seem like such an abstract concept for me."

"I don't know," said Franklin, "I've seen more than enough murdered people now for it to never feel that far from home."

"Are you going to be alright tonight, after work?"

"The police are watching my house. They're none too subtle about it, but it's nice to know they're there. They say I've nothing to worry about. I've given Meredy the day off though; you know how she worries. You don't have to come in today if you don't want to."

"I think I feel safer there, I might spend the evening with my parents though, I haven't seen them in ages."

Franklin nodded but his stomach lurched with guilt. He was still no nearer telling Rowan what he knew.

"For the love of God," spat Rowan as the pair stepped before a pencil etching of the New York skyline, a middle and index finger in the classic pose of insult replacing what had one been the Twin Towers.

"They're kids," said Franklin, "they're expressing themselves, it's just not that sophisticated yet."

"They're not expressing themselves, they're expressing Banksy."

Franklin nodded. The spirit of the elusive Bristolian who'd taken urban art to the masses loomed heavy over the gallery. His presence, stripped down to its most basic components of innocence juxtaposed against ugliness, each vignette throughout the spotlessly white space another comic book panel tracing of a far superior talent.

"Is that Alf's piece?" asked Rowan.

Franklin followed her gaze to where a handful of people had assembled. The visitors could not have numbered more than half a dozen, but something about this work had clearly caught their attention.

Alf had made a coffin. A truly old-fashioned casket, the likes of which Franklin hadn't seen in decades. It was inexpertly crafted along the lines of that which would be found in a Hammer Horror film, but finished surprisingly well with an even coat of varnish. On the casket Franklin saw a framed photograph of himself staring back at him. He was smiling and standing in the visitor parlour of Gallow & Sons, wearing his ceremonial coat tails and hat, completely unaware in that moment what his son's intentions had been.

Beside the photograph, Alf had made a wreath of letters, bound in wire and woven with yellow plastic flowers. The wreath read "DAD".

Franklin's eyes fell to the floor where a small plinth, less than a foot high, informed onlookers that the piece was entitled "Dead Dad by Alfred Duke," alongside a paragraph of text on the work.

Rowan caught her friend's expression. "Franklin don't worry…"

"…Don't worry? Look at it!"

He felt a sudden and near overwhelming urge to cry, which he only barely managed to hold back.

"It's just art," Rowan went on, "it doesn't mean anything. It's like you said, he's just a kid."

"You know it's more than that. Look what everyone else has done – wanky shock pieces to get people talking. Alf's the only one that's done anything about him and it's just… horrible. I had no idea that's what he thought of me, that he wanted me to…" Franklin turned on his heels and marched from the gallery. At first he wanted to call his son and demand an explanation, but the thought of Alf sneering and revelling in the devastating hurt his artwork had caused was too much for him. Instead he called Verity.

"Franklin?" she asked. "What are you calling for? Is it Alf?"

"As a matter of fact it is," he replied, "next time you speak to that git of a boy, tell him that I've seen his masterpiece, and if he wanted to hurt me, it would have been much easier if he'd just come to my door and stabbed me in the gut."

"What are you talking about?"

"The casket, Dead Dad?"

"Oh, the exhibition, yes, I was coming down to see it next weekend."

"What? You knew what he was making? You let him?"

Verity laughed coldly, "I let him? He's a fully grown man, I don't have to let him do anything."

"Well... You knew what he was making; you could have told him it would hurt me. You could at least have warned me."

"D'you know what, Franklin? Even if I could tell him that his art would hurt you, why in the world would I want to do that? You haven't been there for any part of his life, and that's fine, I know you would have if you'd known about him, but he's a young man, who grew up without a father, and how he reacts to having you in his life now is up to nobody but him. You don't like what his art says about you? Tough shit, because this isn't about you, he's the only blameless one in all this and I will not have you telling me how my son is permitted to express himself."

"Blameless? How do you get to that? Are you saying I'm at fault here? You should have told me!" Franklin was roaring so loudly into the phone that passersby were watching.

"Yes he's the blameless one. We were the drunk kids who thought we could risk it without a condom. We made a mistake that night, it turned out to be a wonderful mistake but I decided I would shoulder all the responsibility myself – I let you get on with your life because you once had dreams that were bigger than just doing what your dad told you to, I thought it was right to let you live life how you'd planned. Fat lot of good that did you."

"I would have been there," Franklin said, now much softer and with a heavier soul. "We could have been good together, like a family."

"Oh Franklin, you know it would never have worked," she sighed. "Now, if you don't mind you've all but ruined my lie-in."

"I'm sorry…" but she had already hung up.

Franklin tried his best to shake the horrors of the confrontation from his mind, but couldn't. It wasn't so much that everything she'd said had been completely true, but the terrible, dark acceptance that his own son wished he was dead.

46.

The police descended on the city centre by the van load. With almost all the Bristol force working in riot prevention, additional officers had been drafted in from Bath and Cardiff to provide secondary backup.

As Edison journeyed from the station to St Augustine's parade, a sense of dark excitement mixed with fear seemed to mingle in the dry air of the van as two rows of officers stared anxiously at one another as the vehicle bounced down Park Street in a convoy of identical police vans.

Through the window, Edison watched as temporary bollards were erected between the pavement and the road, protecting not just the Sunday shoppers, but the window fronts of the shops along the way. The road itself was closed to regular traffic as it was the route the anti-fascism demonstrators would take towards their destination. Edison rubbed sweat from his palms; the scale of this protest was even larger than he'd feared.

"This is what it's all about," said Sarah Fry, a butch, brash constable whom Edison could not remember having exchanged two words with in the past, but nevertheless felt free to jostle him in the ribs as she spoke. "You can almost taste it can't ya'. This is the real shit."

Edison tried to smile but found himself struggling.

"'Spose you've 'eard about Trish?" asked Sarah. " What's goin' on there?'

Edison shrugged his shoulders as he caught a glimpse of a shop owner spreading a roll of duct tape over his window. "Something about professional misconduct, I heard."

The group of twelve police officers had been largely reflective and quiet throughout their journey, but Sarah Fry had decided to take it upon herself to speak for them all. She cleared her throat and began. "Now, I know what we're all finking. This is gonna be a bloody hard day, but tha's why we all signed up for this right? To see a bit of action?"

Her fellow officers nodded unenthusiastically.

"Now, we all know what 'appened on 'alloween and we all know we lost one of our friends – this guy 'ere saw it all, so 'e knows what we're fightin' for. D'ya wanna say something, Ed?"

Edison simply shook his head and looked down at his boots.

"OK, this city's on the brink and it's up to the likes of you and me to maintain order. We don't know what's gonna 'appen but we gotta be prepared for it. You guys with me?"

There was a murmur of approval.

"Let's do it for Colin! Show these pricks that they can't ruin our city!"

A slightly more raucous cheer passed through her audience. Edison wondered who she meant by the pricks; was it the barely concealed racists within the "Reclaim our Streets" mob, or the anti-fascists who would be countering them? Perhaps she meant both, along with anyone who sought to unbalance law and order across Bristol – including the killer himself.

As the van pulled into St Augustine's Parade, Sarah Fry slid open the door and hopped out onto the plaza before the vehicle had fully come to a stop. Edison sluggishly followed the trail of officers who clambered out in her wake and found himself beside the angled fountains that he'd so often stood guard over on weekend nights.

They were immediately met by a tactical coordinator, Zachary Bridgewater, a distinguished looking man with an elaborate grey moustache whom Edison could recall only seeing at times where crowd control was necessary.

"Officers," he began and Edison found himself straightening his back and standing to full attention at the bark of the man's command, "this is going to be quite a day, quite a day indeed. We've got two sets of protesters – Reclaim our Streets are coming from Broadmead and the anti-fascists, who outnumber them three times, are meeting at Park Street, so where you're standing now is going to turn into a battleground within the hour unless we do our jobs properly." Zachary took to strolling up and down the line of officers as he spoke with a kind of regimented ease that suggested to Edison that this man was no stranger to military formalities. "Now, we don't want to hem them in, that kind of stuff doesn't go down well these days and just drives the protesters into a rage, however, we will be keeping them away from the Colston statue as that will be the target for the anti-fascist types. We'll be forming two lines, each of about two hundred officers, locked arm to arm and with each line there will be around ten feet of buffer zone. That's three metres of no-man's land."

Edison peered over to the far corner of the St Augustine's Parade, where another cortege of police vans was pulling up and spilling out its contents. On the opposite side of the square, officers, who were rehearsing their elaborate, interlocking formations like ballet dancers, were ringing the statue of Edward Colston.

"You don't need me to tell that you'll be recorded on phone cameras all day, if you so much as place a foot out of line it will be all over the news by teatime. I don't care what any of the protesters say to you, I don't care how much they swear, scream, or spit, you will stand your ground and not react, and yes, everyone wears their ID number over their riot gear – we're not the Met, and I won't have this turn into a fiasco. We're going to do things properly on my watch, understood? Right then, get geared up and head over towards the Colston statue."

A compartment in the back of the police van was opened, revealing row upon row of protective clothing. Edison found the uniform which corresponded with his number and donned his fireproof overalls, padded vest, gloves and helmet with visor. Finally he attached the riot baton to his belt. Silently he prayed to the milky clouds overhead that he would not have to use it.

On his approaching the statue, amid a sea of officers, Edison heard barked orders through a megaphone from another officer on a stepladder. "When you're linked, arm in arm, it's your duty not just to look after yourself, but the officers on either side. Step in line."

From a morass of confusion two lines of officers assembled themselves. The coordinators had obviously performed their calculations well as once linked arm-in-arm, the wall of police stretched the entire width of the plaza, twice over, with a constant gap of no less than ten feet between them at all points. Edison was facing the Broadmead end of St Augustine's Parade, a position he would not have chosen as it put him face-to-face with the racists who he was certain were more likely to make the first move of aggression.

Arms were relaxed but positions were held. Edison switched on his walkie-talkie. From a mire of static came a voice. "We might have underestimated Reclaim Our Streets, it seems that they've teamed up with other far-right groups from across the country. I'm guessing two, maybe three hundred of them…. We have visual of Karl Kitson, he's at the head as expected."

"Come on ladies!" yelled the voice from the officer beside him, unmistakably that of Sarah Fry who had been rendered anonymous and genderless beneath her riot gear. Her voice was gleeful, this was what she'd been waiting for, Edison found himself comforted that he was beside at least one officer who showed no trace of the fear he could barely contain inside himself.

When the drums began, Edison thought at first they might be the sound of his heartbeat, but as they drew louder and nearer it was evident that they were coming from Park Street as the band of assorted anti-fascist demonstrators made their way down the hill and towards the square. Memories of science lessons at school were the strange regression Edison found himself reliving in that moment, imagining a mixing jar over a Bunsen burner, its contents bubbling away until two chemicals were mixed into the water, all it had taken was the slightest heat and the whole thing erupted into a plume of dense, dark smoke. That's where he was.

When the anti-fascists made their appearance it struck him what an uncoordinated jumble they were, he could see CND flags waving alongside rainbow flags, banners supporting freedom for Palestine with those decrying the coalition government. Some wore tee shirts with catchy, funny, even rude, slogans but most dressed as they would on any other day. It was a mess of concepts, which had somehow come together to face a common enemy with a single shared ideal.

240

In Bristol, all people were welcome, they were saying. "Freedom Not Hatred in Bristol," read a sign.

As if they had been waiting for their cue from a stage director behind the scenes, the Reclaim Our Streets mob made their entrance. These were a much more unified group, who had dressed in accordance with their beliefs. They were comprised almost completely of men; bald, beardless and booted with military style fatigues and black bomber jackets. Above them waved huge flags of St George as they marched in unison to the sound of their own boots on concrete. They may have numbered only a fraction of those opposing them, but they cut a far more threatening approach as they drew closer. They were simply more coordinated, and clear with their presentation. They sang a chant with a single, repeated verse: "Let's kept the streets, white! Right!"

Edison gulped nervously as a lone member of the troop stepped before them. Karl Kitson was familiar not just to Edison, but to almost every police officer in the city. He unzipped his bomber jacket to reveal a black tee shirt which bore the words, "I AM BLACKBEARD."

Overhead, news and police helicopters circled. For weeks this had been building, helped by Trish Gladstone and the inflammatory posts from Ellie Sutton, every tweet, every angry YouTube video had helped fan these flames, so that from this chaos something as perfect and precise as a game of chess could be formed. Every piece in place for the battle that would commence. High above them the statue of Edward Colston watched with disinterested eyes.

"This is it," cried Sarah Fry. "Here it comes!"

47.

"This is madness," said Franklin as he watched the live coverage of the protest on the television in his office.

"Is your brother there?" asked Meredy, who was looking over his shoulder in the doorway, her eyes fixed to the screen.

"Right in the heart of it, practically all the police in the city are there."

"Not the ones outside the door though."

Franklin nodded. For the past day and a half the staff of Gallow & Sons had become all too aware of the unsubtle police presence that had taken residence at the edge of the grounds. In a white van four plain-clothes officers were taking shifts in pairs to guard over the property. What they were expecting was anybody's guess, but their presence was of some reassurance to Franklin.

"There's going to be nothing left of the city centre," said Meredy.

On the screen the two tribes had met along two thin blue lines of police officers that were buckling and swaying against the force. Angrily they exchanged insults and plastic bottles were thrown across the no-man's land that separated them. They were inching closer, drawing in to the officers who were attempting to keep them apart. All it would take would be the smallest fracture in the defence and the entire barricade would give way.

"They're a bunch of animals," Meredy sneered. "Fascist scum, this should never have been allowed to happen."

"We all have the right to protest, they're exercising their democratic freedom."

"They don't know the first thing about freedom. Waving the flag of our nation about like that, dressing in that fake military stuff. My dad went to war to end fascism in Europe and these bastards pretend they're the voice of a nation. Not in my name!" Meredy shouted at the television.

Rowan appeared in the doorway. "I put Mr Patel in the freezer," she announced.

Franklin was impressed. "You got Mr Patel's body out of the van and into the refrigerated unit all by yourself? That's a two man job."

"Yes, it's a two man job – or one woman," said Rowan triumphantly and she and Meredy shared a high-five.

Mr Patel had been an elderly nursing home resident the pair had collected earlier that afternoon. "Well, don't make a habit of it, the last thing we want is somebody getting dropped."

"I just wheeled him out of the van on the stretcher and into the unit, it was simple."

Meredy shuddered. "Less of this kind of talk please, I hate it when you talk about the bodies like that… imagining them all in that refrigerator stacked upon each other. It gives me the willies."

Franklin consulted his watch. "Well, I think we're all done for the day, I suggest the pair of you clear off before the whole city goes up in flames."

"You don't think it'll be that bad do you?" asked Rowan.

"No idea, but I'm glad I'm here in Bedminster and not anywhere near St Augustine's Parade tonight," he replied.

"Would you like a lift home?" Meredy offered to Rowan.

"That's very kind of you, but I like cycling back. I can go via Broadmead and cut out most of the centre."

"If you're sure."

Franklin walked them to the door, and once they had left, offered a friendly wave to the white van at the end of the garden path from which two very bored looking police officers returned the gesture. He locked the door behind him and switched the parlour light off.

Upstairs, Felicity had been patiently waiting for him on the sofa. Wheezing and twitching in her sleep, she lifted her head and followed Franklin's path from the living room to the kitchen where he opened a tin of cat food and forked half of its contents into a bowl and placed it beside her on the sofa.

Switching on the TV and turning to the BBC News channel, the live feed informed him that the barricade was still holding. The gap between the two rows of officers had become the perfect spot for news reporters to deliver their coverage and where the cameras could better see the front line through the gathering darkness. They had quickly discovered that what had once been a generous buffer was now being squeezed from the sheer pressure of the people on either side. None of this looked safe to Franklin who scoured the police lines to see if he could catch a glimpse of his brother, but even if Edison had been on screen, he could not have identified him, all the police officers looked the same in riot gear.

Franklin checked his phone, no missed calls and no text messages. Opening up his laptop he was disappointed to find that he'd not been contacted during the day via email or Facebook. He wasn't sure what he expected from either Verity or Alf, but he had hoped one of them would have seen fit to contact him, but there was nothing. Perhaps, he concluded, his actions had been so hasty and his reaction so petty that he had put himself beyond forgiveness.

On the television, the police lines were snaking perilously like Chinese dragons. Occasionally projectiles were hurled from one side to the other, bottles mostly, but Franklin was sure he had seen a rock or two. Of course this was how it would end, he said to himself, there was simply no other way. Perhaps this was what the killer had wished for all along, to turn Bristol upon itself like a serpent devouring its tail. Perhaps this was his master plan, not to destroy the city himself but to hand it over to the people to do it for him.

If there was a debt of blood owed by the city, then it should be the city that offers itself in payment.

The phone rang and Franklin's attention was immediately turned from the television. It was a local number but not one he recognised.

"Hello?" he answered.

"Good evening, is that Mr Gallow?"

"It is."

"This is Detective Inspector George Leach of the Bristol Police, do you have a moment to talk?"

Franklin's mouth went dry. "Is everything alright, I'm watching the news and my brother's there."

"Edison's fine as far as I know, I just have some information that I've been asked to pass on to you regarding the book that was delivered to your house last month."

"The skin book?"

"The what? Well, yes, I suppose that name does rather suit. We've been conducting some tests on it and it's been significantly more difficult to extract the DNA we had been expecting. Now, if I continue, I trust that I do so under the strictest confidence, I'm sharing this information in the hopes that it might offer you some peace of mind and that anything I say will go no further."

"Of course," Franklin lied. Anything he was told would go no further than Rowan.

"The reason we struggled extracting any useable DNA was because we imagined the skin was much newer. The techniques of extracting cells are age dependent and… well, it seems we were making rather a few presumptions given the condition of the skin. It had been tanned semi-professionally, which had helped preserve it, but we now think, well, we now know, that the skin came from a man named Cecil Conway. He was a police officer who was involved in riot control during the 80s."

"You mean the St Pauls Riots?"

"I suppose I do, yes. The thing is, and this is what took us all by surprise, Mr Conway was reported missing in 1981, that's 33 years ago."

Franklin gasped. "Good grief. How long has the killer been planning this?"

"If you ask me," said Detective Leach, "about 33 years, or however long it takes to become an expert marksman with a crossbow."

"Inspector, before that article by Ellie Sutton was published this morning, had the police revealed to the public that Colin Harlow had been killed with fire?"

"I believe not, Mr Gallow. We appear to have suffered quite a significant leak."

Immediately after he had finished the call, Franklin called Rowan.

"Are you still cycling?" were his first words to her.

"Um, yes. I've got you on earphones and mic."

245

"Pull over. You need to hear this."

"Done. Franklin, are you ok?"

"I think I know who Blackbeard is."

"What? D'you want me to turn around, I can be there in no time."

"No, no, it's fine. The police are keeping guard, I'm safe here, but I need to know that you are. With the whole police force covering this riot, it's the last night you want to get yourself in any trouble."

"Franklin, who is it?"

Downstairs, Franklin could hear banging, an angry, constant thud that sounded as if it was coming from the front door. "Someone's at the door,"

"Don't answer it," said Rowan, "the police will deal with whoever it is."

"A policeman just called, he's been working on the skin book. They know who it was – he was a policeman who went missing in 1981."

"1981? That's a whole lot of planning."

"But you know what this means, don't you?" There was more knocking at the door.

"I know exactly what it means. Run to the officers in the van, tell them who the killer is."

"Someone's at the door."

"Then open a window and shout it to them for God's sake."

"Get home and wait for me to call you, just me, nobody else, ok?"

"Of course."

When she was gone, Franklin found himself immediately confronted by the next problem at hand. Creeping downstairs he peered through the open door into the reception, where he was certain the sound had been coming from. There were more bangs, distinct and clear, but most definitely coming from another part of the property, inside the building.

With his mobile in one hand, he used the other to tap the code into the door which led to the death chamber. The lights immediately flickered on as the door swung open, but there were no windows to reveal himself to anyone hiding in the grounds. Pushing the door shut behind him, he once again entered the code "1-7-7-6" and heard the electric buzz of the mechanism lock.

He was just about to phone the police from this fortress of safety when he heard the banging again. Before his eyes the door to the metallic refrigeration unit swung open and from within he saw a body bag wriggling and unzipping itself.

"Put down the phone, Franklin," said the man as he slipped from the unit onto his feet. "Put down the phone and do everything I say."

48.

Any sense of control the demonstration had displayed seemed to have been lost hours ago. It was an exhausting push and pull against Edison and his line of fellow officers as they clashed with the angry faces of the Reclaim Our Streets mob who shrieked vitriol over their heads.

"Rights for whites!" shouted Karl Kitson to the frenzied anti-fascist protesters just feet away from him. His baiting words were answered with a volley of water bottles, one of which struck him just above the eye. The man barely flinched. "Come over here ya fuckin' pussies!"

Any semblance of order had collapsed several hours before when the carefully choreographed chants from the racists had given way to vile slurs and name calling.

When the rupture came, it came so suddenly that Edison didn't at first know what had happened. There was a slackening in his right arm to which he sighed with relief, such had been the tension upon it, but it was when he saw that half a dozen officers had been knocked over that he understood the fatal breach in their defence.

Then, like water bursting through the rivets of a stricken ship, came the protesters, immediately exploiting the weakness and erupting on mass through the gap. Other officers pulled their fallen colleagues out of the way of trampling feet, allowing further gaps in the wall to develop. Now, like the breaking of a dam, the mob flooded through, straight into the frightened hoard of fascists who stood aghast or turned on their boots and fled.

Screams filled the air as the vast crowd pushed into the white supremacists. Edison found himself tumbling to the ground as Sarah Fry dragged him with her as a current of protesters blundered past her. Her head hit the pavement and her helmet was sent spinning off into the road. Edison yanked her to her feet where she found herself face to face with the jeering Karl Kitson.

"Fuckin' pig scum," he growled and spat in her face. Before Sarah could respond, the man punched her square in

248

the cheek. Sarah stumbled backwards, dazed but still conscious. Karl Kitson's mouth dropped open. "You're a lady… I didn't know."

With a flick of her wrist her baton was fully extended. She struck him across his jaw, causing him to cough blood as he dropped to his knees. Sarah circled him and slapped handcuffs across his wrists before forcing him facedown unto a paving slab, riding his back as he fell.

That was that, Karl Kitson had sent himself to prison for a considerable amount of time. Not even the most loyal of his supporters would defend a man who would punch a woman in the face, the courts would look none too kindly on him attacking a police officer either. He was finished.

There was no longer any line to speak of, most of the anti-fascists had seen the fall of the wall as their victory and were now backing away from the scene triumphantly.

Fights were erupting everywhere, with the Reclaim Our Streets either on the run or vastly outnumbered as they were beaten with placards and kicked to the ground. Edison found himself thrust into action pulling a group of teenage girls off of a middle-aged skinhead who was crying for help. Helping the man to his feet, he dragged him through the morass to the edge of the square where a paramedic was hastily piling injured people into the back of an ambulance. One man with a broken nose was arguing that he didn't want to ride with a racist. "Just get in and don't say a word!" Edison barked.

But the man was distracted by something, and, following his gaze, Edison saw people were scaling the statue of Colston, the one at the summit unscrewed a bottle and poured clear liquid all over the monument. It all happened with such speed that Edison couldn't quite understand what was happening, but knew instinctively that they would want to do more than belittle the man with a splash of water.

The protesters hopped from the statue to the ground and one of them lit a rag in a bottle and threw it with force at the statue where it exploded in flames.

 A scream erupted from the crowd, followed by a cheer from some as the statue burned like a beacon above St Augustines Parade.

The statue was made of bronze and would survive the inferno, but the image of him burning would be on the cover of every newspaper for days. The city of Bristol had spoken.

49.

Rowan hung up the phone and scrolled through the images Franklin had taken of the skin book. One of the photographs was of the ornately written poem on the first page, she zoomed in closer and reached into her bag to retrieve the binder in which she kept all official notes from the funeral home.

The signature on the release form was not a perfect match, but she didn't expect it would be, the curls and loops were less formal. The skin book was concise but the signature was much more casual. Nevertheless they were unmistakably from the same hand. Of course they were, Rowan thought, how could she have been so blind when it seemed so obvious now?

She knew she should call the police and she knew they would listen. Even in the midst of a riot the capture of a serial killer would be their greatest priority. They might not ordinarily pay much heed to an untrained civilian, but Rowan had proved herself to be a more than trustworthy source. She'd made a promise to Franklin that her days of lone sleuthing were behind her, yet as she studied the signature she found herself overwhelmed by rage.

She needed to know why, but she also needed to know how. Killing someone with a crossbow took immense skill and accuracy, but that was nothing compared to the huge mental obstacle that must be overcome. How does someone swim so hard against the tide, what kind of person can turn their heart to stone and steal somebody's life? How did the killer do it? She had to find out, she owed it to Ruby and all the victims who'd never had justice.

She called the only person who would not try and talk her out of it.

"Hey, are you on your way home?"

"Jude, I have something to do. It's important, it's about the murders."

"Wait, what? Are you alright?"

"I think so. I hope so... I'll be fine. I just, I think I just need someone to know where I'm going." She read the address from the document in her hands.

"You're not going to go and meet this killer are you?"

"I am. I have to, and if anything happens you have to tell someone. I need to understand, and I need you to tell me I'm doing the right thing."

"I don't know, Rowan, I can't say it's the right thing because it sounds like complete madness, but I know why you're doing it. I trust you."

" I trust you too, now I do, anyway. I know you've secrets and I don't think I want to know what they are, not all of them, not right now. God, there was a time that I even had it in my head that you were Blackbeard, you know, the late nights and strange phone calls."

"I can explain all that," he said with a note of panic in his voice.

"I don't want to know, I just wanted you to know why I need to do this."

"I think I love you, Rowan," he said quickly.

The confession was like a little kick to her heart. "I'll see you later. Please, just stay on the line."

Her ride to Clifton Village would take her past the far end of St Augustine's Parade, away from where the riots had been. In the darkness she could see something smouldering and smelt the faint trace of smoke in the air. People were milling about and slowly making their way from the centre and into the surrounding streets. Rowan rode through the crowds and up onto Park Street.

Once in Clifton, she consulted the address once more before stopping outside the house. She folded her bike and put it under her arm. With her free hand she rang the doorbell.

When the door opened, Lois Roker, the refined elderly woman who had so impressed Rowan with her ageless elegance, was shaking her head slowly.

"You know, I assume?" the woman sighed.

"I know," replied Rowan.

"I was hoping it wouldn't come to this. Now hand your phone over and come inside."

Rowan did as she was told.

50.

Larry Roker stood before Franklin, his crossbow trembling only slightly in his hands. He wore gloves and overalls, covering every inch of his body save for his head.

"It was both of you, wasn't it?" asked Franklin.

" Yes it was."

"How did you get in?"

"Patience," shrugged Larry. "I knew this place would be a fortress so I simply waited my chance. I know how to hide, Mr Gallow. I slipped into the garage when you were parking and then just had to put the corpse under the van and climb into the body bag. Not the most pleasant experience of my life, but a necessary one."

"A Trojan Horse. Very clever of you."

"This whole operation has been clever, but it has also had a great deal of luck. Yes, the costumes have come in handy but I'm quite sure we could have pulled it off without them – it really is extraordinary how invisible being old can make you. We were able to escape without being noticed, because nobody suspects someone knocking on eighty to be a murderer. That's why we needed you – to be our legend…"

Franklin was not going to take the bait and ask Larry what he meant. He knew that his best chance of survival was to remain calm and to keep the old man talking. "That's how you survived. Your wife shot you that night, that's why it was in the leg."

Larry nodded. "We didn't want to kill Jess, she was our friend, but we knew there was a chance she suspected us. That has been the greatest lesson this whole experiment has taught us – if we are creating a monster, we must become monsters."

"But you are monsters. There's no way you can get away with this."

Larry smiled coldly. "We're old people, Mr Gallow, we're quite prepared to die for our cause. This has not been hasty or ill thought out. We're here to change the city, to forge a new legacy of justice. If judgement will not fall on those who most deserve it, then it's up to the people themselves to right the wrongs of history."

"And how do I fit into any of this?"

"I'm very sorry, but you are our patsy. From the start we knew we were inventing more than just a serial killer, we were creating a legend. The story of Jack the Ripper is much more enticing when you think he was a prince than if you believe he was a penniless drunk. My wife and I may have been the true killers, but what better story could there be than an undertaker, so obsessed with death that he reaped vengeance on his own city."

"So," Franklin ventured, "it sounds as if I'm unlikely to make it to the end of your story. What happens to Franklin Gallow?"

Larry nodded slowly. "He took his own life."

Lois Roker poured tea from the fine bone china pot on the table before her. Beside her on the sofa lay her crossbow, aimed directly at Rowan.

"Would you care for a cup, dear?" she asked.

"Why did you do it?"

The old lady curled the edges of her mouth into what could have been an attempt at a smile and sipped on her tea. "My husband is a judge Miss Kaplan, were you aware of that?"

"I was."

"He has played his part for many decades and I've stood dutifully by him. Time and time again he's watched in horror as yet another guilty man has walked free because of some trifling technicality or corrupt piece of police work. Dozens of times, maybe hundreds, the guilty have escaped justice because an idiotic jury were dazzled by a man's smile or the cut of his suit, set free to commit more crimes or just live a blameless life in peace. At first we thought we should take revenge on those who had slipped through the cracks in the justice system, but soon, very soon in fact, it became clear that the biggest injustices were the ghastly crimes of the past for which nobody had ever been held accountable."

Rowan eyed the crossbow cautiously. Lois was stroking it as if it were a beloved pet. "But the people you killed, they didn't deserve to die, they weren't responsible for slavery, or the Queen Square riots or the bus boycott, or any of it."

"Perhaps not, but that didn't leave them blameless. They were representatives of something darker. Yes, I'm sure it's sad for their families but our goal was something much greater. We wanted to start a revolution of thought – that no one is blameless as long as the crimes have gone unpunished."

"You're insane – the pair of you."

"On the contrary dear," she smiled as she dropped sugar cubes into her cup from a pair of tongs, "it was messy, but necessary. Far from being from the mind of a madman, our plan was a labour of love, practiced over decades, calculated in the most precise a detail. We knew our targets and we followed them with the precision of a cat stalking its prey, taking it in turns to claim a life so that we may each claim an alibi, not that anyone suspected us. Did you know that on the night I shot my husband and killed my friend, my word was taken as truth right from the start? I claimed I was drunk and fell asleep at the table, and that was it – no more explanation needed because who would doubt a dear old thing like me. Surely I wouldn't have waited for them to leave, having drunk nothing but fruit juice all evening, and drive across Clifton and meet them in a park; surely my husband wouldn't have walked her intentionally across a well lit park so that I could get a good shot at her."

"How could you do that to her? How could you do that to anyone?"

Lois narrowed her eyes sympathetically at Rowan as if she were a simpleton. "It wasn't easy to begin with. Back in 1981, when we first hatched our plan, we really had no idea how we'd go about it, but after the first murder there was no going back. That policeman was so much easier to kill than either of us had thought. We just picked a name from the list of officers who were involved in the St Pauls riots and followed him over several days until we knew his schedule well enough to know when he would be alone. I played the role of little lost housewife and asked the man for directions and my husband stabbed him in the back. It was as simple as that. The plan was hatched and we've spent thirty years raising it like a child, perfecting our archery in the back garden and selecting who should be our next victim, and why."

"Then you're not mad, you're evil."

"Evil? When the crimes I've committed are put against those that helped build this city, the trading of slaves, the exploitation of the destitute, they pale into insignificance."

"You murdered your own friend," said Rowan, her voice trembling in fear and rage.

"Did I? I fear that's not how the history books will remember it. If I'm guilty of a crime greater than cowardice, the world will never know. I'll gladly take my secret to the grave, as will my husband, and I'll do so without a trace of remorse – it's Mr Gallow who shall be the icon of the city."

"What do you mean?"

"We told him we would come for him when we needed him and my husband is with him now. He will become a legend, a Robin Hood, or perhaps even a Blackbeard. He'll live on forever as both villain and hero; the man who found a city guilty for its crimes and sought his own justice to repay the debt of blood."

"And what about me?" ventured Rowan.

Lois sighed pitifully. "I'm afraid you weren't intended to be part of this. You will vanish from the face of the earth. You shouldn't have got involved, I didn't want to have to kill you."

Rowan fixed her stare on Lois' face. "But you're not going to," she said, "this has been your confession."

Lois Roker straightened her back and twitched her eye. "I'm sorry, dear, what do you mean?"

"You may think you're getting away with this, but check the phone you took from me."

Lois raised an eyebrow and pulled Rowan's phone from the pocket of her waistcoat.

"Jude," Rowan called, "this is Lois Roker, she and her husband are the killers."

"Hello, Mrs Roker," was Jude's cheerful reply at the end of the phone. "Nice to meet you!"

"You deceitful little bitch," hissed Lois. "How long has he been listening?"

"How stupid do you think I am? I called him before I even rang your bell, he's heard everything."

In an instant the kindly mask that Lois Roker wore for a face was transformed by a full-throated screech. Her eyes bulged red with fury, her hands pulled at her chestnut hair until it tore in clumps. Rowan leapt to her feet and kicked the coffee table, sending the tea set spinning through the air.

"That's Limoges porcelain!" screamed the woman as she reached for the crossbow. Rowan grabbed the metal tea tray and used it as a shield. The sound of an arrow clanged against it and sent it spinning from her grasp. Rowan was on Lois in a second with a fearful punch to the face that rendered the old woman unconscious.

"Jude?" she gasped into her phone. "I've just knocked a pensioner out. Call the police and tell them that Franklin Gallow needs them."

Franklin's phone began to vibrate on the steel table beside Larry Roker.

"It says Rowan," Larry informed him as he glanced at its screen. "D'you think she knows?"

"I have no idea, she's probably just calling about her schedule for tomorrow."

Larry pondered the likelihood of this. A bead of sweat began to form on his brow. "Ok. Now... put your hands up."

Franklin did as he was told. "How am I supposed to have killed myself in this scenario?"

Larry's eyes narrowed as he raised the crossbow. "You shot yourself with this – in the chest."

If he could just keep Larry talking, perhaps it would give Rowan time to figure out that something was amiss. "That's rather dramatic, don't you think."

"It's... poetic, I think, yes, poetic."

"That's what the gloves are for then? You're going to get my prints on the crossbow when I'm dead."

"Yes, that's right – and the overalls are for... splash back."

"I see. I suppose there's very little I can do to convince you otherwise is there Mr Roker?"

"No," Larry replied. His voice sounded narrow and high, his face was pale and pouring with sweat. "Now could you please stop talking?"

Something was keeping Franklin alive, preventing Larry Roker from shooting him. "It's not easy though, is it? Killing someone?"

"What are you talking about? I've killed many times before..."

"But not like this. You've shot people in the back or in the dark. You've never killed a man who was looking you straight in the eye before have you? I'm not your legend or your monster, I'm not Blackbeard, or Jenkins Portiere, I'm not Colston. I'm Franklin Gallow, just a man."

"I've killed better men than you, Mr Gallow. All of this could have been avoided. At Jess' funeral we gave you a chance to tell us all you knew. We asked you to investigate to see how honest you were with us, you never once mentioned the book, you lied to us!"

The skin book. Perhaps that was how he'd survive. "The police know about the book," he said. "They know whose skin it was, a policeman called Cecil..."

"...You told the police? We told you not to!"

"They know I can't be the killer, I'd have been six years old when you murdered that man. The secret's out, you won't get away with this."

"You're lying!" he squealed.

"Then how do I know who the skin came from?"

"Stop lying to me," Larry screamed, his face red with rage, "I can't stand liars! There are liars in my courtroom and liars in the city, stop... stop lying to me!"

Franklin saw the man flinch as the arrow left the crossbow. When it hit him it struck with the force of a mighty blow, like a punch. A memory of being a boy and being struck by a neighbour's cricket ball flashed before his eyes as he dropped to his knees.

"I told you I could do it," Larry whimpered with the voice of a child.

Franklin looked down at his wound. The arrow jutted from the centre of his ribcage like the flag on a sandcastle. It quivered as blood bubbled from its base. "You bastard," was his reply.

As Franklin slumped on to his back, Larry Roker stepped around him and pushed at the door to the death chamber, when it didn't give he rattled it on it's hinges.

"You stupid, stupid old man," said Franklin blearily, as his blood trickled out on to the floor. "You don't know the password. You're stuck with me now!"

A smile spread across Franklin's face. As the room turned black he was content to know that his last thought in life would be one of triumph. He had caught his killer.

51.

Franklin had always known death was real. From his earliest memories, death was not a far away concept, it was an ever present being, the fifth member of his family that kept itself hidden away in the shadows of his home.

He had seen how death could come at any time. There were the strokes and heart attacks, aneurisms and kidney failures. Flu could claim the young and old alike, cancer could strike with staggering speed, and then there were the violent ends, the car crashes, the suicides, the murders, the random acts of fate, like choking on a grape or tumbling down a staircase. For Franklin, death had always been just one mistake away, one wrong turn and everything would be gone forever.

Where was he? He was certain he couldn't be dead yet for he felt a nub of consciousness, a lucidity. Perhaps these thoughts were simply the random firings of neurons; a final firework display as each brain cell burst out of existence, to be replaced by oblivion. He opened his eyes. He was under water in a murky, silty lagoon where fish swam before his face. A cormorant broke the surface and darted after them, leaving little ripples in its wake. He could see a cloudy sky overhead and the huge mechanical cranes of Bristol's waterfront silhouetted against it. He was in the harbour, bobbing like a log beneath the surface, but slowly rising out of the murky darkness, higher and higher as if being lifted on a jet of bubbles, until his face broke through the surface and into the daylight.

The clouds above turned milky white and the sun dimmed into the coil of a light bulb. He gasped. He was indoors; he was in bed.

Like waking from a dream, Franklin realised there was somebody else in the room. As his eyes focused on the figure beside his bed the face of the stranger was reconstructed and his features slid into place.

It was a young man with shoulder-length blonde hair and a handsome, angular face. His mouth fell open and he began to shout: "Rowan! He's awake!"

Rowan, he remembered that name. Rowan was his friend – had she died too? A moment later her familiar face loomed overhead with a broad smile and a single tear rolling down her cheek. "Franklin, you're alive!"

"Am I?" he replied, drowsily.

"Jude, get the nurse. Go!"

Franklin watched the young man leave the room. "Who's that? He looked like an angel."

Rowan laughed. "Bloody hell, they really did give you some strong stuff. That was Jude… he's my boyfriend, I suppose."

"Where am I? What happened?'

"You've been here for two days. You've had an operation to have the arrow removed. They said if it'd been just an inch or so to the left it would have gone straight through your heart."

Franklin looked under the blanket to his bare torso where a bandage was stretched across his nipples and taped in place. Just the sight of it brought back memories of Larry, and with them came a sudden stinging pain in his ribcage. "Ouch. It hurts."

"He broke a couple of ribs, and the surgeons had to remove one to get at the arrow. We could have lost you."

"How long have you been here?"

"Today? About six hours. Your parents and Edison stayed the night with you and Alf was here for a little while yesterday."

"Alf came to see me?"

"He's been pretty upset, believe it or not."

"Good," Franklin smiled. "I should hope so too."

"Even Peterman dropped by with some flowers. You should get attacked every day, people realise they really like you when you almost die."

Franklin breathed deeply and felt the stitches in his chest expand painfully. "Did I really almost die?"

"It was pretty scary. I had just had a run in with Lois Roker – did you know that she was involved too?"

"I worked it out, in the end anyway."

"Jude helped. He called the police while I was cycling over. I've never got across the city so fast, I can barely remember the journey. By the time I got there the two policemen on watch were trying to knock down the door to the death chamber, but I knew the code. Larry Roker was trying to kick his way through the wall to get into the garage – he was in such a frenzy and kept on saying he didn't do it. Turns out that he was actually a bit of a coward when it came to facing justice himself."

"How did I look?"

"You really don't want to know, but let's just say I've seen you looking better."

Franklin nodded and offered a smile. "And Lois Roker?"

"She's confessed to everything, according to Edison. Once she came round anyway." Rowan flashed her bandaged hand at him.

"You punched an old lady?"

"Punched and knocked out," Rowan confirmed.

Jude returned with an excited looking nurse who gave Franklin a brief examination "Mr Gallow, it's so good to see you back. You're something of a hero by all accounts, it's all over the news, I'm so happy to meet you; it's been an honour to look after you. Please may I have an autograph when you're up to it?" The nurse offered him some pills with water, which he drank feverishly.

"What are the press saying about me?" he asked Rowan once the nurse had left.

"It was a huge story for a few hours. I think they were expecting the killer to be some young radical though, as soon as they learned it was an elderly couple all the sexiness went out of it."

"Bloody hell," Franklin sighed. "Even our serial killers have to be bright young things nowadays."

Jude cleared his throat. "Hello, Mr Gallow." He offered Franklin his hand, which he shook as firmly as he could muster.

"I believe I owe you some thanks."

"It was all Rowan really, she saved you, and herself. I just called the police."

263

"Well thank you nonetheless." Franklin turned to Rowan. "I like him, and he's very handsome too."

"Thank you," Rowan beamed. "He's not usually like this Jude, I think the painkillers are still taking effect."

"Jude. I like that name," said Franklin dreamily. "What's his surname?"

Rowan simply looked at her boyfriend, suddenly ashamed of her ignorance.

"Jude Tyndale," Jude replied, offering Rowan a wink.

"I think I need to sleep," Franklin said softly. "Thank you for being here when I woke up."

"I'll always be here Franklin," she replied as another tear rolled from her eye. "Hey, it's all over now."

"Yes it is," he replied. "And guess what. We won."

Rowan kissed his forehead and Franklin fell into a dreamless sleep.

52

"It burnt itself out in the end," said Alf to Franklin. "After that, everyone got a little scared. Things were just a little too real."

"So you were here, for the protest?"

Alf nodded, "Of course."

Franklin looked over the statue of Edward Colston. Its bronze skin had bubbled and cracked and his once benign features had turned into a gruesome mask of outraged agony. "I think I rather him like this."

"I agree. There's something rewarding in seeing the old bastard like that."

"I wonder what they'll do with him. It seems like asking for trouble to repair him, won't the same thing just happen again?"

Alf shrugged his shoulders. "No idea."

"I expect he'll be taken down and the council will claim that he's not salvageable and lock him away to never see the light of day again. I imagine they'd rather him stay out of sight and out of mind."

"Probably. That'll teach him," said Alf.

"I don't think you can really take revenge on a statue, can you? Whether we like it or not, he's part of our history – maybe we need reminders that the way we live now is partly due to past sins. We can't keep paying for our mistakes forever, that's what the Rokers didn't understand. We can try to understand though and stop it from happening again."

"You sound like Mum. She's always going on about how we repeat history if we don't remember it."

"Your mother is a very clever woman," said Franklin as they turned away from the statue and strolled towards the waterfront.

Alf had requested this meeting. It had been a wonderful surprise and an awful worry, but his son had soon reassured him that he meant no malice. Perhaps a brush with death made people realise how much they meant to one another.

Franklin buttoned up his coat. November winds were rushing through the streets as if dragging winter behind them. The cold hurt his wound but it seemed to be getting better with each passing day. What was more uncomfortable were the stares of passersby. Much to his chagrin, Franklin had become an unlikely local celebrity.

"Don't worry about them," Alf said, kindly. "They'll be on to something else as soon as the next celebrity scandal breaks, or Ellie Sutton tells them what they're supposed to be outraged by."

"She's been trying to contact me," Franklin informed his son, "I'm supposed to be meeting her right now. As childish as it may seem, telling her to drive all the way to Cardiff to interview me has given me an enormous amount of pleasure."

Alf smiled. Franklin told himself that he saw the smallest trace of pride on his face.

"It's this way, this isn't too much for you is it?"

"Not at all," Franklin lied, "but where are you taking me?"

"Mum said you were upset by my art piece. She said you thought it meant I wanted you dead, so I wanted you to look at it again – properly this time."

The thought scared Franklin, but only mildly. "Ok, I'd really like you to tell me what it does mean."

"Dad. I'm gay." Alf suddenly blurted out and the pair stopped in their tracks.

Franklin cleared his throat. "Thank you for telling me, it really means so much that you trust me enough to tell me, and honestly, I couldn't be more proud of you if…"

"…Franklin, I know you know. You've known for months."

"What? No I didn't."

"You don't understand what it's like to have a kid, do you Franklin? The day you told my mum that you knew I was gay but you wanted to wait until I was ready to tell you, the very first thing she did was tell me. I just wanted to see how long you could wait until you asked about it."

"Damn it!" Franklin grumbled. "I had a whole speech rehearsed. I'd practiced it and everything, I was going to get it so right and sound like a really cool dad."

Alf laughed. "From what I just heard, it didn't sound that brilliant, a little trite in fact. But anyway, I'm glad it's done now."

"So, are you seeing anyone at the moment?"

"We're not ready for that kind of chat yet, Franklin."

At the gallery Alf pushed his way through the door and nodded to the dozing man at the table by the entrance.

"Hey, Alf," he said as he rubbed his eyes.

"Hey, Percy. Mind if I just show my friend around?"

Percy shook his head. "Go nuts. We haven't had anyone in all day. I don't know why I even bother opening up." It was then that he took a double take at Franklin. "No way, are you that guy?"

Franklin just nodded sheepishly and sloped past the table. As he approached the sculpture of the casket, surrounded by flowers and wreaths of letters, he did so with the apprehension one might reserve for a live grenade.

"See. It's not that bad is it?" asked Alf.

"The art, or how it makes me feel?"

"I don't know. Maybe a bit of both." Alf glanced around the gallery. "Well, at least I managed to evoke an emotion in someone. What a load of pretentious tosh."

"See, if I said that I'd sound like an idiot."

Alf said nothing but watched as Franklin inched closer to his artwork. Just as he'd hoped, Franklin crouched down and read the small note he'd agonised over when the sculpture had first gone on display. A little description was all it was supposed to be, to help give clarity to the intentions of the artist.

Franklin read it softly aloud. "Dead Dad, by Alfred Duke. (wood, wire, synthetic flowers.) Growing up I knew only the smallest things about my father. I knew he met my mother at university and that he had gone on to become a funeral director, but other than that, he was a stranger to me. He lived only in my mind, not unlike someone whose father has died. I wanted to use the iconography of his trade to depict a kind of eulogy, separating the ghost of a man I had never met from the one who I had started to know. We don't get to see our own funeral, so my offering to my father was that I would give him a ceremony to welcome him into my life; to be among the living and no longer just in my mind. My piece is dedicated to him and the life I hope we can share."

"Well?" Alf asked nervously.

"Good grief, boy. You do have feelings... you don't hate me." Franklin found himself incapable of resisting the urge to hug his son. He opened his arms, but Alf sidestepped out of the way of the embrace.

"I'm not ready for that either," he said, "I'm taking baby steps towards actually even liking you, but hey, I bet you never thought I'd call you that." Alf pointed to his sculpture before he turned and walked away to Percy at the table.

At first Franklin didn't know what Alf had meant, then he saw it. Formed in wire and bound in plastic flowers, the word was there for all the world to see, as proud and true as it could be.

"DAD" it said.

53.

Rowan woke to the sound of eggs frying in the kitchen. Stirring, she looked across the open plan flat to where Jude was humming to himself and dancing naked before a pan.

"Veggie fry up?" he offered.

"Oh yes please. It smells delicious." Rowan sat up in bed and opened her iPad. The world had survived another night, the news informed her.

"I think I just heard the postman," said Jude. "Could you be a sweet and get it for me? I'm waiting for some guitar strings."

Rowan nodded and climbed out of bed. She threw Jude's dressing gown around her and revelled in the sense of being swathed in the smell of her boyfriend.

She skipped down the stairs with the keys to the delivery boxes for both their flats. As expected, Jude's guitar strings had arrived along with an assortment of threatening looking bills. She pocketed his collection and unlocked her own box.

Inside was a single letter in an unstamped envelope. It had been posted by hand that morning. Rowan eyed the piece of mail sadly, as she always did when this happened.

Before she returned to Jude's flat, she stopped off at her own, and sitting on the edge of her bed, opened the envelope and read the note inside. "ROWAN. YOUR FATHER KILLED YOUR SISTER." It had been written in capital letters on an old fashioned typewriter.

Sighing, Rowan reached under her bed to the shoebox she kept there. She dropped the note inside, along with the dozens of others she had received over the past two years; each with an identical message: "Your father killed your sister."

Burying her thoughts, just as she always did, she closed the shoebox and returned to Jude.

Printed in Great Britain
by Amazon